ALSO BY KATY EVANS

MANWHORE

The REAL Series

REAL

MINE

REMY

ROGUE

RIPPED

manwhore
+1

KATY EVANS

G
Gallery Books
New York   London   Toronto   Sydney   New Delhi

G

Gallery Books
An Imprint of Simon & Schuster, Inc.
1230 Avenue of the Americas
New York, NY 10020

First Gallery Books trade paperback edition July 2015

GALLERY BOOKS and colophon are registered trademarks of Simon & Schuster, Inc.

For information about special discounts for bulk purchases, please contact Simon & Schuster Special Sales at 1-866-506-1949 or business@simonandschuster.com.

The Simon & Schuster Speakers Bureau can bring authors to your live event. For more information or to book an event, contact the Simon & Schuster Speakers Bureau at 1-866-248-3049 or visit our website at www.simonspeakers.com.

Cover design by Damon
Cover photograph by Shutterstock

Manufactured in the United States of America

10   9   8   7   6   5   4   3   2

Library of Congress Cataloging-in-Publication Data is on file.

ISBN 978-1-5011-0155-7
ISBN 978-1-5011-0157-1 (ebook)

To the biggest leap you will ever take.

PLAYLIST

GRAND PIANO by Nicki Minaj

OUT OF MIND by Tove Lo

THOUSAND MILES by Tove Lo

SURRENDER by Cash Cash

DO I WANT TO KNOW by Arctic Monkeys

BEGIN AGAIN by Purity Ring

TALKING BODY by Tove Lo

SKY FULL OF STARS by Coldplay

SUGAR by Maroon 5

I LIVED by OneRepublic

GOLD DUST by Galantis

THINKING OUT LOUD by Ed Sheeran

MY HEART IS OPEN by Maroon 5 and Gwen Stefani

PEACE by O.A.R.

EXPOSING MALCOLM SAINT
By R. Livingston

I'm going to tell you a story. A story that managed to pull me
apart completely. A story that brought me back to life. A story
that has made me cry, laugh, scream, smile, and then cry
again. A story I keep telling to myself over and over and over
until I have memorized every smile, every word, every thought.
A story that I hope to keep with me forever.

The story begins with this very article. It was a regular morning
at *Edge*. A morning that would bring me a big opportunity: to
write an exposé on Malcolm Kyle Preston Logan Saint. He's a
man who needs no introduction. Billionaire playboy, beloved
womanizer, a source of many speculations. This article would
open doors for me, gain a young hungry reporter a voice.

I dove in, managing to get an interview with Malcolm Saint to
discuss Interface (his incredible new Facebook-killer) and its
immediate rise to popularity. As obsessed as the city has been
with his persona for years, I considered myself lucky to be in
this position.

I was so focused on revealing Malcolm Saint that I let my
guard down, unaware that every time he opened up, he was
actually revealing *me* to me. Things I had never wanted were
suddenly all I wanted. I was determined to find out more about
this man. This mystery. Why was he so closed off? Why was
nothing ever enough for him? I soon discovered he was not a
man of many words, but rather a man of the right words. A man
of action. I told myself that every inch of information I hunted

was for this article, but the knowledge I craved was actually about myself.

I wanted to know everything. I wanted to breathe him. Live him.

But most unexpectedly of all, Saint began to pursue me. Genuinely. Wholeheartedly. And relentlessly. I could not believe that he would be truly interested in me. I had never been pursued like this, intrigued like this. I had never felt so connected to something—someone.

I never expected my story to change, but it did. Stories tend to do that; you go out searching for something and come back with something different. I wasn't looking to fall in love, I wasn't looking to lose my mind and common sense over the most beautiful green eyes I have ever seen, I wasn't looking to drive myself crazy with lust. But I ended up finding a little piece of my soul, a little piece that isn't really that small at all: it's over six feet tall, with shoulders about a yard wide, hands more than twice the size of mine, green eyes, dark hair, and it is smart, ambitious, kind, generous, powerful, sexy, and has consumed me completely.

I regret lying, both to myself and to him; I regret not having the experience to recognize what I was feeling the moment I felt it. I regret not savoring each second I had with him more, because I value those seconds more than anything.

However, I don't regret this story. His story. My story. Our story.

I'd do it all again for another moment with him. I'd do it all again with him. I'd leap blindly into the air if only there were even a 0.01 percent chance that he'd still be there, waiting to catch me.

FOUR WEEKS

I've never been so hopeful as when I board the pristine glass elevator at the M4 corporate building. A handful of employees ride along with me, murmuring perfunctory greetings to each other and to me. I think my mouth must be on vacation because I can't seem to force it to speak. But I smile in reply—my smile nervous, nervous but hopeful, definitely hopeful. My riding companions step out on their floors one by one until I'm alone, riding up to the executive floor on my own.

Toward him.

Toward the man I love.

My body is raging. My blood is pumping—my blood is *storming*—my thighs are shaking. My stomach feels filled with little earthquakes that just won't quit, then they turn into a full-fledged roil when I hear the elevator *ting* at his floor.

Stepping out, I'm in corporate nirvana, surrounded by sleek chrome and pristine glass, marble and limestone floors. But

I hardly have eyes for anything except the tall and imposing frosted glass doors at the far end of the room.

Framing those doors to each side is a pair of sleek designer desks, for a total of four.

Behind these desks are four women in identical black-and-white suits, sitting behind their gleaming dark-oak desks, working quietly behind their flat-screen computers.

One of them, the forty-year-old Catherine H. Ulysses—right hand of the man who owns every inch of this building—stops what she's doing when she sees me. She arches her brow, then seems both tense and relieved as she lifts the receiver on her desk and murmurs my name into it.

I. Am. Not. Breathing.

But Catherine doesn't miss a beat as she motions me toward the huge frosted doors—those intimidating doors—that lead into the lair of the most powerful man in Chicago.

The human being with the most powerful effect on *me*.

This is what I've been waiting for, for four weeks. This is what I wanted when I left a thousand messages on his phones and what I wanted when I wrote a thousand others that I left unsent. To see him.

For him to want to see me.

But as I force myself to step forward, I don't even know if I'll have the strength to stand before him and look him in the eye after what I did.

I'm wracked so hard with nervousness and anticipation and hope—yes hope, small but bright, even as I shake like a leaf.

Catherine holds the door open, and I struggle to hold my head high and walk into his office.

Two steps inside I hear the *swoosh* of the glass door shutting behind me and my systems halt at the familiar sight of the most beautiful office I've ever been in.

His office is all vast marble and chrome, twelve-foot ceilings, and endless floor-to-ceiling windows.

And there he is. The center of its axis. The center of my world.

He's pacing by the window, speaking into a headset in a low, low voice—the kind he uses when he's pissed. All I can make out are the words *have to be dead to let her fall into his clutches* . . .

He hangs up, and as if he feels me in the room, he turns his head. His eyes flare when he sees me. His green eyes.

His achingly familiar, beautiful green eyes.

He inhales, very slowly, his chest expanding, his hands curling a little at his sides as he looks at me.

I look back at him.

Malcolm Kyle Preston Logan Saint.

I just walked into the eye of the most powerful storm of my life. No. Not a storm. A hurricane.

Four weeks, I haven't seen him. And he still looks exactly as I remember. Larger than life, and more irresistible than ever.

His striking face is perfectly shaven today, and his sensual lips look so achingly full I can almost feel them against mine. Six feet-plus of perfectly controlled male power stands before me, in a perfect black suit and a killer tie. He's the very devil in Armani; strong-boned, square-jawed, gleaming dark hair and those penetrating eyes.

He's got the best eyes.

They twinkle mercilessly when he teases me, and when he doesn't tease me, they're mysterious and unreadable, assessing and intelligent, keeping me guessing about his thoughts.

But I had forgotten how cold those eyes used to be. Green arctic ice looks back at me now. Every fleck of ice in those eyes gleaming like diamond shards.

He clenches his jaw and tosses the headset aside.

He looks as approachable as a wall, his shoulders stretching his white shirt, which clings to his skin like a groupie. But I know he's not a wall; I've never wanted to throw myself at a wall like this.

He's walking toward me. Every step he takes makes my heart pound as he moves with that quiet and confident own-the-world stride of his.

He stops a few feet away and shoves his hands into his pants pockets; and he seems so big all of a sudden, and he smells so utterly *good*. I drop my eyes to his tie as the little candle of hope I walked in with starts to flicker with doubt.

"Malcolm . . ." I begin.

"Saint is fine," he says quietly.

I catch my breath at his words.

I wait for him to say something—to tell me how much I *suck*—and ache when he doesn't. Instead I hear a voice from the door.

"Mr. Saint," Catherine announces, "Stanford Merrick's here."

"Thank you." I hear Saint's quietly powerful voice and a tremor rolls unexpectedly down my spine.

I stare down at the shiny marble floor, embarrassed. My shoes; I wore something I thought would make me look pretty. God, I don't think he's noticed or is interested at all.

"Rachel, this is Stanford Merrick, from human resources."

I feel my cheeks grow hot hearing him say *Rachel*. I still can't look into his eyes; instead I focus on shaking Stanford Merrick's hand.

Merrick is a medium-height man, with a smile that gives the impression of friendliness and a calm presence that is all but swallowed by Saint's.

"A pleasure to meet you, Miss Livingston," he says.

I hear the sound of a chair being pulled out, and my knees feel like soup when I hear Saint's voice again. "Sit," he says, his voice low.

I move to obey, still avoiding his gaze as I sit down.

While Catherine goes around the office pouring coffees and refreshments, I keep him in my peripheral.

Popping open his jacket button, he lowers himself onto the center of the long, bone-colored leather couch directly across from where I sit.

He looks so dark in that sable suit.

So dark against the sunlight, against the light color of the couch.

"Mr. Saint, would you like me to go on, or would you like to do the honors?" Merrick asks.

He won't take his eyes off me.

"Mr. Saint?"

He frowns a little as he realizes he wasn't listening, only looking at me, and says, "Yes."

He leans back and extends his arm out on the back of the couch, and I feel touched by his eyes as Merrick takes out files and paperwork from a folder while I sit stiff and tight in my seat.

Saint's energy field is massive and overpowering and so unreadable today. All I can think is: Do you hate me, my Sin?

"How long have you been at *Edge*, Miss Livingston?" his man is asking.

I hesitate, and notice the slow buzzing of Saint's cell phone resting beside him on the couch. He reaches out to power it off with one hand, his thumb swiftly stroking once across the screen.

The corner of my mouth tingles unexpectedly.

I shift in my seat. "Several years," I answer.

"Only child, correct?"

"Correct."

"Says here you won a CJA award for commentary last year?"

"Yes. I . . ." I search for a word through all the *I'm sorrys* and *I love yous* foremost in my head right now. ". . . was really humbled to be even considered."

Slowly shifting in place and folding his outstretched arm, Saint absently strokes the pad of his thumb over his lower lip, studying me with a gaze that gleams with intelligence, surveying me in silence.

"I see here that you started working at *Edge* before you graduated from Northwestern, correct?" Merrick continues.

"Yes, actually, I did." I tug the sleeve of my sweater, trying to keep my attention on his questions.

In my peripheral, I still can't stop being aware of what *he* is doing; Sin. How he sips from his glass of water, how he smells, how tightly his fingers curl around the glass.

His dark hair, the crescents of his eyelashes, how they frame his eyes. His lips. So unsmiling. His eyes, so untwinkling.

I turn my head to face him, and it's almost as if he was waiting for me to turn.

He stares at me, so deeply into me the way only *he* can, and green becomes my whole world. A world of purely arctic, untouchable, unbreakable green ice.

Nothing this cool should have the ability to make me this hot. But there is heat in the ice. Ice burns just as much as heat does.

"I'm sorry, I lost my train of thought." I jerk my eyes away.

Flustered, I shift in my seat and look at Merrick. The man is staring at me strangely and with a bit of pity. There's a slight movement in the direction of Saint as he shifts his shoulders on the couch to face Merrick better, and I notice *Saint* is looking at *Merrick* with a dark but controlled look of displeasure.

"Cut through the bullshit, Merrick."

"Of course, Mr. Saint."

Ohgod. The fact that Saint has noticed his man is making me nervous makes me blush tenfold.

"Miss Livingston," Merrick begins again, pausing as though he's about to say something monumental. "Mr. Saint has an interest in expanding the services we offer our Interface subscribers. We're offering fresh content from specific sources, mainly a group of young journalists, columnists, and reporters we're planning to take on."

Interface. His newest enterprise. Growing like a monster—a force to be reckoned with on its own, it's been breaking through all the technological and market barriers in its expansion. I'm not surprised that Saint is taking it into this next step; it's a genius move, from an admirable businessman, the next logical move for a company just named among the top ten places to work for.

"I love it, Malcolm. I love the idea," I tell him.

Ohmigod!

Did I just call him Malcolm?

I seem to catch him off guard. For a fraction of a second, his eyes shadow. It's as if there's a storm brewing inside him . . . but the next instant, he cools it back down.

"Well, that's wonderful to hear," Merrick says then. "Mr. Saint has an eye for talent, as you know, Miss Livingston. And he wants to make it very clear that he means to bring you on board."

Sin has been watching me the whole time Merrick speaks. He watches as the smile leaves my face, replaced by shock instead. "You're offering me a job?"

"Yes." Merrick is the one who responds. "Indeed, Miss Livingston. A job at M4."

I'm stunned speechless.

I stare at my lap as I register what I heard.

Sin doesn't want to talk to me.

He's barely affected by me at all.

He called me, after four weeks, for *this*.

I lift my gaze to his, and the instant our eyes lock, I feel a crackle in my system. I feel it like a jolt. Forcing my gaze to stay on his face, which is beyond unreadable, I try to keep my voice level. "A job is the last thing I'd expected you'd offer. Is that all you want from me?"

He leans forward in a fluid move, elbows to his knees, his stare never leaving me. "I want you to take it."

Oh.

God.

He sounds just as stern as when he called *Dibs* on me that night . . .

Knotted up inside, I tear my eyes away and stare out the window for a moment. I want to call him Malcolm, but he's not Malcolm anymore to me, I realize. He's not even Saint, who teased me mercilessly until I caved. This is Malcolm Saint. Looking at me as if he never held me in his arms.

"You *know* I can't leave my job," I tell him, turning.

He doesn't seem bothered. "We'll meet your price."

Shaking my head with a little laugh of disbelief, I rub my temples.

"Merrick," is all he says.

And Merrick instantly continues.

Sitting tensely in his seat, a huge contrast to Saint's lounging form, Mr. Merrick explains, "As I was saying, we'll be offering news content to our subscribers, and Mr. Saint has been a longtime fan of your voice. He appreciates its honesty and the angles you take."

Red-hot color spreads up my body. "Thank you. I'm super flattered," I say. "But there's really only one answer," I add breathlessly, "and I've already given it to you."

Mr. Merrick forges on with a look from Saint. "This is the proposal for the job and we need an acceptance or decline within the week."

He fans a set of papers over the table.

I stare at them, unable to register, to comprehend, what this means.

"Why would you do this?" I ask.

"Because I can." Saint looks at me levelly. His gaze is intense. Matter-of-fact, even. "I have more to offer you here than where you are."

He's not moving, he's utterly motionless, but he's just set my world spinning to the thousandth degree.

"Take the papers, Rachel," he says.

"I don't . . . want to."

"Think about it. Read it before you say no to me."

We stare for a beat too long.

He stands with the grace of a feline uncurling. Malcolm Kyle Preston Logan *Saint*. CEO of the most powerful corporation in the city. Obsession of the ladies. Elusive as a comet. Relentless and ruthless. "My people will contact you by the end of the week."

I wonder all of a sudden if there will ever be a time when this man stops surprising me. I really admire his composure. I admire many things about him. If I thought for a moment that we could fight it out, I was wrong. Saint won't waste his time on that. He's too busy reaching for his never-ending ambitions, conquering the world.

And me? I'm just trying to piece mine together from all the debris on the floor.

Inhaling, I gather the papers quietly. I take them and don't say goodbye or thank you or anything at all, just hear my shoes as I leave.

I open the door and can't help but steal one last peek into his office; my last glimpse of him is leaning forward on the couch with his hands on his knees, exhaling as he drags a hand over his face.

"Will you be needing anything else from me, Mr. Saint?" asks Merrick with a tone that is almost *begging* for more work.

When Saint lifts his head, he catches me watching him. We freeze and then just stare. At each other. He looks at me warily, and I look at him with all the regret I feel. There are so many things I want to say to him, but this is how I leave, all my words morphed into silence as I shut the door behind me.

His assistants watch me leave.

I board the elevator quietly and stare at my reflection on the steel doors as I ride to the lobby. I suppose I look pretty, my hair down, my attire draping, soft and feminine, against my body. But as I stare into my eyes, I look so lost that I want to dive inside to find myself.

And I realize that love is as ever-changing as a sky or as an ocean: always there, but not always sunny or clear or calm.

Outside, I flag a cab, and as we drive off, for a second I turn and stare at M4's beautiful mirrored façade. *So regal. So impenetrable*, I think, until my phone buzzes.

WHAT HAPPENED?!
Did u KISS AND MAKE UP?!

TELL US! WYNN IS LEAVING IN 3 MINS AND WANTS TO
KNOW

DID HE READ YOUR ARTICLE? Did it make him MELT?

I read Gina's texts and can't even summon the energy to text back as the cab pulls into traffic.

"Where to?" the cab driver asks.

"Just drive for a bit, please."

I look out at Chicago, a city I love and that frightens me because I never seem to feel quite safe in it. Everything looks the same. Chicago is still busy, and windy, electric, modern, wonderful and unsafe. It's the very same city I've lived in all my life.

The city didn't change. The one who changed was me.

Like a thousand women before me, I fell in love with the city's favorite bachelor billionaire player.

And now I will never be the same.

After what happened, he will never be mine, just like I always feared.

FOUR WEEKS + 1 HOUR

"I couldn't get a read on him. I just couldn't. I was too over-whelmed just by seeing him and having all these things to say and knowing that he must hate me and didn't really mean to talk to me at all." I glance away, inhaling.

"Rachel."

That seems to be all that Gina can say. She falls morgue-quiet after that.

A few minutes ago, I finally asked the cab driver to drop me off at a Starbucks simply because I didn't want to go home. Gina immediately caught up with me, and now we're at a table in the back, in our own little world.

"I am so sad, Gina." I hide my eyes behind one hand for a minute, my elbow propped on the table. "It's really over now."

"Fuck this." Gina purses her lips. She's scowling as usual. "Does he even care that you fell in love regardless of him being a player—a manwhore and whatnot?"

"Gina!" I scowl.

She scowls back.

I shouldn't even be talking to her about this. Gina warned me a thousand times that this would happen. She'd said *Don't get involved with him* until she tired of it. Because Saint has a record and I was on assignment. But could I have stopped myself from being swept away?

He's a cyclone and I walked straight into the eye of it when I agreed to write that exposé.

Falling hadn't been in the plans. Falling for a guy had never even been in my *life* plan. Gina and I were supposed to be single and happy forever—workaholics, best friends for life, and tight with our families. She'd gotten her heart broken before and she'd passed on all the tidbits to me so that I didn't have to go through that too. And like that I had protected myself. I was never as interested in men as I was in furthering my career. But Saint is not just any man. He didn't seduce me in just any way. And what we shared wasn't just . . . anything.

I'm a columnist and I should have a concise word to describe him, but I have nothing other than "Sin."

Exhilarating, addictive, he is a player who plays it right, a billionaire who is used to being asked for things from people—and in the end, I hate that he must have felt that I was just like everyone else in his life, wanting to get something from him.

No, Rachel, you're not like everyone else. *You're worse.*

He sleeps with one groupie for four nights, or four groupies for one. He gives them nothing of himself. Maybe he gives them a check for the charities they ask for, as I once heard one ask him, but this doesn't put a dent in his account. He lets them feed him grapes in his yacht, if they want to; he's too spoiled by women to stop them. But he doesn't give them another passing glance when they leave. But with you, Rachel? He let you *in*. He fed *you* a grape in his yacht. He came to your campout not because he likes sleeping outdoors but because he knew *you* would be there. He told you about *four,* his lucky number. The number that symbolizes him going above and beyond the norm. Oh god, I have never been so aware of how deep he'd let me in until I stood before him today, completely cast out of what had become my own personal paradise.

"I would've said so many things to him if his man hadn't been there discussing a position for me." I pull out the papers and pass them over. "I could hardly concentrate on this with Saint in the room. Even his man was affected."

She reads under her breath. "An offer of employment for Rachel Livingston . . ." She lowers the paper and stares at me with those sultry dark eyes that are now as puzzled as I feel.

"Interface is expanding into news," I explain.

She stares down at the papers. "If you don't want this, I do."

I kick her under the table. "Be serious."

"I need more sugar." She goes to the condiment table, returns, and settles back down with a little packet of sugar she adds to her coffee and stirs.

"What's a man like him, the CEO, doing in a meeting like that?" She frowns. "Saint is too smart, Rachel. He wanted to make sure you showed up. He fucking *wants* you there. He is offering health insurance for your next of kin. Your mom. Do you realize what this means for you on the work front?"

My mom is my weakness.

Yes, I do realize.

Saint is offering me . . . the world.

But a world without him is nothing now.

"Rachel, though *Edge* has been getting good press attention since . . ." She throws me an apologetic look because she knows I don't like remembering the *article,* then adds, "But how long will that attention last? *Edge* is still hanging by threads." She sips her coffee. "And Interface is *Interface*. It's not going anywhere but up. M4, Rachel, it's like . . . huge. None of us have ever dreamed of working there. It hires, like, geniuses from all over the country."

"I know," I whisper.

So why does Saint want *me* on board? He can get anyone he wants. In any capacity.

"I bet Wynn would say for you to take it. We need her advice; she's the only one in a relationship."

"Gina, I said *I love you* to a guy for the first time in my life. I would never, as long as I live, choose for him to be my *boss*." I add, pained, "And Saint doesn't get involved with his employees."

Her eyes cloud over with worry. "And you want him more than the job."

I'm so ashamed of saying yes, because I don't deserve it. Not even to want it. But I duck my head and nod.

I have a hole in me. So huge and empty, every pleasure in my life feels like nothing without him.

Gina rereads the letter, shakes her head, folds it, and hands it back to me. And all the while I'm still at M4. At the top floor, inside that marble, chrome, and glass office. And I can still smell him in my nose. My brain synapses won't quit firing off, replaying the scene in his office. Every word he said. Every word I had hoped he'd say that he did *not* say. Every shade of green that I've seen in his eyes lost to me—except for this new cold shade of green that I had never seen.

I remember his gaze on my profile as Merrick interviewed me. I remember his voice. I remember what it feels like to stand close to him.

I remember how he exhaled when I left, as if he'd just engaged in some sort of physical battle.

And how his eyes latched on to me after that. Roping me in.

As Gina and I walk back home, I am so grateful I didn't tell my mother I was seeing *him* today. She'd have raised her hopes on my behalf and I'd hate to dash them now. I tuck the papers back into my bag, and when we finally walk into our small but cozy two-bedroom apartment, I go to my room, shut the door, drop onto the bed and pull out the papers again.

It's just your regular offer. I scan every page now and it lists the benefits, a salary that I do not deserve and is usually what much more experienced, award-winning columnists make . . . but then I hit a spot that really affects me.

Saint's signature, on the bottom of the contract.

I hold my breath and stroke his signature a little bit. There's an energy on it, like a stamp, somehow making the document feel heavy.

Crawling under my bed, I pull out my shoebox where I keep little things I treasure. A gold R necklace my mother gave me. On impulse I put on the necklace to remind myself of who I am. Daughter, woman, girl, human. I shift some of the birthday cards from Wynn and Gina aside. And find a note. The note that was once attached to the most beautiful flower arrangement that arrived in my office.

I take the ivory-colored card and open it . . . and read.

It was the first time I saw his handwriting. He signed the message, *A FRIEND WHO THINKS OF YOU, M.*

Still dressed, I curl up on my bed and stare at it.

My friend.

No. My assignment, the story that I thought I'd wanted, the city's playboy who became my friend who became my lover who became my love.

Now he wants to be my boss, and I want him more than ever.

MY LIFE NOW

I'm lying in bed and he's dropping delicious, shivery kisses all along the back of my ear. I'm breathless as I absorb the feel of his tanned skin against mine, the strength of his muscles, the ripples of his abs against my tummy. Oh god. I can't take him. I want to eat him with kisses and I want him to eat me back, every inch of me, I don't even know where I want him to start.

He takes my hands and pins them to his shoulders, leaning over to buzz my mouth with his. "Open, Rachel," he murmurs, and his green eyes, his green eyes are looking at me in the dark.

"Are you real?" I breathe, my heart in my throat, my lungs working madly in my chest.

He's looking down at me so familiarly, I'm not sure if this is a dream or a memory as he drags his fingers up my arms, sinuously, and I close my eyes. Oh god, *Sin*. He feels so good. I murmur his name and shakily trail my hands up the hard planes of his chest. God, he feels so real. So excellently real. He feels just like he used to feel, moves like he used to move, kisses like he used to, takes control of me like he used to.

He pins me with his weight and I struggle to get closer, wiggling and arching and shivering, his long, strong body stretched out on top of mine.

I close my fingers around his shoulders like he seems to want me to do as he circles his hands around my waist now and continues to set slow, tingly kisses on my neck, and need slams into my midsection, my skin screaming while I burn. I want. Want his hands all over me, his touch covering me, head to toe. His mouth. Oh, please.

"Malcolm, please now, please now . . . inside . . . now," I hear myself beg.

He's not in any hurry. He never is. He curls my legs around his hips, kissing his way up to my mouth. It's been forever since I felt this, his lips at the corner of my mouth. I feel my eyes well with tears. Every inch of him is missed by every inch of me. One second I'm rocking my hips in silent plea, the next he's driving inside me.

It's the sound that wakes me. A soft mewling sound that I make. A sound of absolute pleasure, such absolute pleasure it borders on pain. I'm soaked in sweat when I bolt upright in my bed. I look around, shakily wiping the wetness on one side of my face, but no. He's not back in my bed. I'm still crying at night, my body's still aching for his at night.

I wrap my arms around my legs and put my cheek on my knee, exhaling as I try to push the part-dream, part-memory out of my mind. I go into the bathroom, splash my face, look into my eyes and I'm still the lost girl in the elevator. When did I become this girl? I'm not this girl, I think in frustration as I stamp out to my room.

I go back to bed and cover myself with the sheets all the way to my neck, rolling my cheek into the pillow and punching it as I stare unseeingly in the direction of my window. A stream of streetlight filters inside. If you listen hard enough, you can hear the sounds of the city outside. I wonder where he is right now.

You're fucking haunting me, Sin.

You're fucking haunting my every second.

I can't sleep, can't think of anything but the way I feel when I stand close to you. When you look at me. When we're in the same room.

The way you were in your office . . . I couldn't *read* you. I couldn't *read* you and it's killing me.

Turning on the light, I lose a battle I've been waging with myself for a whole month.

I go get my laptop and boot it up in the darkness, then I do something I haven't done in a while. Gina had forbidden me to. I had forbidden myself, for survival. And sanity. I haven't checked in so long it's not even coming up in my browser. But now I brave Saint's social media and brace myself for what I find as I skim through. I don't know what I'm looking for. Or maybe I do. I'm looking for anything, *anything* that links me to him.

Hey @MalcolmSaint I'm Leyla, Danis' friend ;)

@MalcolmSaint Hey bro meet us at Raze

@malcolmsaint is better off without that bitch who betrayed him

Marry me @malcolmsaint!

@Malcolmsaint I'll be your slut and I'll mud wrestle your lying
bitch ex to the death, if need be!

@MalcolmSaint are you going to forgive your girlfriend? PLS
forgive her, you look beautiful together!

Speaking of bitches @MalcolmSaint should know

@malcolmsaint please tell me you told your exgirlfriend to go
fuck herself! YOU DESERVE SO MUCH BETTER YOU DESERVE
A PRINCESS

Interface wall:
Bro! Call us when you're in town, there's someone we'd like
you to meet

And then, there's the picture of a woman blowing him a
kiss.

I scowl over her protruding nipples, clearly visible in her
wet designer top.

Then, I scroll over his tagged pictures and find one of him.
Him flipping off the reporter who asks him about my betrayal,
a pair of cool aviators shading his eyes, his jaw as tough as a
granite slab.

God help me. Now that I've started looking I can't seem to
stop. On a famous local vlog, I find this:

"Indeed there has been speculation on whether his
daredevil attitude for the past month has anything to do with
the recent breakup with journalist Rachel Livingston, what is
rumored to be his first relationship ever. Livingston, who had
been investigating Saint when they met, had a huge fallout
with the tycoon when her investigation leaked and her own
version published shortly after on *Edge*. Rumors of whether

M4 is integrating a news section into their Interface media
website were abuzz when Livingston was spotted back at
M4 . . ."

"In the meantime Saint himself has been skydiving, and,
according to a witness, taking over businesses at a speed that
has been alarming to the members of his board . . ."

And on Facebook:
#TBT ThrowbackThursday: remember this picture? We had
bets going on how long it'd last but nobody bet on it lasting
as long as it did! I know it seems she played you but we know
better than that, nobody plays as hard as you do—hope you
used her good!

I stare at my computer screen. I'm suddenly sick with dread
wondering what *he's* read too. Is this how he thinks of me? A
bitch? I'm a bitch and a slut, who "whored" myself into his bed
for information? I'm stunned to realize that even when I poured
my heart into my article—it was, like Helen says, a love letter
to him—the words I wrote didn't matter. My actions trumped
it all.

Saint values truth and loyalty.

I can't take it.

I open up an email and search through the several emails of
his I've got.

Even if it's suicidal.

Even if he's the most unobtainable thing in the world,
placed so far off, I'd need a satellite to hoist me up high enough
to snatch him. He's my own personal moon . . .

In End the Violence, I'm always waiting to see what I can do to help those who've been exposed to loss. I always seem to be waiting to see if my mom's health is stable. Waiting for the right story.

I don't want to wait anymore.

I don't want to wait for the story, wait for the right time, wait for the muse, wait to forget him, wait to be wanted by him, wait to see if time will be on my side and help me fix things with him.

With all the nerves in the world but a determination to match it, I select his M4 email. The early one we used to use when I started to interview him. I have no idea who will read this email, but I keep it business and type out a message, knowing that keeping it simple is the best chance I've got.

Mr. Saint,

I'm writing to let you know how much I appreciate your offer. I'd like to discuss it further with you. Would you please let me know if there's any convenient time I could stop by your office? I will adjust my schedule to yours.

Thank you,
Rachel

WORK & WRITING

I'm running on three hours of sleep, but I'm determined to make something good out of my day the next morning. I even smile at a few strangers as I get out of the cab, take the building elevators, and walk into *Edge*. I chitchat with a few colleagues as we get coffee, call my mother to say good morning, answer a few emails from my sources.

But there's that tiny little buzz still in my body.

I still stare at green eyes whenever I stare at . . . anything, really.

I see a full mouth.

A full mouth, smiling in the way he used to smile at me.

I exhale slowly, do my best to push the thought of yesterday aside, and stare at my computer screen.

My very blank, very white computer screen.

Keyboards are clacking, reporters talking over their cubicle walls. *Edge* has been doing a little better after my love letter to Saint. The job cuts have stopped, two new journalists have been hired, and although there are only a dozen of us, we still some-how manage to make noise. Oh boy, do we make noise. We're the specialists of making every event of the day seem more monumental than it is. It's our job to hunt for news, after all. Create stories.

Write something, Rachel.

Inhaling, I put my fingers on my keys and force myself to write one word. And one word becomes two and then, my fingers pause. I'm out of juice. Out of ideas. Empty.

I read what I wrote.

MALCOLM SAINT

It's the first time in my career I've hit a dry spell. All the love I had for telling stories—a love that was born when I was very young, piecing together stories about my mother—left the day one of those stories took something priceless away.

Something called . . .

MALCOLM SAINT.

I've been begging Helen to give me the good stuff. A good piece that could motivate me, make me realize the words I write can make a difference. But she's been stalling and popping out excuses by the dozen. She tells me that if I'm having trouble with the little pieces, then it's definitely not the moment for an-other big one.

Hitting the backspace, I watch the name disappear.

MALCOLM SAIN

MALCOLM SAI

MALCOLM SA

MALCOLM S

MALCOLM

Oh god.

I squeeze my eyes and erase the rest.

On impulse, I reach for my bag, slung on the back of my

chair, for the folded paper I carry inside. Taking it out, I unfold it and scan right to the bottom. To the very elaborate, male signature on it.

Malcolm KPL Saint.

The guy who sends my world into a tailspin. The sight of this signature on the page gives me all kinds of aches.

"Rachel!" Sandy calls from across the room. Tucking the paper back into my bag, I peer out of my cubicle and see that she's pointing into the glass wall separating Helen, my editor, from all of us.

"You're up!" she calls.

I grab my notes that I also emailed her recently, then go and stand by Helen's open door. She's on the phone, signals for me to wait.

"Oh, absolutely! Dinner it is. I'll bring my best game," she assures, then she waves me in as she hangs up, beaming.

Well. She's in a good mood today.

"Hey Helen," I say. "Did you look at the story options I sent?"

"Yes, and the answer is no." Her smile fades and she levels me a look. "You're not writing that." Sighing, she shuffles the papers on her desk. "Rachel, nobody wants to know about any *riot*." She says the word *riot* like one would say *excrement*. "You have a lively, energetic voice!" she goes on. "Use it to bring happiness, not focus on what's wrong in the world. Tell us what's *right*. What's the right thing to wear when dating a hot man? Use what happened with that hot ex of yours to teach girls how to date properly."

"I'M SINGLE, HELEN—*hello*? Nobody wants dating advice from someone who screwed her only chance at . . ." I trail off and rub my temples. "Helen, you know I'm having a little problem."

"That you can't write?"

I wince.

It hurts because for twenty-something years, writing was all I wanted to do.

"Go on." Helen points at the door. "Write me something on how to dress for the first date."

"Helen . . ." I take a few steps forward instead. "Helen, we discussed this before. Remember? How very much I want to write about things that are wrong in the world, in Chicago. I want to write about the underprivileged, the violence in the streets, and while you promised me opportunities, you have given me zero. In fact, lately, the Sharpest Edge column is all about being single and dating in the city. I have no boyfriend and no dating life. I'm not interested in the dating life, especially after what happened. I keep wondering if maybe you gave me a story that impassioned me again . . . I'd hit my stride. In fact, I'm sure I would," I plead.

"We can't always write about what we want, we must think of others, and your audience," she reminded me. "The loyal audience who's followed you throughout your career is interested in *dating advice* from you. You dated a very physical and renowned man; don't throw all that life experience away. Other opportunities will come, Rachel. We're barely catching our first breath of fresh air. And I need you on more stable ground before we shift your direction again."

"But weren't we all about taking risks now in order to take us somewhere?"

"Nope. The owners don't want more risks right now, while things are stabilizing. Now please. Can I get a break from this riot and safety talk for a few weeks? Can you do that for me?"

I force myself to nod, pursing my lips as I turn to leave. I try not to feel angry and frustrated, but when I come out and hear all the keyboards clacking and watch all my colleagues writing their stories, some with bored faces, some with happy or engrossed faces, I can't help but ache to write something that gets to me so much, you could see it on *my* face too.

"Hey. You, there. With the golden hair, gorgeous body, but absolutely gloomy face," Valentine calls from his cubicle as I walk by.

"Thanks," I say.

He motions me forward to his computer and I end up standing behind him and bending over to peer at his screen.

And there's Sin.

A video, which shows the power in even his smallest gestures. I'm melting when I hear him answer a question in some sort of interview about his opinion on the state of the oil prices. *Stupid,* stupid melting bones.

After we both watch for a moment, Valentine says, "Your ex."

He's not my ex, I think sadly, wishing that even for a blink I'd have had the courage to wear that title.

"He really knows how to fill up a room. He's keynote speaker this weekend at McCormick Place. I'm thinking of asking Helen to let me go. Unless you want to?" Val peers at me over his shoulder.

I shake my head, frustrated. Then shrug. Then nod. "I'd love to, but I couldn't."

Valentine's eyes cloud over at that; I'm sure it's because he remembers all the hate mail that came through the servers after Victoria's article. "You need to get out more. Want to come clubbing with me and my current this weekend?"

"I'm going to camp out this weekend. But proceed living dangerously for me. I'll find a way to bail you out of jail."

He laughs as I go back to my corner and settle down in my chair. I'm determined to work past this glitch. I want this to be an excellent dating piece, one that can help every girl like me meet and attract the guy she wants.

Inhaling, I pop open my browser and search the dating forums. I mean to find out the most major concerns girls have when going out on a first date, for starters, but before I know it, I'm opening another tab. Then a press conference link. Then I plug in my earphones and hike up the volume and stare at Saint on the video.

He's behind a podium erected outside. People are standing in the back—every chair is occupied. Most especially with businessmen. Though I spot a few fawning fangirls nearby too.

His hair moves a little with the wind. His voice comes through the speaker, low and deep. Even though he's talking through a computer and not talking directly to me, my skin prickles in response. Stupid, stupid skin.

When the camera zooms in, I look into his eyes as he connects with the audience, and feel an ache. The look in his eyes as he talks to all those strangers, so much more personal than the wariness in his eyes when he looked at me yesterday.

But I think of how his eyes would burn so hot when he peeled his shirt off my body that I'd be in cinders by the time I lay naked and waiting for him to touch me . . .

And the way his eyes would glimmer with teasing, boyish hope as he looked at me when he asked and asked, patiently and ruthlessly, for me to be his girlfriend.

I hate that I will never, ever be his "little one" again.

I play the email roulette all day . . . and there's nothing from him.

I end up with two sentences for my dating article. Valentine and Sandy are hitting a nearby sandwich place and as we cross the building's lobby, Valentine says, "Come with, Rachel."

"I think I'll just . . ." I shake my head. "I'm going to try to get some work done at home."

"Bullshit," he says as we hit the sidewalk.

Sandy stops him. "Let her go home, Val."

"I worry about this girl. She's been kind of blue lately."

"Don't worry about me, I'm perfect," I assure them as I flag a cab. "I'll see you two tomorrow."

FRIENDS

Valentine isn't the only one "concerned." So are my friends. And later that night, they insist on Girl Time.

Wynn was adamant we discuss this "job issue." I assume Gina's told her about the job offer on the table from Malcolm since nobody else knows about my other writing problem. Not even my friends. I just really dislike being the one knocked-out on the floor after life struck her out. I'm *trying* to get back to normal even though I don't know what normal is anymore.

But at least one of the fixtures in my life is drinks with Wynn and Gina during the week. We sit at a high table near the windows. It's comfortable.

Still, I've been refreshing my email like mad.

"I don't know why you thought he'd want to talk to you about what happened so soon, it's only been four weeks and what happened was kind of . . . well, it could take *years*," Wynn says.

"Wow, Wynn," I groan.

"Well, I'm being honest, Rachel!"

I toss back the rest of my cocktail. My mind flashes to his hand, reaching for my leg under the table . . .

Twinkling green eyes, teasing me until I can't bear it . . .

I love my friends; we've been together forever. They call my mom "Mom" and know everything about me, but now as Wynn asks me to relate the "job issue" and Gina tells her all about it, I keep draining my cocktail in silence, sadder than I'm letting on. My friends know everything about me, but at the same time, they don't know it all.

They don't know that as I sit here I remember all the ways he used to tease me about how I play it safe. He used to tease me to come out of my box, that he'd catch me. But would he catch me now?

"It doesn't matter why he took four weeks," I cut in when Wynn and Gina keep arguing over why he took so long to contact me. "I just want him to talk to me. I want to know if I hurt him so I can make it better. I want a chance to explain, apologize."

"You doubt you hurt him?" Wynn asks, aghast. "Emmett told me there's no way he'd give you the time of day right now if you weren't under his skin."

"Interesting," Gina says. Then, looking at me, "You're not the only one haunted by Saint, do you think that you're haunting him too?"

"I don't want us to be ghosts for each other. I want us to go back to the way we were when he . . . trusted me."

Wynn whistles admiringly. "You can get that man in bed, maybe he'll reluctantly love you, but you won't get his trust if his life depended on it now."

I wince at the thought of that. "True, trust is important to him; if I can't prove to him I'm trustworthy I'm doomed to be one of his four-night girls."

"Did you get the impression he'd give you another chance?" Wynn asks.

I stay quiet.

"Rachel?"

"No, Wynn. He doesn't want me anymore. But I need to apologize. I just . . ." I shake my head. "I just don't know what to do." I look at Wynn when my refill comes, frowning as I realize something. "So you and Emmett have been talking about it?"

"Um. Well, yes," she says uncomfortably. "Everybody's touched on it, you know? It was public."

I press on, "Did Emmett have any advice for me?"

Wynn shrugs. "He doesn't think a man like Saint would give you another chance. But then, he did offer you a job, so . . ."

"What does Emmett the *chef* know about a guy who literally owns Chicago?" Gina tells Wynn, rolling her eyes. "Plus Emmett's a guy. He's telling *you* this so that you, Wynn, don't turn out to be a reporter and reveal that he wears pink undies and shit."

"Gina." Wynn scowls.

Gina grins, then turns to me. "Tahoe says—"

"*Tahoe?*" Wynn and I say in unified shock.

"Tahoe ROTH?" Wynn asks. "The oil tycoon and Saint's *bestie?*"

"He's not Saint's *only* bestie, Callan Carmichael is too," Gina specifies, then she cuts me an apologetic look. "I'm sorry, Rache. I'm not supposed to talk to you about this. But he's concerned and so am I. And . . . well, from what Tahoe told me, Saint's pretty messed up. Colder than usual. Really withdrawn."

I sit here listening, aching.

"He loves Saint as much as I love you," Gina says, and when Wynn opens her mouth to ask about the obvious elephant in the room—her plus Tahoe—Gina holds up a hand to stop her. "I don't care for Tahoe, but he hasn't enjoyed your breakup any more than I enjoy watching you mope. He called me to ask what was up, 'cause of course Saint's not talking and he says he hasn't seen Saint like this since his mother died."

Knowing what I know—that his mother was the only one who probably genuinely cared for Malcolm while he was growing up, how he felt he'd failed her, how he'd failed *himself* in failing her, how he's been trying to fill up an empty hole ever since—Gina's words wreck me.

Wynn chides, "Stop talking to Tahoe, he's just using this as an excuse to have sex with you."

"I know, right?" Gina laughs.

"So? Are you going to let him?" Wynn asks, curious.

"No! He's gross. I mean, he's *hot*, but his attitude is gross."

I stare at my cocktail and wonder if I'm already getting drunk to the point where I'm getting emotional too easily.

I've cried so much I don't even have to try. The kind of crying where the tears just spill. With no warning. With no effort. They just come. I cry at the thought of never being with him again. And I cry because I know I hurt this beautiful, ambitious, intelligent, generous, caring man. I used to rest my cheek where I could hear his heart. Now it's locked behind iron doors and ten-foot walls that *I* put there.

"Rachel, men like Saint never commit. Not for the long term. But . . . he reached out to you. Offered you a job. If you reach back, maybe . . ." Gina trails off and sighs. "Hell, I don't know. I don't know how to help you, Rache."

"Saint is very physical. You know what would do you and

Saint a world of good? Tyrannosaurus sex: mean, violent, delicious, painful, and cathartic." Wynn adds, "That will lead you then to spooning. Emmett and I are still so new though, we can't even spoon. It's more like sporking."

"What the hell is that?" Gina asks us, frowning.

"When they're hard when they spoon you!" Wynn rolls her eyes. Then she looks at me and giggles. "Did he do that to you too?" she asks me.

"He used to . . . um, pull my ear." I tug one of my ears absently, helpless not to be drawn into my memories.

"Now that's because you have really small, cute ears. Emmett likes kissing my nose." Wynn crinkles hers for emphasis.

My heart has turned into an empty eggshell. It feels ready to crack as my fingers fly up to brush one corner of my mouth. "Saint used to give me these torturously slow ghost kisses . . ."

"Oh, you two!" Gina says in dismay. "You're making me want to barf."

Wynn laughs, but I fall quiet as the hurt and the regret and the heartache come back with a vengeance.

"Say, have you heard from Victoria?" Gina asks. "She lost her job after Saint canned her reveal article and all she does is tweet now and complain. She's just some Tweleb now, but I bet she buys likes for her tweets, 'cause who's even reading her?"

Then, alarmed by what she said, she adds, "BUT DON'T GO ON SOCIAL MEDIA. Nothing good can come out of that."

I purse my lips and don't tell them that I've already had a social-media fest recently and now I can't stop.

"I don't understand why he didn't can my article too. Why just hers?"

"Obviously he didn't care what they said about him." Wynn

shrugs. "Maybe that's why he only canned Victoria's, because she talked about *you*."

I play email roulette again several times, refreshing and refreshing, checking to be sure I have all the signal bars lit up.

"Rache, we worry, you and those sad panda eyes," Wynn says.

"I'm not a sad panda, come on."

"The only times you don't have the panda eyes is when you get the googly eyes from thinking of him."

"That, or the screen-saver face when she thinks of him," Wynn counters.

"Ha ha," I say, rolling my eyes and pushing my cocktail away. "It's just that I love him. I love him so much. It breaks me to think I hurt him. I'm so confused, I just don't know what to do."

They fall quiet, and I find myself back at M4.

Trapped again by forest-green eyes, cold as winter.

MESSAGE

I wake up in the middle of the night to hear the soft buzzing of my phone on my nightstand. Feeling for it in the dark, I tap it awake and my heart pumps when I see the message icon and then the name "Saint" on it.

Wings flap against the walls of my stomach.

Rachel,

Thursday at 2:15 works for me, I trust we can wrap this up before my 2:30.

M

Oh god, he answered me himself.

A part of me doesn't miss the time he's answering. It came in at 3:43 a.m.

Was he out?

Turning on my lamp, I lean back in bed and check Tahoe's Twitter because that man is a living newscast.

My man @malcolmsaint has a new babe crying for his attention

My heart stops in my chest. I feel like a horse just kicked me. *A new babe?*

I groan and bury my face in my pillow. Holy god. He's ruined me. He's ruined my sleep. He's ruined the word *dibs*. And elephants, and grapes, and men's white dress shirts—and suits. He's ruined me for other men. He's ruined sex with anyone else—something I don't even want to try—and he's even ruined sex with myself. I can't go back to sleep.

I reread the tweet—my stomach squeezing painfully—and I force myself to click the link once and for all. And then, I stare at a picture of a beautiful car with shiny wheels that looks like it could sprout wings and fly.

I smile to myself, exhaling in relief.

Tahoe goes on to say the "beauty" is a Pagani Huayra Gullwing. Pagani Huayra is an all-handmade, top-of-the-line luxury sports car, only six cars produced a year, worldwide. Worth close to $2 million, Saint's has a black interior with red stitching, and a shiny red outer color. By the revealing way in which the doors, the hood, and the trunk open, the car is a real-life equivalent of a Transformer—designed to showcase what lays within it by cracking open.

I'm not a car buff, but even to my untrained eye, it's exquisite.

Chosen with exquisite taste by a man who wants and appreciates the best.

I think of Malcolm and how he loves using his cars fast, and a pang of longing to be with him hits me in the chest. What I'd give to sit again in his passenger seat as he takes me on the ride of my life, driving those fast cars like a young billionaire with too much confidence and too much testosterone does. And me, just holding on to my heart while he steals it.

TRUTH

I'm early to *Edge* on Thursday. Using my First Date piece as a distraction, I avoid a group of gossiping coworkers as I go get coffee, then I settle down in my spot and get to work.

I review all my notes, specifically the notes on women's first date concerns. They range from *Should I let him kiss me on the first date if I'm interested in something long term?* to *What do I wear that will give out the right signals?*

Typing up a rough draft, I start saying definitely you want to wear something that will tell your guy, *I'm not a slut, but I'm good in bed.*

I follow that with tips about wearing something that hints at your curves but isn't completely skintight.

Then I continue forward with the next thing you want your outfit to say: *I'm a woman, not a girl.*

Something with a little cleavage, a little waist, I type.

If you like this guy, you want him to want you as much as you want him. So your outfit should hopefully say, *Hey, I'm cov-*

ered up a little more than I'd like, but wouldn't you like to know what I'm wearing underneath?

On that, I elaborate on the psychological studies proving the less revealed, the more a man wonders.

I type out two pages and edit for the next hour, hardly noticing the newsroom is even noisier than usual today. By the time I'm ready to go home at noon, Valentine drops a copy of the *Chicago Tribune* on my desk.

"Read it," he says.

It's dated for today, but it looks so read already, the pages are soft as tissue.

LINTON CORPORATION INTERESTED IN ACQUIRING A NEW *EDGE*

Speculation abounds that the newly minted Linton Corporation has been actively considering the possible acquisition of a small local magazine, *Edge*. Linton Corporation's director of acquisitions, Carl Braunsfeld, comments that *Edge*, mostly known for its fashion and culture pieces, has gotten quite a bit of press after renowned Chicago darling Malcolm Saint's first ever-known girlfriend was caught investigating him for an exposé. The young director said, "We're in the process of considering many investments, but there are no firm details on any *particular* directions we might go, yet . . ."

Ohgod.

I squeeze my eyes shut and loathe my stupid exposé with a passion now.

"Is there truth to this?"

"Helen knows nothing about it." He shrugs. "Hell, I kinda wish it were. Or not."

I frown, thoughtful as I read the article again and wonder

if Saint knows this Carl Braunsfeld. I memorize the name before Valentine carries it over to the colleague in the next cubicle, then I gather my stuff and head home to change.

After all morning writing about First Dates, I'm buzzing as though I'm going on one now. And wouldn't that be a dream? A fresh start with my guy?

Look pretty, Livingston!

I settle on a loose silk blouse with a V-neck, paired with a knee-length, high-waisted black skirt that hugs my waist rather nicely and emphasizes my slight, but pretty, top and bottom curves. I add a pair of tan pumps that blend with my legs and make them look longer, then a small, delicate necklace with an R that sits right where my pulse flutters. I add an ankle bracelet just to look sophisticated and female and young, then I add a layer of coral lipstick on my lips.

I've looked far more seductive for Saint, true.

But I'm going to M4 and I can't be looking like a club kitten. What I have to say is serious and I need him to take me seriously today.

Running my comb over my hair one more time, I make sure that my shirt is nicely tucked, my bra blending with my skin and not see-through, and once I am happy with the way I look, I grab my bag, make sure I have the contract pages inside, and head out.

I ride the cab in silence. This thrill of exhilaration doesn't lie. I'm excited to see him, nervous. Afraid.

Months ago, the first time I set foot in his building, I arrived at M4 thinking it would be the story of my life. This isn't just a story now; this *is* my life.

M4 is as shiny and imposing as ever as I get out of the cab and stare at the building. I can't even see the top from where I stand. I've never in my life felt so little. "Oh god," I breathe as I smoothe my hands down my skirt.

I check my phone for the time—and it's 2:08, so I'm officially seven minutes early for my appointment.

I start forward when I notice the gleaming silver BUG 3 just up ahead, and a man emerging from the driver's seat.

There's a sudden stutter in my heart. My body temperature hikes. I watch the decadent powerhouse that is Saint toss the keys over the car top to the driver waiting on standby. As he pulls his jacket out of the backseat and straightens to shrug it on, his hair is ruffled by the breeze.

Holding my breath, I watch him storm into the building. And still, for long seconds afterward, I stand here. Staring at the spot where he was. I decide to give myself half a minute between us, then I inhale and follow him into the building.

"Hi, Rachel Livingston for Malcolm Saint," I say at reception, my eyes heading to the elevators.

Oh, fuck. He's still there.

This isn't how I imagined starting the meeting.

But when the blonde behind the desk verifies my name and efficiently points me to the glass executive elevator bank, I realize I can't just stand here before her, waiting for him to go up.

Stomach knots.

Saint is standing there like an energy tower, as dark as the marble around him is light. He's checking his phone as he waits for the elevator to arrive. Two men stand behind him—silent. Respectful. Kind of staring at the back of his head in awe.

I approach nervously and remain a few feet away too.

Once the elevator opens and the people shuffle out, many murmur their greetings to him, "Mr. Saint," as he boards.

The men follow. I keep my eyes downcast as I board too and go into the first corner to the right.

Saint is standing right in the middle, taking up triple the space his body really occupies.

"Mr. Saint"—one of the men breaks the silence—"I'd just like to say, it's an honor to be working with you. I'm Archie Weinstein, one of your new budget analysts—"

"Don't mention it, it's a pleasure to have you." I hear Saint's voice.

I'm pretty sure Saint shakes his hand. And now I'm pretty sure he's looking at me. I swear he is. I can feel his gaze on the back of my head. I could hear it in his voice in the way he answered the man. The men disembark on the nineteenth floor. Just thirty-nine more to go.

Oh fuck, I wasn't prepared to ride an elevator with him.

The moment the doors close, there's a crackle in the air.

"I'm expecting you'll join M4 too."

I close my eyes. I can't believe how his presence stirs me. How, even while merely feeling him watch me, his looks still burn me. And how—when he speaks—his voice still ripples through me. I force myself to turn halfway around. He's looking at me with those green eyes of his. His gaze is so endless. And looking at me as if he's trying to find some sort of answer written on my face.

I flush. As *usual.* "I . . ." Clear my throat. "It's a very generous offer but—"

Ding!

He signals for me to go out, and I force my legs to work, and when he comes out himself, I almost stumble over myself to catch up with his long strides.

His assistants get flustered as they receive him. Catherine, his head assistant, leads them all with a string of messages and a pack of Post-its.

"Mr. Saint, India and UK called," Catherine murmurs only for his ears as she comes around the desk, then she mentions a long, long list of other callers and rescheduled meetings and people asking for appointments with him.

"Update on the Interface board meeting?" he asks as he shuffles through the notes she hands out.

"Report's on your desk, sir."

"Good."

He finishes scanning the notes, and when I catch one of his assistants blatantly checking me out in these clothes, I start rethinking everything.

Oh god. I want to turn around, go back down to the lobby, go home, and change.

Instead I stand here as, now, two of his assistants eye me. Thoroughly. Head to toe.

I feel a touch of nerves when he gives one last command to Catherine and then he opens the door to his spacious office and a muscle flexes in the back of his jaw before he speaks to me. "Come in, Rachel."

If I thought I could keep my shit together when I saw him today, I was so very, very wrong. All my systems are faltering as I walk forward. His eyes are on me. Straight on me, and oh so green.

"Um, thank you."

Survival instincts beg me not to touch his body as I pass through.

He secludes us inside and we head to his desk. He signals to the two chairs across from his desk. "Take your pick."

I waver between both options, tense.

He sounds like such a . . . *businessman*.

I choose the chair on the right, closest to where his own is aimed; I watch as he removes his jacket and drapes it over the back of his chair. I feel a rather big kick in my heart at the sight of that torso—which I know is hard and cut and beautiful—shrouded in his crisp white shirt.

He takes his seat and leans back as the stock tickers continue shifting and Chicago surrounds us through the windows.

Saint's office is huge, but the center of its axis is where *he* is. I tell myself that the man he was with me is still there, under the intimidating businessman and under those cool green eyes. But he looks so much like the ruthless, ambitious Malcolm Saint right now. How can a girl find her courage like this?

"Anything to drink, Mr. Saint? Miss Livingston?" Catherine asks, coming through the door.

He waits for me to answer. I shake my head, and he adds without looking at her, "I'm set. Hold all calls."

She leaves, but the static between Saint and me remains.

And where do I even start to apologize?

"How are you?" he asks.

I start when he speaks. It's only three words and such a normal question. But that he cares to ask makes the arteries in my heart tie around like a pretzel.

"I'm okay. I'm trying to distract myself with work and my friends."

"Distract yourself from what?"

"Well," I shrug. "You know."

Silence.

"What about you? How are you?"

"Good. Staying busy too."

"Busy getting the moon?" My lips quirk.

His lips quirk back. "Always."

My smile quickly fades because I don't like him across a desk. I don't like him to look at me as if he's seeing me for the first time, because he's seen me so many others. The only guy who truly sees me when he stares.

"Are you still doing those campouts?" he asks me, leaning back in his chair.

"Of course. I take everything but the tent."

He laughs softly. "You can pretend you didn't like the tent, but it shielded you from the elements."

I remember.

I remember that there was no rain or earth or wind, only him.

Suddenly, the now-familiar ache in my chest branches out from my heart, reaching all my extremities.

"You must hate me. Why do you want me here, really?"

"That you're good isn't enough?"

I blush. "I'm not that good." I tuck a strand of hair behind my ear. "Saint . . ." I peer up at him. "Why are you still protecting me from . . . the elements?" *Or your enemies?*

He leans forward, his expression confused again. "Because I need to. See, I really need to. And you need to let me, Rachel."

"I can't," I choke out.

"Yes, you can."

I want to tell him that I would say yes to anything, anything he asked, except *this*.

I cross my legs—inhaling, slowly—and try to look proper and calm when I finally speak. "I can't take the job. It's a dream job, with a dream salary, except that . . . I don't want to work for you."

"And I want you to work for me. Very much," he says quietly.

God, this man. He's a Bermuda Triangle of my life and I got lost there, never to be found. Why is he doing this to me?

"I don't want the job," I repeat, laughing lightly over his

stubbornness. Then I add, a pleading whisper, "I want you, Malcolm. Just you. Like before."

The calm in his eyes fades, replaced by something wild and stormy that makes me feel as if the entire room is shuddering.

"When we talked for the last time on the phone and I told you how I felt about you . . ." I start.

I'm knotted up inside as I force myself to look into those eyes, eyes that are carving into me with anger now.

"I wanted to tell you, but I never got the chance before you returned. You see, I have ambitions too. I wanted . . . well, *want* to give my mom a bit of financial security so she can focus on painting and won't have to be stuck at a job she doesn't love. She's on Medicaid but it's not that reliable. I guess . . . Saint, I just wanted to feel secure knowing I could take care of her. I wanted to save my magazine because it's all I've known. I wanted a story but after I started, I just wanted to spend more time with you."

My heart is pounding so hard in my ears, I can hardly hear my own words.

"When I took the assignment, I never imagined that you'd be the way you are, Malcolm." I shake my head a little, full of shame. "I was supposed to find out why you had an affinity . . . to number four. And it was supposed to be an article, four things about you . . ."

My eyes well with unshed tears.

"How to stop at four? You know? I never expected . . . I never expected you to be the way you are . . ."

The heat is stealing into my face and I can't bear having his eyes on me. It makes me anxious that I can't read them so I stare at his throat, at his beautiful, perfect tie.

"I wasn't going to write the article anymore. I told my boss

I wouldn't, except Victoria—I told you about her. Remember? She's . . . she's the one who always seems to do better than me. She released her article and I was desperate for you to hear my side."

I inhale shakily, my eyes still on fire.

"I can't bear to think what you think of me but I need you to please believe me when I say not one moment with you was a lie. Not one."

With a slow, deliberate move that makes me breathless, he stands from his chair and walks to the window, giving me his back.

Oh god, what must he think of me! How he must hate me. Think I used him. Lied to him.

I stand and take a few steps but I stop when I hear him take four deep breaths, and just like that, I crumble, and a tear rolls down my cheek.

"Malcolm, I am *so* sorry," I say.

I quickly wipe the tear away before he can see it. He's still facing the window as he mutters *fuck me* under his breath and shoves his hands into his pants pockets, his anger like an incoming hurricane in the room. It seems to be costing him everything to keep that simmering energy of his on a leash. I have never seen him like this. Not ever. He's under control, but there's a storm inside him and I can *feel* it.

Finally, he speaks, and his voice is so low and controlled that I'm afraid of the force of the anger it conceals. "You could've talked to me. When you kissed me. When you told me about Victoria. When you needed my comfort, Rachel. When your neighbor died. When you couldn't see eye to eye with your family and friends. You came to me when you needed me. You came to me when *I* needed you . . . you could have talked to fucking me, trusted fucking *me*." He turns and leaves me breathless when I feel the full force of his flashing green eyes on me. "I could've made this go away so fast." He snaps his finger. "Like *that*. With one call."

"I was afraid of losing you if you knew!"

A flash of bleak disappointment crosses his face, and as he stares me down, his green eyes could melt steel. "So you kept on lying instead."

I wince and stare at his throat.

An eternity passes.

"There's nothing more here for you, Rachel. Except a job. Take it." He goes back to his chair and drops into his seat.

I can hardly speak. "There's you here. Don't shut me out because I made a mistake."

As I walk back, it's the first time I feel his eyes run over me, evaluating what I'm wearing. They were supposed to make me feel powerful and good, these clothes, and I feel tender and naked and fake. So fake. Thinking any clothes would make him see me differently. Thinking something so superficial could hide the real me—the flawed me.

I'm blushing when I sit again, and Saint doesn't say anything at all. He's stroking his thumb slowly over his lower lip, the only part of his body moving now.

"Consider my job offer," he says.

I shake my head. "I don't want you as my boss."

"I'm a fair boss, Rachel."

"I don't want you as a boss."

I wait a moment. His gaze smolders with frustration.

"You shouldn't want me here," I blurt out. "I am not a good journalist, Malcolm. If you want to know the truth, I lost the heart for it. I'm worthless to you. I'm not someone you will probably ever trust again."

He cocks his head with a slight frown, as if curious over this development. "Take a week to think this through. In fact, take two." He watches me as I struggle for words.

"I don't want to hold you up—"

"You're not."

The way he studies my features causes a thousand tiny pin-pricks of awareness inside of me. I know this stare. It's a stare that makes my heart race because I can tell he's trying to get a read on me.

"What's so wrong about working with me?" He narrows his eyes.

I shake my head with a soft laugh. Would I even know where to begin?

I think of his assistants, half in love with him or worse. I don't want this to be me. I don't want to be forty, in love with a man I can never have. At least when I had my career goals, ambitious as they were, I always imagined I'd be able to attain them someday. But him? He's already as unreachable to me as all of the sixty-seven Jupiter moons.

"Even if I dared leave *Edge*, which I won't, but even if I did, I'd never accept a job I was unsure I could even do."

"You can do it," he says, firm and calm.

"I'm telling you, I can't." I laugh a little and lower my face.

When he speaks, his voice is soberly low. "I'll stop asking you to work for me when you prove to me you can't write any-more."

"How am I supposed to do that? Write you something bad?" I scowl in confusion.

He seems to ponder that for a moment. "Write one of my speeches. Write the one for tomorrow. You're familiar with Interface, its business model, objectives, cultural footprint."

I narrow my eyes.

"If it's as bad as you say, I'll back off," he adds with the kind of lazy indulgence only people who hold all the cards emit.

He sits behind his desk with a familiar little twinkle in his eye, so powerful and tanned and dark-haired and green-eyed and toe-curlingly masculine, challenging me to rise to his bait. The temptation is so strong, I have to fight it.

"I can make it bad enough you'll stop asking me to work for you."

"But you won't." His eyes gleam, and his lips form a smile that causes all kinds of visceral tugs inside me. "I know you won't."

I sit here, struggling.

I want to see him. I want to have an excuse to see him.

"This wouldn't mean I'm working for you. You won't pay me for this. It's just so you can see that writing is . . . hard. I'm not who you need at M4, Malcolm."

I'm feeling tingles in my stomach from the smile he wears. "I'll be the judge of that."

"When do you need it by?"

"Tomorrow morning."

"And the event is at noon?"

He nods slowly, eyes glimmering in challenge. "Get it to me by ten."

"Mr. Saint, your two thirty is here," a female voice says from the door.

I come to my feet when Malcolm uncoils from his seat. He eases his arms into his crisp black jacket. "Ask Catherine for the guidelines the other speechwriters were working with." He buttons up, and pauses. "I'll expect to see your email."

"Malcolm," I start, but then stop. After a moment, I whisper, surprising myself, "You will."

As I watch him head to the door, adrenaline courses through me, every part of me shaking except my determination.

When I get back to *Edge*, I walk to my seat like a horse with blinders, avoiding everyone. I print out some stuff for the speech and then head home. I haven't told Gina I met with him, or my mom, or Wynn, or Helen. He's my secret, somehow, too precious for me to share, my hope too raw and too tiny to survive the questioning of anyone else.

I don't want to hear if what I'm doing is dangerous. Wrong. Or right. I'm doing it because I have to—I *need* to—because he asked me to, and this is the only way I can be close to him for now. *Yes,* I could accept his job offer and be closer for longer—but I'd define myself as his employee for possibly forever. That's not what I want to be to him.

I stare at my laptop once I get home. Only seconds after I boot it up, a familiar dread starts creeping into me, as it does when I sit to write now.

But I think of Interface. Malcolm. How relentless he is, how ruthless, how innovative, and he's right.

My pride won't let me write something I don't like. I want to dazzle him. I want him to read it and, even if he hates me, I want him to feel awe or admiration for my words. I want to talk to him through the simple act of writing his speech and if he trusted me with this little thing—I don't want to fail him.

Before I start writing, I call my mother to say hi, check up on her. Then I tell Gina, "I'm going to write!" so she doesn't just burst into my bedroom. Then I turn off my cell phone, close my browser, and look at my Word file as I put in the first word: *Interface . . .*

SPEECH

After a night spent writing draft after draft after draft, I'm at *Edge* early on Friday, quickly sipping an orange juice as I boot up my computer, then diving straight in to edit the best of what I wrote.

Using the brief guidelines Catherine gave me, I also applied what I've learned about Interface and double-checked my facts, then I marked those facts in bold so he pays extra care to double-check those.

My body's in knots by the time everyone arrives at the office around nine, and I open an email, search his name, and attach the file.

To: Malcolm Saint
From: Rachel Livingston
Subject: Your speech

Here it is. I promised you it would be bad, but please know that I can't bear for it to be—I hope, actually, that it's good.

Good luck.

I would have loved to be there.

Rachel

I don't expect a reply, but I get one nonetheless.

To: Rachel Livingston
From: Malcolm Saint
Subject: Re: Your speech

Your name's up front, you're welcome to come.

I'm halfway through reading his email and the butterflies are already flapping against the walls of my stomach.

He just *invited* me to his speech.

I exhale and try to calm myself, but god, it's so hard to. I've got to turn in my article for the Sharpest Edge column and, suddenly riding on the momentum of Saint's speech, I finally churn out the piece on what to wear on the first date. I think of the ways his eyes change and I write down things I've secretly believed since I met him. That men like women to look feminine, so wearing a soft color, or a soft fabric, or a soft wave to our hair, really makes a nice contrast to all that hardness of a man. Soft lipstick might work better for long-term interest rather than bold colors, which speak mostly about sex.

Once I finish the article, I go toward Helen's office with my printout, when Valentine swings his chair around to stop me.

"*Yo!* Captain!" he calls, saluting me like an army general.

He's really got his salutes mixed up, among other things: he's wearing a yellow vest today with a purple shirt beneath.

"Helen's having a ball with you. She's basically selling the idea to young girls that *you* know what it takes to snag the hottest bachelor in town."

I frown at that, because it's definitely what Helen is doing and so far off the mark, it's absolute bullshit. "That must be why she keeps looking at me like I'm the goose that lays golden eggs," I say, just to make light of it.

But maybe . . . no, *probably* . . . it's why she's been so forgiving about my "writing issue."

Val smirks. "Well, you're the goose with the eggs Saint could have fertilized."

I'm too hyped about Sin's message and enjoying my writing high too much to let Valentine's jibe have any effect.

I merely roll my eyes and ask, "Are you going to McCormick?"

"Nope, she wants me to revise all this bullshit." He signals to his screen, then winks. "But the truth is, she needs to bully me to feel alive."

"I'm glad you seem to enjoy it." I head to Helen's office with my printout even though I've already emailed the piece.

I set it on her desk, and when she directs her attention to me, I say flat out, "Saint's speaking at McCormick Place about Interface, and he got me a place in the reporting pool. You mind if I go, even if it's just to observe?"

Helen looks at me levelly. "I expected you'd ask me after yellow-vest did. Yes," she agrees. "But not as a dormouse. Ask a question! Let people know we're covering."

Seeing my hesitation, she quickly adds, "Getting out there and acting normal is the only chance you've got of things actually going *back* to normal." A pause; a frown. "What? You're not sure now?"

No, I'm not sure. I'm not sure about anything these days.

Your name's up front.

"Come on, go! Hurry out there and make some inquiries that make us sound smart!" Helen says. "Someone who will make up for Val's clothing."

Bracing myself for the worst but hoping for the best, I nod and head back to my seat. Helen's right, I need to go on as normal.

I care about him more than what anyone can say about me. I won't pass on a chance to see him.

Five minutes before the conference begins, I pay my driver and ease out of the cab. Keeping my hair out of the wind, I hurry into one of the four main buildings of McCormick Place.

This is the grandest convention center in the country, so massive that it takes several minutes to wind through the walkways and halls to reach the auditorium where Saint is keynote speaker.

The press is already in position near dozens of steel folding chairs: neighborhood papers, community radio stations, five local news teams. It's a big deal, apparently. Hundreds of professionals fill up the room, sharp and prepared with cameras, notepads, microphones.

As I wait in line at reception and try to discreetly comb my hair with my fingers, a small group of new arrivals near the entrance spots me. I'm given a thorough examination and then, the whispers start.

Fuuuck me.

Red down to my toes, I force myself to stand in line until I reach the woman with the clipboard. "Hi, Rachel Livingston with *Edge*, here for Malcolm Saint."

"Honey, they're all here for him," she mumbles without looking up. She locates my name on her page and I silently thank Saint's press coordinator for the favor—or Saint himself.

I notice how reluctantly the woman locates the badge, until she finally hands it to me. I fake confidence as I take the badge with my name and head inside.

There's a crowd gathered already, applauding when a bald presenter in a gray suit takes the stage. "Welcome," he says into a microphone.

Though I try to keep my attention on the stage as I search for a seat, there's no missing the stares coming my way.

I feel an uncomfortable squeeze in my stomach when I think of Victoria and wonder what she's doing, if she's covering for that stupid magazine whose blog she exposed me in. She must be thirsting for my blood after Malcolm killed her article.

I don't see Victoria here, thank god. But people see me. And suddenly, I. Don't. Care. What they say.

I'm impassioned here. He impassions me. Just thinking of watching him speak today lights up my writing fire, so I should let him light me up and let me burn.

I stand before an empty chair at a back row, next to a long aisle.

That's when a commotion from the entrance draws my eye, and the sight of Saint walking inside hits me with a jolt of feminine awareness as he takes the room with a trail of businessmen behind him. Malcolm owns every place he's in, every floor he steps on. More virile than any man I have ever had the pleasure of staring upon, he uses that eat-you-up stride as he heads to the front of the room.

It's impossible, but I swear even the air shifts—dynamically, energetically—with him in the room.

The presenter speaks his name into the microphone, and then, behind the wooden podium, stands Malcolm freaking perfection Saint.

"As many of you know, since inception, M4 has experienced record-breaking growth across all platforms . . . but there's been an area among the M4 holdings that has captured my attention the most. For over the past year, a team of more than four thousand specialists and I have been laboring to bring to you Interface, which, in its short time online, has beaten every social-media site in the areas of engagement and user signup," he says, and then he eyes the audience with a pause.

He's so much larger than life that my eyes are wide as I absorb the full impact of him up there—owning the room. Owning everyone in it. Especially me.

But . . .

He's not reading my speech. I'm a little bit confused, then I realize—I really did lose it. I've lost my spark, I've lost it all. He believed I could write well, maybe. Enough to want me to work at his company. He gave me a chance, and now he's realized I'm no good. He won't want me, even for a job. He won't want me at all.

I'm stressing so much, I regret that I miss some parts of his speech, until the room bursts into applause.

I swallow. Look up at him.

I feel his presence in the knees. He smiles, waits for one of the reporters to ask him a question, his eye contact direct.

Noticing the enraptured looks of my companions, I can already predict the words used to describe his presentation and him: *Mesmerizing. Concise and sharp.*

Abraham Lincoln's Gettysburg Address was only 270 words long. Likewise, Saint seems to embrace brevity and run with it.

As he starts to answer questions, I also notice that most everyone is standing, even when they have chairs, a phenomenon not many people accomplish.

God, what would it be like to say yes—yes—and work for

him? See him at work every day, taking on the world, chasing and attaining his every ambition?

No, I could never do this.

NEVER work for a man who's seen me naked.

It has to be a rule.

But it would also be complete and utter torture to never see him again . . .

A reporter from *Buzz* asks a multipart question, and after Saint lists down the answers and the man continues looking eager for more, Saint adds, "Now, what part of your question did I not answer?" His voice is low and deeply solid, the crowd hushes as though affected by its timbre.

"Saint! Saint! They say you couldn't fit all your followers on your Facebook page and before it exploded, had to create your own Interface to fit them all."

"If I'd created Interface for myself, I would've called it My-Face."

Laughter.

He calls on someone else.

"Speaking of you, Saint, is it true you have as many men followers as you do women?"

"I haven't been following the statistics." He smiles. "But it *is* true the world is made of both."

My stomach, which had been all gnarled up, seems to like that smile.

"Your M4 conglomerate is the most powerful corporation in the state. Is it true a lot of your employees aren't college graduates?"

He keeps eye contact with the silver-haired, bearded reporter who asked, and succinctly answers, "We hire people who want to make things different. We encourage education and partner with educators across the country, but we prize free thinkers and people who can get things *done* above all else."

He scans the crowd then, and suddenly a shockingly brilliant pair of green eyes lands on me. I had forgotten I'd been standing there with my arm raised. He calls on me.

"Rachel Livingston from *Edge*," I hastily identify myself, as is customary, but when I hear gasps in the audience—*fuck*—I just forget what I was going to say.

Scrambling, I blurt out the second question that comes to mind, bypassing the real one I want to ask: *Why did you not read my speech?* "Interface, as a word, is a shared boundary across which two separate components of a computer system exchange information. In choosing this name, did you mean to make fun of how dispassionate relationships can become through online communication, the loss of personal contact?"

A hush spreads.

The room blurs as he holds my stare from the podium; everything blurs but the chiseled perfection of Saint's masculine face and the shockingly personal look in his gaze.

"No, I'm not poking fun at relationships, especially since I admire anyone who can endure one." He looks directly at me with a challenge in his eyes.

When finally some people laugh, a trickle of warm heat burns in the center of my tummy, spreading down my thighs.

What does that mean?

Dibs, I remember.

It had annoyed and confused me at the time. Now, I would give a billion times more than any other woman in the world for him to call dibs on me.

He scans the audience afterward and I don't remember being this shaken since the first live press conference I attended as a journalist.

The answers continue, along with the questions, and then Saint thanks the crowd. Their applause is enormous as he leaves the stage, and the emptiness seems greater after his commanding presence. Reporters rush to edit their videos and write their stories.

I'm lingering in the room, I don't know *why* exactly, when Catherine approaches me in her usual brisk, professional way. "He wants to see you. Follow me to the greenroom."

I follow her to the back of a hall, then hear her announce me.

When she waves me in, I step inside and it's full of beautiful furniture, new Persian rugs, technology, and classical background music, a huge fruit basket and chilled wine, as if only the best will do for this man, even if he's here for only a few minutes.

I look at him. Glorious in the room. Sucking the space around him, like a beautiful, commanding, energetic black hole. Sucking me so that all I know right this second is *him*.

He looks at me. "I see you made it."

His voice rumbles through me.

"Yes." My lips tug upward and I laugh a little. "Wonderful speech," I mumble. "Are you taking one-on-ones?"

"No. I leave for a meeting in . . ." He checks his watch, then raises his brow as if the time flew. "Five."

His assistant hands over a couple of note cards; his dark head bends downward as he quickly skims them. She leaves after a questioning look in my direction, and I take the moment he's distracted to regroup.

I'm embarrassed to look at him. Amazing how we've spent so much time together, shared so many things, and he still manages to make me feel more girly than anything because he's so masculine. And more shy than anything because he's so confident. And also because I like him and care about his opinion so much.

Which is why admitting the following hurts: "You didn't read my speech."

He lifts his head at that. "I didn't read your speech," he agrees, leaving me no choice but to laugh a little joylessly.

"I'm not surprised. I *told* you I've been struggling. Would you give me pointers as to what would've made it work for you? Was it too impersonal or too fact-oriented . . . ?"

He sets the note cards aside, frowning a little, his eyes a little bit amused. "Nothing like that," he assures soberly. "It was merely too unique. It had your stamp all over it." He looks at me with smoldering, intense eyes again, eyes that hold me motionless. "You couldn't write for anyone else. You're too unique to adopt someone else's point of view; you're too impassioned about yours. You should be writing about exactly and precisely what interests you, Rachel. That is what I'm offering you at M4."

I'm stunned by the unexpected praise. He speaks honestly. In fact, I detect no flattery in his words or in his gaze. Only the truth as he sees it with those eyes that have seen more than they should by his age. Eyes that have seen everything and that somehow I can feel right now, seeing into *me*.

"I want to write, but . . . it's the first thing I've written easily in weeks," I admit.

Other than Helen, I haven't admitted my block to anyone but him.

"It was good."

Pride fills me at his words, a pride I haven't felt for my work in a long time.

I'm almost weak with it when Saint steps forward and lifts his arm as if he's about to touch my face.

I wait for the touch, my body tightening.

He stops himself, laughs mockingly under his breath, and then he stops laughing, admitting with sober intensity, "You can write. You won't ever lose that."

Yes I did, I lost it when I lost you.

I remain looking up at him, and then my eyes flick down at his hand as he lowers it to his side, his fingers—how they curl into his palm. His scent is filling my lungs and I don't want to expel a breath just so I don't lose that decadent smell. His hand is at his side, but how is it possible to feel his fingers in places they once touched? I'm crying out for them in every cell.

"You did it on purpose, didn't you?" I ask. "To get me writing? You didn't need a speech. You just wanted me to realize I could work past my block."

I'm almost weak when a smile touches his eyes so lightly, it's barely there. "You think so."

"I know so, Saint." Then, looking into his eyes, eyes that watch me as if he knows what I'm thinking, I force out a little, "Thank you." When he nods, I add, "I'd hoped not to embarrass myself completely in front of you. I'm glad you at least . . . liked what I sent."

"Even if this means I still want you at M4?" he asks, a soft challenge.

I feel excitement surge through me. "You do?" I shake my head. "I couldn't."

"The offer's still open," he insists. Suddenly, unexpectedly, he looks at my lips—really stares at them—for three long heartbeats. *Thud, thud, thud.*

"Thank you." I clear my throat. "Until when is it open?"

"Until you say yes."

He walks away, leaving me aching, hopeful, happy, hurting, all at once.

He stops by the door, and looks at me again.

Making love was never as simple as him and me having sex.

Saint made love to me with his smile. There's a smile in his eyes now.

"Are you available Saturday?" he asks.

I'm . . . hallucinating. I'm making things up, I'm this desperate.

"What do you mean?" I croak.

"There's an all-day business event. I'd like to introduce you to some of my Interface crew."

I don't hesitate, not even a little. "I'm available."

He grabs the doorknob. "Next Saturday. Someone will pick you up at noon."

It's late when I get home to find Wynn and Gina watching a movie in the living room. "Hey," I say as I go to the kitchen and pour myself a glass of water.

I plop down to watch some TV with them, replaying what he told me about my writing today.

"What did you do all day? Why are you so quiet?" Wynn asks.

I grin a little and shrug.

I used to tell them everything about Saint. They were my accomplices. My sidekicks as I went underground to infiltrate the player's lair.

Now Saint is my treasure. He's so precious and I have so little of him, is it wrong I want to keep him to myself?

"Rachel! Share! All right, she's gone mad!" Gina exaggeratedly declares to Wynn. "We need to get this girl some serious help."

I grin as they both shake me.

"You dicks, let go!" I squirm to get free. "I saw *him* at McCormick Place today. He was keynote speaker at some social-media thing." I keep replaying the looks we shared down to the very end. I snuggle my head into the back of the couch and sigh happily. "And he invited me over to this business thing," I add.

"What business thing?" asks Wynn.

"What do you fucking mean? This should have been yelled out since you stepped in the door!" Gina cries, indignant.

"Oh god." I moan into my pillow, then toss it over to them, red. "I can't talk about it. I need to process! Good night, guys!"

I hear them murmur to themselves and speculate, I sit on my bed and scroll my contacts in my phone.

Do it, a part of me prods. *No, don't do it*, another part goes. *Yes, ask him something he needs to answer.* But I can't. I can't push that hard. I need to take a page from his book and be patient.

I hug my pillow instead. *Saturday*, I think, making a mental list of things.

I need to look perfect.

I need to *not* make a fool of myself.

I need to remind him of what great friends we were even when we weren't deliciously fucking.

I need to win Saint back.

SATURDAY

When a shiny silver Rolls-Royce pulls over outside my apartment building on Saturday, I fairly shoot out the door.

I'm wearing a pair of white slacks with a cardi and silk top, and I colored my cheeks a little bit, and glossed my lips, opting to look professional, and I tied my hair back in a braid that hangs down my back. When I walk out and see Otis standing there, guarding the Rolls as he waits, I can't control the excitement surging in me.

"A pleasure, Miss Rachel," he says, beaming.

"It really is," I admit with a smile.

I settle in the backseat and Malcolm's familiar scent reaches me. Clean and expensive. I take a good whiff of his aftershave and cologne and am sure I just stepped into heaven—a heaven ruled by a green-eyed devil.

The scent lingers strongly, along with a whiff of top-quality leather. I feel butterflies. Eat your heart out, Pretty Woman.

Soon the car pulls up at the driveway of a 5-star resort

hotel, where Catherine H. Ulysses greets me at the door. As she leads me across the sumptuous lobby, she explains the situation. "Every summer, Mr. Saint's winemakers invite him, along with a few of his choice business partners and employees, to a wine tasting so he can select his favorites for the yearly M4 gala. He wanted you to meet them, considering . . ." She shoots me a disgruntled look. "He wants you at M4."

As we walk down the hall, a group of men come forward, one of whom rushes to catch up with us. "Cathy! We really want Saint to place an order with us at South Napa Vineyards."

"I couldn't sway him either way." Catherine keeps walking with a clipboard to her chest, and I try not to break stride either.

"Please put in a good word for us, we've brought *all* of our best whites."

"What can I say, Richard? Some days he likes reds, others he likes whites, others he's up for pinot noir rather than the cabernets. He likes his variety; what can you do?"

"Catherine, we've been doing this for years. By now we'd *love* some sort of commitment. It would speak highly of us if we were to be the prime supplier this year."

"And I'll tell you what I told the rest of them: good luck. May the saints be with you."

We wade into a beautiful restaurant already full of people. The space boasts twenty-five-foot ceilings and is set up with long tables, each one draped in white linens with elegant silverware and sleek chrome centerpieces holding long, lone orchids.

Pure luxury surrounds us.

At the far end of the room, expansive glass doors open all the way to the walls, revealing dramatic views of a golf course to one side, and a pool, waterfall, and pergola to the other.

After we cross the room, we head into another section, even

more luxurious than the first. This area is strategically scattered with white-upholstered conversational seating, lines of delicate folded menus standing open at the centers of the sleek glass coffee tables. Wine racks line one side of the room while the other side reveals a beautiful view of a terrace and golf course.

Catherine is checking out the area while telling one of the waiters who approaches, "This turned out perfect. Mr. Saint likes the view. He also likes his privacy. Nice little area here. Good job, thank you."

Holy god, it's all so beautiful. It reminds me of his apartment, his cars.

Everything about him.

I'm letting my eye appreciate every inch of this place, when I see Saint walk in. My eyes hurt.

Catherine lifts her head too. "Excuse me," she tells the waiter. "Excuse me," she then tells me, flustered as she heads for the door.

As Catherine threads through the crowd to greet him with her chart to her chest, there's an almost imperceptible hush in the room.

The people who were closest to the doors immediately walk up to him.

He's wearing black slacks and a white shirt, no tie, his hair slicked back to reveal his stunning face. He looks hot multiplied by a million.

I'm a little embarrassed to realize my nipples ache painfully beneath my top and bra, and I'm more than a little uncomfortable by the fact that I can get aroused at the mere sight of him. I have no right to that little stab of jealousy I feel when he talks to the people who approach. But I dearly wish that it were me alone that he spoke to.

I stare at my shoes and tuck my hair behind my ear and inhale. I promise myself I'm going to look up and not look at him, but when I lift my eyes, it's him they look for. He's greeting a couple who just approached, the woman wearing an especially awed smile.

I watch as he then ducks his head to Catherine and asks her something. She lifts her head and points at me. Green eyes slide down the length of the room to find me. I feel a helpless leap in my heart as our gazes lock—and I realize with dread how I must look to him. Standing alone at the far side of the room, gaping at him. He untangles himself from the crowd and starts walking toward me.

I can't swallow. His face is unsmiling, and he moves with the fluidity of water but the force of a tsunami.

Under his shirt, I can see the indentations of his flat, ripped abs, the flex of his arms and shoulders, his long legs, so muscled and strong, walking toward me. My heart is whacking in my chest so hard I can't hear anything but the noise it makes.

"I'm glad you could make it."

"Thank you, I am too."

He takes one step closer. "Has Catherine explained the day to you?" He looks down at me expectantly. God, we're standing *so* close he's in my personal bubble and I'm within the protection of his.

Talk, Livingston! "Yes, thank you."

I don't want him to leave me yet, I find myself searching for something to say.

"I wasn't sure what you'd require of me today but I hope I dressed all right."

He doesn't even look at my clothes when he nods. And then he says, "I'd like you to meet some people."

"Of course."

He waves a hand and I get to greet Dean, his PR person,

and then he introduces me to his other assistants, a few members of his board, and two key Interface design members. "Nice to meet you," I say to them all.

I remain talking to one of them. A young man who didn't finish college but his work as an innovator and application designer has been lauded across the world.

Saint has been praised for having a great eye for talent. He brings out their talent, their determination, and their mettle. The M4 conglomerate is proof of that. They all truly follow their leader.

"Oops, time to sit down." The young man heads to search for his name on the tables. I scan for mine and, once sitting, I survey the menu at my place for a while as the room finishes filling up.

There's an impressive array of wines on the list. I'm trying to find one I may be familiar with when Catherine comes and moves the card next to mine and sets the name *Malcolm Saint* there instead.

Oh.

Saint is coming over?

My heart starts pounding. I can't even breathe when he takes his seat. One second the chair is empty and the next he's there.

I can smell him in every breath, especially his aftershave. Oh god, how can you miss a smell so much?

He takes his menu quietly and reads, and my concentration is nil as I pretend to do the same. Then some guy comes over to say hi, and Saint and he discuss oil prices. Saint's hand is on the table, resting there, idle—his big tanned hand. That's all I'm looking at—I'm this pathetic.

I think about reaching out. Touching his hand and linking

my fingers through his. Sending a message that says, *Dibs on this. Dibs on you.*

I am obsessing about it. I slowly set down the menu but don't dare do anything. I offered to work the weekends; this isn't a date and I want to respect the distance he seems to want to keep between us. But I still can't stop staring at his hand and remembering how it feels, how thick it is and strong and warm. Malcolm shifts in his seat then and shoves his hand into his pocket, scanning the menu again when they drop the conversation.

"It's getting cold out and we're barely out of summer," I say.

"Yes," he agrees, lifting his eyes to me for a long, long second. Then, he sets the menu down and shifts his shoulder to face me a little more.

His gaze is fiercely direct and a bit stormy. Oh god.

Chills down my arms, my legs, my feet.

"So. Wine tasting," I say.

"A man shouldn't let another man choose his wine," is all he says.

"Only make it?" I quip.

He looks at me as if for the first time tonight. And then, he smiles. Full on, mega-watt, grab-on-to-your-panties-sweet-bitch smile.

God.

There's no wine, no drug this powerful.

His *smile.*

We remain seated as we start the tasting.

After the fourth wine, I notice that Sin makes a signal to a waiter, and soon, the waiter sets a blindfold over my place settings. "For the lady newcomer," the waiter tells me with a little grin.

I watch as Malcolm's long, tanned fingers take the blindfold. He lifts it up and looks at me, a frank question in his green eyes.

"May I?"

Oh god. "I . . . um, sure."

He starts to lower the blindfold over my face. I'm not breathing when he covers my eyes with the velvet material. All the darkness in the world engulfs me. I hear the clink of glass, the sound of footsteps, of chairs. I catch my breath when warm, long, achingly familiar fingers guide my own to curl around the stem of a wineglass.

Saint's touch is so familiar to my body, I'm raging right now. All my systems on *go*.

"Noel isn't going to ever drop his issues with you, is he, Kyle?" a businessman sitting very close asks in a low voice, clearly meant not to be overheard.

Saint is quiet beside me.

Kyle.

Is the guy addressing *him*?

Saint's thumb pauses on the back of mine until he's sure I'm holding the glass on my own. His nearness is so disturbing and exciting it takes me a moment to get a good grip.

"Ever going to address the rift between you two?" the voice speaks again.

"No," Malcolm answers. Then he whispers to me, "Smell it."

My senses fire up. All but my eyesight. Sin's voice feathers down my spine as I scent the wineglass he still hasn't released even though I'm holding it too. I can smell the soap on his hand. I can hear my heartbeat. My skin prickles as I drag in the scent and almost taste it.

"Taste it," he says, in my ear, and when he speaks again, his tone is different. Colder. "Whatever I had to say to my father, I said it long ago."

"But he blames you." The man is still whispering, but Saint is not.

"He can blame himself."

One more whisper from the businessman: "So is that why you've never tied yourself up to a woman? You suspect it's going to be like father like son?"

He lets out a long, rumbling laugh. "I'm not anything like him," he murmurs dismissively.

I'm quiet, trying to make sense of what I'm hearing, sipping the wine, when I feel Saint take the glass from me, whisper, "How was it?"

Fuck. How was it indeed? Too curious for her own good, is the lady? "Fruity, I think. Dry."

I lick my lips and there's a silence. Is it odd that my stomach feels warm when I feel, sense, his eyes on my lips as I lick them one more time?

Then warm, gentle fingers on my hand as he gives me another glass. "Smell it again," he tells me, the touch of his fingers lingering on mine. The tone holds a degree of warmth and command as well as curiosity.

I lift it to my nose and sniff, the aroma opening my lungs somehow.

"Now taste."

God, his voice is all man. All sensual. Pure Sin. He makes the command sound coaxing to the point you never consider not obeying.

"His phantom corporations," the man goes on, speaking words that sound important but that I have trouble registering in my dizzied mind, "all those overseas, hiding money, rumors of corporate espionage going on? Aren't you concerned these snoops could be around M4?"

"Nobody gets into M4 without a thorough screening. Procedures too lengthy to discuss here," he says.

Then Saint, to me, "Do you like it?"

"I love it," I breathe.

Saint speaking: "Catherine, we'll order three cases of each so far . . ."

I'm listening to everything but at the same time focused on this second wine. I'm loving the way it rolls down my throat, swirls in my mouth. Dry but sweet.

"One more," Saint coaxes quietly as he hands me a third. His whisper tickles my ear when he takes the glass from me. "What's the lady's verdict?"

I smile and go up in knots at the teasing in his voice.

God, I can't take it when he teases me. "It's a little dry and earthy. The tastes really come alive with this." I touch my fingers to the blindfold.

"Hence the purpose of wearing it," he explains.

He takes it off me so gently that I hardly feel his fingers unwrap it from around the back of my head. There's something quiet in the air between us as he lowers it. Like a secret. His eyes shine on me with intimate knowledge. Somehow, I can tell he likes the trust I placed in him just now.

Trust.

God, was this a test? He's so beautiful and he was once a little bit obsessed with me and my windpipe swells with the force of the feelings he gives me.

We smile at each other before he's forced to return to the

conversation. I lean against the back of my chair, relaxed and drowsy, other parts of me tense with awareness.

"Revenge is a dish best served cold," one of the men finally says.

I watch Saint, this ever-changing mystery to me. I watch his mouth as he talks, quietly, to them about something, and I watch his mouth as he takes a drink. The mouth I haven't kissed in so long. As he talks, I tune out and wonder if I could be that wine, that glass. He reaches out with this knowing male smile and lifts it to his lips again, glancing down at me quizzically.

The lights from above hit his tanned face, the quiet melody providing the ambience. But no soothing background music can detract from the pulsing energy of this man beside me.

He's a complicated man.

He never really mentions business, or anything about himself. He's unselfish. Some men love to talk about themselves or brag—never him. He teases you instead, he baits and challenges you. And I know that when he's quiet, and looks the calmest, that's when you should be most scared.

He is very calm and quiet beside me now.

Like a nuclear weapon, charging.

"Enough talk about my father. Rachel, would you like to go to the terrace?" he asks.

I realize suddenly he was playing along with these men until this moment, when he firms his voice and snaps the door shut on their curiosities. He indulged them for a while, but he's the most powerful man in the room, and he'll indulge them no longer.

When he stands and instructs the waiter to carry our wines outside, I stand and excuse myself from the men, taking a moment to head to the terrace to regroup before he joins me.

"He has a temper."

Turning at the voice, I find a gray-eyed young man in a navy suit approaching me, speaking with a bit of a slur. "You don't want to see him lose it and you definitely don't want to make him lose it," he says, coming over with a full glass of wine. "Only reason he can be so contained is if he gets it every time he wants. That's all he wants a woman for. Lucky bastard." He offers the wine to me.

"I'm glad he's found something that works," I say noncommittally, shaking my head, declining the offer. But if Sin needs to work out something, I wish he'd work it out on *me*.

"Try it," he insists.

"Oh no."

"Come on, try this one, it's a 'seventy-three." He hands me the glass, and as I take it, he moves around behind me.

"Thanks, but pass," I say, shaking my head as I try to set the wine down, but he's already put his hands over my eyes.

"Come on, indulge me," he says in my ear.

I sip a little, just to get him off my back, and say, "Good. I'm done now."

I notice, through a slit in his fingers, a very broad, muscular chest in a white shirt suddenly blocking my line of vision, and the guy's hands drop from my face as he croaks, "Mr. Saint. I was getting acquainted with . . . well, this young lady here. She seemed so lonely just now."

Green eyes look at me and something feels stuck in my windpipe. "Are you lonely?" he asks, as he studies me, and I swear I've never, ever, seen such a look of challenge and jealousy in Saint's eyes.

"No," I whisper.

Without looking at the other guy, he tells him, in a chillingly low voice, "You can go now."

The guy looks paralyzed. Saint looks at me with complete calm and gestures around the terrace. "How about we move over there?"

As if expecting me to obey, he starts walking, and I follow him across the terrace. It's more private here and a bright fireplace flares at the end. Still remembering the crestfallen look on the pale guy's face when Saint dismissed him, I burst out laughing. "Sin!" I chide. "You were so mean. So intimidating. He didn't do anything."

His voice is calm, but his expression is all steel. "He touched you," he says simply.

"Whaaat?" A disbelieving laugh leaves me.

He faces me fully, frowning in curiosity as he leans against a stone wall and crosses his arms. "I remember that laugh." He looks at my smile with a sober expression, and his eyes grow dark. My laugh fades.

I hear myself whisper, "I guess I don't laugh all that much anymore."

A silence. He's still looking at my lips as though waiting for them to smile again. "That's a pity," he murmurs. He lifts his finger and traces my lips, corner to corner. "I do like that laugh."

I look at him, breathless.

I've never had a vice until him. His aroma hits my senses, making my mouth water. He's my only vice. My only longing.

This longing, I bet he can see it in my eyes as he drops his hand. My smile is gone, but the feeling of his touch remains on my lips.

We stand here, and though I want and crave, we stand looking at each other like strangers.

As if you never knew his arms, and how they held you; his lips and how they pressed onto yours . . . always the corner of your lips first.

A breeze hits me, and I know that I have never hurt like this, or had so many regrets. I know that I might not be okay until the first part he touched forgets what it was like to feel his fingertips. But will I ever? I feel like his fingertip just branded my lips for another eternity.

A woman comes over to greet him. He clenches his jaw as if the interruption frustrates him.

"You stunningly beautiful man," the woman gushes with a manicured hand fluttering up his hard chest. "I tell everyone I know you're the only man who looks as stunning in his passport picture as he does in real life. Let's do Monte Carlo again!"

She leaves and I find myself smiling in amusement. "Is that where you've been traveling?"

He shrugs disinterestedly. "Among other places, yes."

"But not with Callan and Tahoe?"

"They had business. I traveled with other friends."

"Socialites? And . . . playboys who have nothing to do?"

"People who wanted to get away for a while."

Away far from me, I think sadly. I kick a leaf from the terrace floor and realize that somewhere during the night, my braid came undone. Now I try to keep my hair from flapping around me and tilt my head to study his face. "It felt like you didn't even want to come back to Chicago."

He's studying me with equal intensity, watching me fail to catch the flying wisps of my hair. "Nothing to come back to in Chicago."

"M4," I tell him.

He reaches out to seize most of my flapping hair in one fist and holds it in control against my nape. "M4's a big boy. I've taught it to stand on its own two feet without me." He smirks. "At least for a little while."

But you didn't teach me how to survive the storm that is you, I think as I reach up and use both my hands to keep my hair still.

When he eases back and drops his hand, I shiver with the breeze—the loss of his body heat cooling me too fast.

"Cold?" he murmurs.

I shake my head—because it's so much colder in Chicago in winter—but he heads to the end of the terrace, where there's a pile of blankets.

I wrap my arms around myself and sit down on a couch near the fireplace and I try not to look at him like I have nothing else to do. Then I try not to look at the couple kissing on the other corner of the terrace. They're making out by the railing. It's not a full-on juvenile make-out but rather a long adult kiss that seems to go on and on and on.

I shiver and tighten my arms around myself. Malcolm brings a blanket and hands it over, silently looking at me.

He's standing there, beautiful beyond the imagination. He oozes power and class, sophistication. He oozes testosterone and every woman inside has noticed him—even the ones here with other men. I notice that too. My stomach squeezes unhappily at that. I drop my gaze and I see his shoes as he lowers himself down next to me.

"You all right?" he asks me, pulling the blanket over me.

I shake my head, then nod, then want to groan when I realize maybe the wine is bubbling a little too high into my brain.

When he stretches his legs out, before I can think better of it, I lift the blanket. "Here, it's cold," I say, scooting to make room for him.

He grabs me by the waist and slides me next to him so he doesn't have to move, then he lets go and leans back and doesn't seem cold at all, the blanket idle by his waist as he sips wine and studies its contents.

The move was easy and natural . . . and Saint looks so calm right now. But I'm floored. *He wants me near?*

Holding the blanket a little higher with one hand, I watch him drink his wine out of the corner of my eye.

I think of all those long dreams I had, only to wake up alone in bed. Needing. Needing him. And now my shoulder touches his. I sit helpless. I should move away but I'm stealing this touch and I can't stop myself.

He reaches out to grab a new wine from a passing waiter.

"Do you want to take a break upstairs or do you want to stay here for a while?" he asks me, his tone casual, but his deep stare is somehow not the least bit casual.

"I'm enjoying the terrace very much right now."

He smiles. And god, that smile.

"Do you want to try this one? It's a cabernet, 'sixty-eight." He offers the wine to me.

"I'm heading into the woozy department, so maybe not," I admit.

"Just a taste?" He watches me with those eyes full of mischief and dips his thumb into his glass. I watch as he lifts it. My heart stops when he rubs my lips with it and at the wet caress, desire drizzles over every corner of me, every shadowed place.

"What are you doing?" I ask breathlessly.

"Something I shouldn't," he husks out, his eyes dark and somber but with a devilish glint.

Holding my breath, I part my lips and suckle a little. His

eyes darken even more, and my body contracts when the taste of him—Sin, the only guy I've ever wanted, ever cared for—reaches me. Opening up my every memory, my every need.

His voice like silken oak, he whispers, "One more, Rachel?"

We're playing with fire and we both know it. I can see the devil in his eyes and I can feel the heat that's going to turn me to cinders and I can't stop it; I won't stop it. I nod, but then, when a little fear screams at me that he's going to hurt me, I say, to protect myself, "Just one."

This time when he dips his thumb into the wine and brings it up, I suck it delicately, not wanting him to know how much I crave his taste more than anything.

I give it just a tiny suck, as if I'm only interested in the wine slipping down my tongue. But it's his thumb, square, clean, familiar, that I want to bite into, that I want to kiss, taste, make love to. There's a moan in my throat, trapped there. A need inside me, trapped there. A love inside me, so very trapped there he might never get to know how much, how very much I've come to love him.

Watching me for a moment in disappointment, as though he wanted me to latch on to his thumb longer, he sticks it into his mouth and sucks the rest with one pull. Then he whispers at me, "This one's sweeter than the rest."

"I . . . yes."

There's a silence after this is done. He's looking at me with a bit of amusement and a strange yearning I've never seen in his eyes and I'm flustered to death.

My voice is thick when I can finally manage to speak. "What those men said . . . about your father."

"They were business associates of my mother's. They know my father." His lips curl sardonically, and his eyes shutter until there's no more of the fleeting tenderness I just saw. "Don't worry. I don't associate with friends of his."

He brings out his phone. Changing topics.

"Remember this picture?" he asks and turns the screen to me.

I'm both ashamed and excited at the discovery as I peer closer to see. "You still have it."

With the click of a button, he's showing me a picture of me on his yacht, *The Toy*. I was staring out at the water the first time I was there, thinking of . . . well, how endless the water looked. And wondering why I was so distraught over watching some floozies feed him grapes and hearing about all the fun he'd had at an after-party I was never invited to.

There it is—that picture of me, my profile pensive as I stare out at the lake. "You were supposed to erase it!" I accuse.

"I erased the one I showed you. I took two."

"Two, not four?"

His smile appears, but it doesn't quite reach his eyes. His eyes, instead, look endlessly deep and thoughtful. Then he clicks and there's another one of me. I'm sitting on a street bench with a magazine on my lap. *The* magazine. In which I published the article about him. I'm staring down at it with a look of such loss—as if I lost my whole world that day and all I had left was that single magazine with his picture on it.

I don't understand where he got it but I'm surprised, embarrassed, and in my heart, so very sad that that picture—that moment—exists at all. "Where did you get it?"

"Online." His eyes darken a little as he looks at me, a muscle tightly flexing in the back of his square jaw.

"Do you keep photos of all the people you employ on your phone?"

"I don't employ you yet, remember?" He goes back to the

yacht picture. "Nor was I employing you when you were here." He looks at me.

"Saint," I say, breathless at his proximity and getting scared by what it's doing to me. "You never will. I could never look at you as my boss."

"I wanted to show you this one," he says, then plays with his phone before turning it back to me again. I see an email from a zoo, and he opens the attachment to show me. I see a huge elephant with its trunk up in the air, almost as if saluting the camera.

"That's your elephant," he tells me, watching me closely.

"Rosie," I say, and when I look at him, I can't believe the kinds of kisses I want to put on his face and body, on his lips and on his lovely and hard-to-read green eyes.

He lifts his wineglass, cocking his eyebrow, and drinks, then he hands it over since I don't have one to toast with. I take his wineglass, and—holding his gaze—I set my lips where he drank, finishing it.

The smile he'd been wearing is completely gone when he noticed what I did.

"To Rosie," I say, lowering the glass.

His phone sits idle in his hand, while the wineglass sits empty in mine.

And Saint sits next to me. He's staring at me with such intensity, it almost feels like he doesn't know if he wants to kiss me, spank me, or fuck the hell out of me.

Yes, please.

Handsome and dark-haired, Saint is among the youngest of everyone at the tasting. We both are, but he looks distracting as a comet.

He sits here, overwhelmingly sexual and physical, casual but strong and sophisticated in the clothes he wears, compared to the older men in their suits walking by. I'm conscious of his body heat under the blanket and how, combined with mine, the air is hot enough.

I'm so aware of the hardness of his thigh against mine, of the crackling air and the magnetic pull between us.

Does he feel it too? Does he hate me, but want me still?

Could I compartmentalize like that? Be physical with him while I love him so completely?

I'm not sure I could.

So I sit here stiffly and look at him quietly, looking away when it's too much to bear, and then back to find him still watching me.

Maybe he doesn't want me the way I want him anymore. But even when he wanted me, he had the patience of a saint. And I'm afraid he's going to wear me down until I agree to everything and anything that he wants. Even employment.

"So when is this event at M4 that you're purchasing all this wine for?" I ask, searching for safer ground.

"Six weeks from now."

I nod and smile a little, then tap at his glass I just drained. "This one," I confirm. "I'm obsessed with this one."

"Okay," he concurs with a curve of his lips as he calls a waiter and asks for a similar one. "Try this one now, Rachel."

He puts it in my hand, but I push it back into his, delighting that I have an excuse to touch the tips of my fingers to the backs of his.

"No." I shake my head and push the glass deeper into his hand, prolonging, stealing the touch of his hand. "I don't want another. I want this one." I lift the empty glass, and he laughs and asks for a refill.

I ask him, as we sip, "Why hire me? I'm still battling with myself to write every day."

He shrugs and looks at me devilishly. "All right," he concedes. "Then I need a wine taster."

"So determined, are you, to get me under your command?" I tease.

He looks at me. He looks at me so deeply, I haven't felt this *seen* in a while.

"You have no idea."

JUST A LITTLE DIZZY

It's dark outside when we head back into the event room and toward the hotel lobby.

"It's a good night as always for you, Saint!" he's told by one of the businessmen as we head out.

He doesn't answer. Vaguely, I notice the speculative stares coming our way. The men are checking me out, but the women have eyes only for the green-eyed god beside me. They look ready to charge him and get on with the baby making.

"Mr. Saint!" Catherine stops him at the door. He converses with her about the wine orders. He takes my arm in his hand to steady me as we head back into the event room and I discover the world is spinning a little too fast.

"You okay?" A corner of his lips is curled as he looks down at me.

"I'm perfect."

I don't think he believes me, because he secures me against

the wall of his side with one arm around my waist. And it's so familiar, so . . . right.

He's more relaxed than he's been all night after all the wine we imbibed, and so am I. My defenses are wavering. His presence is intoxicating. He shoots me a smile to melt whatever hasn't melted already.

"You really are drunk," he murmurs, as if to himself.

He walks me over to the elevators.

And I don't question that.

Because . . . because he mentioned there's a room upstairs where we can chill out for a bit. And I said *yes, let's chill out for a little bit.* Because I can't bear to leave, not when he's still here and every other woman in the room has been waiting, *waiting* for me to leave so they can have him.

"You drank more than me," I chide him. How come he looks as in control as always? "I bet you drank wine in the crib, only accepting vintage bottles even then."

He's suddenly wearing this secret smile. "You know me so well, Rachel."

We head into the elevator and it takes me a moment to realize he's teasing me. I laugh a delayed laugh, but then I'm silent and sleepy and I would have usually stood apart, but I'm cold and he steps impossibly close. So close as he presses the top-floor button, that I can feel his body heat, smell the warm, familiar scent of his skin and the scent of wine on his breath as he stands there, staying close as if offering himself to lean on.

He stretches his arm along the wall behind my back and stares up at the numbers. I don't know what to do but I lean against his arm.

"I'm sorry, it's cold," I whisper, blushing.

"It's okay." He curls his arm around me then, and holds me, lightly but close.

God. *Malcolm* . . .

The very idea I had about desire and sex and love, he completely turned it upside down until they're all mingled now. He is the embodiment of them all to me now. I can't love him without desiring him, wanting to be physical and show my feelings for him.

This touch is light—only around my waist. But it doesn't touch what I really need. That touch—*all over*, please.

I want to press my cheek to his chest, and when I do—because, well, I just went ahead and did it—I hear his heart beating under my ear . . . beating nowhere near as fast as mine is. I fist a hand on his delicious-smelling shirt.

"I'm dizzy, Malcolm," I say apologetically.

"Watch your step." As we exit the elevator, he keeps his arm around my waist and leads me to the room.

He opens his room, and I'm stunned by how huge it is, containing lounge areas, bar, dinner table, breakfast table, and the most perfect, beautiful views. On the bar there's a bouquet full of flowers, champagne, and chocolate-covered strawberries. And a note to *Mr. Saint*.

I feel like I'm in a dream, in a dream where I'm his girl and he brings me to these kinds of hotels when he travels for the weekend. I kick off my shoes and drop down not on the couch, but rather on the floor at its feet, leaning my head on the couch seat for support.

He flicks on a lamp and sits down beside me, kicking off his shoes and stretching out his legs. His scent surrounds me and just looking at his long, lean body, all six-plus feet of him sprawled next to me, I feel safer than I have in such a long time.

I want to make him smile.

He's so serious right now. His voice a little gruff, his hair rumpled. I tease him about his having ordered several whole vineyards, and finally, I seem to draw him out.

There's a playful gleam in his eye as he teases back, "A man's got to have ambitions."

He sits with his head back on the seat of the couch, studying the ceiling.

"What if you reach all your ambitions . . . by the time, say, you're forty. Or fifty. Then what?" I ask him.

He faces me again, and suddenly our noses are inches apart. "Then I'll come up with new ambitions." He lowers his voice as if he's just realized I'm sitting super close.

Kissably close.

"And a few new groupies?" I whisper.

His nearness is making me ache in tender places I didn't even know I had. I turn and stare at the ceiling, my stomach hot.

"I can already see you. You'll be in one of your sports cars, brought in from somewhere exotic so it's unique and nobody has it but you. It'll be faster, grander, so shiny. Two girls in the back, your cell phone riding shotgun. One's a Victoria's Secret model and the other is a TV series actress—BUT they have nothing interesting to talk about."

"Well, what are they doing?"

"Hmm?"

"If they're not talking, what are they doing? Are they kissing me? Caressing me?"

"They're kissing each other—in the back while you drive. They're also one-clicking on their phones, spending your money."

His lips curl a little higher and his eyebrows lift too. "I no longer have drivers to keep my hands free for the girls?"

"Nope, they quit. It had to do with the scandal of an orgy in the back of the car, and their families were devastated."

"Rachel," he chides. "Where do you get these ideas about me?"

"The internet." I laugh a little. "Everywhere."

His eyes drop to my lips for a second. My breath catches a little and my laugh drifts into silence. I feel his gaze squeeze my stomach.

He seems to check himself and lead his eyes firmly back up. "What about you? What are you doing when you're forty?" He shifts to look at me more intently. His shoulder grazes my shoulder and I can barely stand the buzzing down my arm.

"I guess . . . I'll be working. Writing, hopefully," I say.

"Nothing changed?" he asks me.

I actually consider what I would like to change. But how impossible it would be. Him? He can't even commit to a wine, how can I expect him to ever want me for long?

My voice is soft as a breath. "What I want isn't known for . . . committing."

"Known by *who*?"

"I don't know." I laugh again, then I glance out the window and inhale slowly, feeling his gaze on my back as the sadness of my circumstance overwhelms me. "Why do you want to hire me? You're so smart. You always think out your actions. For the salary you're offering you could get three journalists with much more experience and prestige."

"None of which would be you."

I sigh. "You're dangling an apple before me. It's hard not to take a bite."

"Now you know how I feel."

"With what? You don't need a bite; you can chow down anything with one swallow. You can take anything you want."

"No. I work for what I most want. I win it, or I don't feel like it's mine at all."

"You didn't feel like your money was yours until you earned it on your own?"

"That's right."

"You like the chase."

"Relish it."

"You like a challenge."

"I live for them." He looks at me with more emotion than I've ever seen in a guy's eyes. I'm melting, warm.

"You're enjoying me saying no then? That is your challenge with me now? You get me to say yes, and you win."

"No, Rachel, we need to get you some glasses. Because you're not reading me right." He looks at me, smiles to himself, drags a hand over his head. "I can never seem to win with you."

"Well . . . I lose," I whisper.

"What did you lose?"

I lost my mind and my heart, my muse, and, I think, my soul to you.

It's the combination of the wine and him. This man who weakens me like this. "I lose. I'm falling asleep now."

I wasn't supposed to yet. But I'm warm and relaxed, over-sensitized to him; his warm breath across my forehead, his hard, thick thigh close to mine . . . the square of his shoulder nearly touching mine.

"I used to play this with Gina . . . first one to fall asleep loses. I bet you never lose . . ." I mumble.

There's a thoughtful silence. Then, in my ear, sending shivers down my spine, is his voice: "I don't like to."

I smile a little and am dozing when he takes my arm and helps me up slowly. "Come here. There's a bed here with your name on it."

"Oh. You can afford a bed."

"Yeah. Do you want me to teach you how to use it?" he mocks me.

"I use a bed for sleep . . . but I don't know what *you* use it for."

"You know. A little fun here and there."

He walks me to the bed and then eases me down there. I sleepily watch him go to the bathroom and search for a toothbrush.

He's still in his shirt, washing his face with big hands, scrubbing his square jaw, then ramming the toothbrush into his mouth and washing fast and hard. He flicks the lights off and comes out, and I close my eyes and exhale before I open them again.

He spreads out on top of the bed, over the comforter while I'm under it. Slowly, he sets his phone aside and curls an arm behind his head as he studies me with an unreadable expression. I smile shyly.

He looks so handsome lounging in that shirt and his slacks on that big, white bed; I want to tease him. I want to see him smile again and again and again. "Sure the entire wine cellar is enough to feed your M4 minions?" I frown.

I feel a couple butterflies when his lips curve, and he shakes his head, then he drags one hand over his dark hair.

"I've heard the M4 annuals are such an event. Do you already know who you're going to go with?"

"Just a friend."

"Oh. A bed friend?" I lift my brows tauntingly, and tease: "Someone you can teach *how to* use a bed?"

He looks at me.

And slowly arches *his* brows. "Do you really want to talk about this?"

His expression has gone from relaxed and flirtatious back to serious again.

Taken aback, I turn to my back and exhale. "I . . . no."

Fuck.

Why did I ask that?

Saint says nothing for a long time.

Then: "Do you miss me?"

He rolls to his side and the fabric of his shirt is about to tear open under the flex of his muscles as he searches my face. He leans close to my ear, and says, "Do you think of me sometimes when you don't want to . . . do you need me . . . do you still feel me?"

"I feel you everywhere."

He curls his hand around my throat, leaves it there, hot and enormous, pinning me down on the bed with gentle firmness.

For minutes and minutes he stays there, with his forehead on my temple, his lips on my ear and his hand on my throat, owning me.

"I can't breathe when you're near, but I can't live without you," I pant, quietly, and he squeezes his eyes shut, drops his head on mine, and we say nothing else.

We lie here with his body leaning over mine, strong and hard, and me, panting in bed, weak and warm. We lie here as if we broke and there's no more glue to put us together no matter how much I wish for it to . . . but we also can't pull apart, as if something else entirely different from glue keeps us together.

It takes forever to fall asleep.

I should go home, but I don't want to. I'm in hell but I don't want to leave if he's in hell with me. My awareness is so heightened that every sound awakens me, every shift beside me on the bed. Even the loss of warmth at the merest shift of a leg stirs me awake and urges me closer to the warm, hard wall beside me . . . but when I sleep, I lose all restraint.

I'm unzipping his pants and devouring him with kisses, dragging my mouth down his square abs, trailing my fingers across his chest muscles with a thirst that is unquenched. When I finally curl my hands around his hard length, I do so reverently. I stroke up and down his shaft as I lower my mouth and kiss him there, right where he's most man. I make love to him with my mouth because I need to claim him. Feel him. Love him so that he loves me.

He lifts my chin. "Look at me." The words have a bite, harsh with need.

My eyes lock with his and his are stormy green. He sees something he wants in my gaze because I sense he doesn't want me to close my eyes. I blink and look back at him as I drag my tongue along his long, hard length. The crown of his cock is thick, swollen, pink, and as beautiful as the rest of his length. His sex is full for me, gushing for me. Between my legs, I'm gushing for him.

I murmur his name around his flesh.

"*Malcolm.*"

He tugs my face up close and slides his lips over mine in a tender kiss.

"Is this what you want, little one?" he asks, pulling me up so I feel him between my legs.

In a world where he can buy anything he wants, I'm his littlest thing. And he's my biggest, grandest thing.

Full, lush lips feather over my cheek before pressing against mine. Soon he's parted and tasted me, his tongue thrusting powerfully inside, seducing me.

He eases me back and parts my thighs, and I feel the gentle tug of his teeth on my clit. Every sensation coming to the surface. I feel my orgasm build, and I beg him, *please Malcolm please*—when I hear a door close, and I bolt awake.

I'm sweating in bed, soaked, shivering. I glance around, confused, when I recognize the hotel suite and hear the shower water start with a squeaky, angry jerk. I close my eyes tight and my stomach drops. Oh god. Malcolm heard me. He heard me say his name. He heard me lose my shit.

I put my face in my hands as I hear the slap of water and I know he's showering. A cold shower?

I try to calm my breathing. Pretend nothing happened, right? I'll pretend I never woke up and pretend I don't remember my dream tomorrow.

No. I can't. I can't stay here, so close . . .

Oh. GOD.

Quietly, I climb out of bed, gather my shoes, and then cross the room. I stop to hastily scrawl a message on the hotel notepad:

Full day tomorrow. Thanks for today.

R

And then I set the pen silently next to the note and head out the door.

ON *EDGE*

I'm so embarrassed. So, so embarrassed I may give new definition to the word. I go back home and sit there, on my bed, smelling his soap and cologne on my clothes, completely sober and unable to sleep. If Saint had any doubts, any at all, that I still wanted him, I'm sure he's pretty sure of how hopelessly I *do*.

Oh god.

And it turns out, I'm not the only one worked up about Saturday; social media seems just as frenzied about it.

My presence at the wine tasting seems to have sparked another kind of wildfire in Saint's floozie circle on Monday.

IS IT TRUE? ARE THE RUMORS OF YOU GETTING BACK WITH YOUR GIRLFRIEND TRUE?

And back to Twitter:

@malcolmsaint spotted with HER

@malcolmsaint is it true? Are you getting back with her?????

They say you were together Saturday

@tahoeroth is it true @malcolmsaint is seeing his
ex-girlfriend? He's staring at her from the podium and WTF
with the look he's giving her!!

I click on the link and stare at a picture of me standing inside McCormick Place as he was getting to my question. I didn't
even *see* anyone take this picture of us. In fact, at that moment
I hadn't noticed that he *was* giving me a very toe-curling look
without regard for anyone watching.

Sighing, I tuck my phone away and search through my
"ideas" file.

I'm mulling over topics when Helen tings me at my desk.

I lock my computer—something I never did before. I used
to think my riches were in my brain and whatever was in my
files was not as valuable as what I, myself, contained. But after
Victoria copied my research file, I realized everything you value
has to be locked well. Oh, life, how jaded you make us, I think
as I lock it—and then I head over to Helen.

When she sees me, she gives me a big grin and gestures to
one of her chairs. "Sit down."

I shake my head and start to tell her, "No, I'm good. Helen,
I'm finally having a breakthrough—"

"We're being bought out," she cuts me off.

"I . . . excuse me?"

So . . . there's truth to the rumor?

Helen clucks. "See, Rachel, you should've taken the chair."

We stare at each other across her desk. Helen looks about as
incredulous as I, but far happier about it.

"We've got an offer and it's apparently your article that caught our investor's eye," she continues. The look she's sending my way practically pets me with appreciation.

Helen's marvel and delight are apparent, but I'm getting more baffled by the second. "Well, who's buying us? *Edge* hasn't been attractive for years."

"No, it hasn't. But it looks like it is now," she says. "The offer's from a big one. It's actually someone you might know. Linton Corporation." She waits as if I know anything about it and expects me to guess.

When I remain silent, she adds, "Noel Saint's new media corporation."

My stomach hits the floor.

I shake my head and brace my forehead on my hand for a minute as I count to . . . well, actually, to four.

"Noel *Saint*?"

"The very one." She smiles. "And you don't need to be worried. He might be making changes, but the current owners assure me you'll be staying. Noel Saint is very intrigued by the woman who captured such prolonged interest from his son."

I want to throw up. I feel so physically sick that I can't remain standing for much longer, much less keep talking about this.

Staring mutely for another moment, I finally say, "If you don't mind I'm going to try to get a column started . . ."

I head out the door and, back at my computer, the memory of an overheard conversation just this weekend teases me.

Espionage . . . he'll never leave you alone . . .

Noel Saint is buying *Edge*.

Because of my article.

Why?

What does he want with *Edge*?

With *me*?

I sit staring at my computer. When Saint pursued me before, he bought my mural . . . he sent me flowers . . . he helped End the Violence take new, technological safety measures . . . but I never imagined that offering me a job at M4 could have a similar underlying reason.

Is Saint protecting me from his father?

I war with myself for the next hour. I lose, and shoot him a text: Can you talk?

Too impatient when he doesn't answer by lunchtime, I grab my bag, toss my afternoon apple inside, and call Catherine on my way to the elevator.

When she answers, I ask in a rush, "Is he in? Can you get me five minutes with him?"

"I'm sorry but he's out of the office today."

I exhale and stop at the elevator. "Thanks." Disappointed, I go back to my seat and think of Sin as I eat my apple.

He didn't sound worried during the wine tasting when he was questioned about his father. He seemed more concerned over what I thought of the wine than what the businessman whispered.

Even so, his father is dangerous.

As dangerous as Saint himself.

And then a bolt hits me, and I remember hearing him tell someone: "*. . . have to be dead to let her fall into his clutches . . .*"

It all starts to click with lightning-fast speed in my head.

Oh.

My.

Oh my oh my oh *my.*

Feeling a spike of adrenaline as I remember the grade-A ASSHOLE Saint's father is, I surf the internet for information on the man.

I find a few articles about lawsuits from employees, and inevitably, I bump into one of those few video interviews he gave the press, when Saint started M4 while his father kept assuring everyone that he gave his son "no more than three months to bankruptcy."

"You are such a top-level douche-bag, and I am so glad Saint keeps proving you wrong," I mutter at the man behind the podium.

Feeling worse and worse the more I see, I start to seriously consider my options and what I'll do if Noel Saint succeeds in acquiring *Edge*. Jumping to my inbox, I scan the emails that I received when my article broke out and I wonder if those who reached out still want to interview me. Then I open another search engine and scan the job boards.

"Why are you checking the online ads?"

I lift my head distractedly to spot Valentine peering at my computer screen. "What?" I ask him.

"The ads. Why are you looking at online ads? Are you leaving?"

I glance around to make sure nobody else is hearing, then close my search, determined to make some calls later.

BOX

When I get to my apartment, I've got a ton of research for my article but I can't stop thinking about Noel Saint, Malcolm Saint feeding me wine from his thumb, and my *embarrassing* dream. After a quick shower I opt to add a mayonnaise treatment to my hair and let it sit under a shower cap for a while when I get a ring from the landlady who lives on the first floor. She says that there's a package downstairs for me but it's quite heavy so she'll have someone bring it up.

The package, when it's brought to my door by her burly bear of a husband, is a huge case of wine. *My* favorite wine.

And a note taped to the top in such familiar writing, my world tilts upside down.

RACHEL,

I COULDN'T KEEP ALL THESE TO MYSELF. I'LL NEVER FORGET THE LOOK ON YOUR FACE WHEN YOU MET YOUR NEW OBSESSION.

M. S.

I reread it several times. I read even the white spaces between the letters. I read the M and the S and everything he wrote.

God. My obsession is YOU.

Exhaling shakily, I bend and heave a little as I carry the box inside, lock the door behind me, then I head to my room and lift my cell phone in trembling hands, press SIN, and call.

I'm wracking my brain for what to say.

It rings three times before I hear him pick up and say, "Saint."

I literally feel the butterflies in my throat. "Hey, it's me," I say, trying to sound casual as I glance at the note in my hand, the want for my own obsession eating me inside as I talk to him on the phone. "So," I begin, trying to not sound breathless, "some guy I know wants to get me drunk. I have a case of delicious wine right on my doorstep with the address to AA for when I'm done."

"Bastard."

I chew the inside of my cheek to keep from laughing. "Help me with this someday?"

The soft and unexpected chuckle on the other end of the line does something to me, and I have to stop pacing and sit down on the edge of my bed. I pluck nervously at the comforter as he tells me, "There are seven days in a week and none of them is someday. Tell me when, Rachel."

A flush crawls up my cheeks. "I'd hoped this week, but I have to write after I did nothing but imbibe wine this weekend."

"I have a better idea. Come downstairs."

"What?"

"Come downstairs," he repeats.

"You're passing through the neighborhood?" I ask in disbelief, turning to gape at the window.

"I'm not *passing*; I'm in the neighborhood for *you*."

Crossing the room, I pluck the curtain aside and see a shiny crimson car pulling over in front of my building. *His* big-shit new car.

"Come down," he says, and then he cuts off. I drop the curtain and text him: Give me 5.

Tossing my phone on my bed, I hurry to the bathroom and yank off my shower cap and stare at my mayonnaise hair. *Oh fuck, Rachel, why did you do a hair treatment today?!*

Gina leans against the doorjamb and asks drolly from the door, "Shall I tell him you've got icky white stuff in your hair and to come back?"

Trembling, I open the faucet and stick my head under the running water, hurrying to wash the mayonnaise out of my hair.

Once done, I drape a towel over me and run it quickly up and down, trying to dry it as much as I can. Sin is downstairs. Sin is in the neighborhood. Sin came to see me.

Finally I toss my hair back, run a brush over it, tie it into a bun, slip into a pair of navy blue leggings, a clean gray T shirt, my easy slip-on Uggs, then rush outside.

Gravity.

Gravity is the force of attraction that exists between any two objects, any two masses, any two bodies. Gravity isn't just an attraction between an object above being pulled toward the gravitational center of the earth. Gravity is an attraction that exists between all objects, in all of the universe—the closer they are, the stronger the pull.

There has never been such gravity as that which I feel to an object parallel to me. This man.

My most powerful gravitational pull—the one that makes me feel like I'm falling even when I'm standing still.

Square jaw, that edible mouth, broad, big, tall and dressed in a suit, surrounded by the raw force of a determination that whirls around his body.

We're inside his car, parked outside my building. Quiet, toe-curlingly beautiful, noble, bold, controlled, and relentless, Saint is once again looking for me, as relentless as the M4's sole proprietor and CEO that I know, and as uncatchable as a storm. A womanizer. A benefactor. A champion of his causes. An enigma.

Everybody dotes on him. Women make fools of themselves over and over in an attempt to attract his eye. He inspires lust, love, and everything in between.

Even obsession.

Even . . . from me.

He was standing by his car when I came out.

"Hey," I said, feeling myself blush. "This is what I do now in my free time." I pointed at my wet hair in its bun.

He stared at me and opened the gullwing door to his stunning car. "I was hoping we could have that talk now," he said.

Now we're in his car and he's settled behind the wheel and I'm nervous.

Everyone wants something from him. He's got a warrior's instinct and is used to being asked for things. He rarely says no.

He . . . takes care of you.

He took care of me once and as I look at him in the dark with the streetlight casting shadows on his chiseled face, I remember how independent I wanted to be but how easily he overpowered me.

I remember the first time I saw him vividly. His slow,

easy-spreading smile that caused a fire to churn in the pit of my belly. He's a man whose fingers once spent hours memorizing the curves of my shoulders and back as we kissed.

The sharp edges of loss haven't been dulled. Being in his car only heightens the ache.

I remember every moment with him, like a treasure and like a punishment.

He's quiet, physical, and thrilling. He's also tender, consuming my world with incredible power and at hurricane speed.

I've never wanted anyone like this, and had never waited for someone's call. Wanted to see someone. I told him about the hole, about sometimes feeling like you wanted something to fill it. It has never been as big as it is now that I see him and hopelessly fear that I cannot have him.

But I want him nonetheless.

I guess reason has nothing to do with it anymore.

"Are you leaving *Edge*?" he asks me.

It's almost unbearable, the intimacy of his voice in the close confines of the car.

One arm draped over the wheel, he shifts sideways to look at me even more directly. "Why are you leaving *Edge*? It's doing better. Isn't it? After that piece you wrote?"

"You mean . . . the love letter?" I ask, then lower my gaze. "That's what my boss calls it."

His voice lowers. "Yeah, the love letter." A beat passes, charged with tension. "Why are you leaving?"

"Because."

He curls his thumb and forefinger around my chin and the contact electrifies me. I jolt a little and lean back against the seat when he crowds me in, studying me. "You're not coming to M4?"

"No." I look at his mouth.

"So . . . ?" he presses, still holding me by the chin. "Why are you leaving *Edge* and not coming with me to M4?"

"How do you know all this?" I turn away to inhale and break the touch because it's so, so painful.

"I have friends everywhere, Rachel."

I turn back to him. "I only looked at a few ads and called to inquire."

He's so close his scent surrounds me like a cloak, heady like a shot of morphine in my veins. Hazy and nervous, I glance at the street behind him, and I shrug. Then admit, blushing, "I know your father's interested."

"And?" he presses, his green eyes capturing me.

"And I won't work for anyone who's against *you*. I'm Team Malcolm," I whisper, flushing horribly.

"If you're Team Malcolm, why don't you come work for me?" he presses.

"Because . . ." I lower my voice. "Even if I'm Team Malcolm, I don't want to be something to you that a thousand others already are."

His eyes shine as he cocks his head. "Really. What is it that you want then?"

"You know what I want," I whisper, lowering my face.

"I want to hear it," he murmurs intensely under his breath.

Say it, I think.

Don't be scared.

You cannot fuck things worse than you already have.

"I want you," I whisper, unable to look up at him.

I hear the sound of his low exhale, and when I peer into the shadows, his face is all I see.

"I'm so mad at you," he murmurs to me, growling a little as he drags a hand over his face.

I'm breathing hard, as if I just threw myself off a cliff, and maybe I did. I can feel the yearning inside me trying to claw itself out of my eyes and toward him.

"Saint," I breathe helplessly.

"So . . . fucking . . . mad . . ." His eyes are heavy-lidded, incredibly so, his jaw jutting out. "So mad I can't see straight." He stares at me as if there are a thousand fires of hell burning inside him. "I close my eyes and see you. Rachel. Your eyes. Your hair. Your blushing face."

"Malcolm . . ." My eyes blur, and I add, pleading, "I'd do anything to prove that I'm loyal and truthful to you."

His jaw clenches just a bit tighter.

"You hurt me," he growls out as he looks at me. "I'm angry at you." His jaw squarer than ever, his eyes brilliant as ever. "But I can't give you up. I can't give you up even when I want to. I don't want to back off. I don't want to give you up," he says.

"Saint, I don't want you to exorcise me, because nothing can exorcise me of *you*," I say.

He looks at me. We're at a stalemate. He flexes his fingers on my arm.

"You said you could make what I did go away. Make it go away, give me a clean slate," I plead.

I reach out and touch his face. His gaze flashes. Eyes burning with desire and possessiveness.

"I want a chance." I open my mouth to beg; instead I lift his hand from the steering wheel and press a kiss to the back of his hand, his knuckles. I nuzzle it and close my eyes, afraid to see him look at me in disgust when his hand smells so clean and good. "Saint, please."

I lift my head and my lungs seize when I see his expression. He looks almighty, and all hungry, like a man returning home after being shackled away from it for decades. My pussy is damp and swollen.

He couldn't look more dominant and possessive. But he hasn't stopped me. So I kiss the center of his palm next.

His gaze is blazing like there's a fire inside him, like he's in the fires of hell and I'm the one who put him there. He takes my face and kisses the edge of my mouth. He draws me over the separation between our seats.

He takes the other edge of my mouth and lowers me to his lap.

Am I feeling a huge erection against my abdomen?

Yes, yes I am.

He wants me.

He wants me so much I shiver with the knowledge. He pulls me close as he drags his mouth up my jawline and toward my ear, taking his time, typical Saint. *You smell good*, he whispers in my ear, his fingers running up my belly, causing shivers all over me. He wants me, lust humming between us.

"I want to forget you, Rachel, but I know you're right, you weren't lying. At least not to me. You were lying to yourself. You told yourself you'd get to the truth of me and all that time, you wouldn't admit that you were falling in love with me."

I hold his gaze, my lungs leaden in my chest. "And if that's true?"

"It's true, Rachel." His eyes gleam with tender possessiveness.

I blush and lower my face, and when he reaches to slip his hand under my shirt and his fingers skim up my abdomen, I whimper and halt him by the wrist. "No, Malcolm, no. You're going to take me to the edge, and then I'll be there alone."

He groans. "If I go to the edge with you, I'll never come back."

"What happened to my risk taker?"

"It's not just myself I'm worried about. It's my cautious girl who, like my fine wine, comes tightly wrapped and packaged."

I lift my fingers, touch the hard square of his jaw, abrading my fingertips with his five-o'clock shadow. "Break me. As long as you're touching me. Shatter me. Use me. Just want me."

Malcolm. Powerful and in control. I touch his lips with my fingertips, he's tense and still. I shudder inwardly touching him, but he doesn't move.

I lower my hand, burning red that he doesn't move his hand on my bare skin.

He rasps out, watching me through narrow eyes, "You still respond to me like before."

"I'm the same. I never lied to you." My heart pumps in fear of his rejection, but I can't stop myself from needing his for-giveness. "I wanted to be with you and to see you. I didn't want to stop," I admit, easing my hand up his silk tie. I feel his abs bunch under my fingers.

I let my fingers wander, never once taking my eyes off his stormy green ones.

He lifts his hand to tug on my ear. I squeeze my eyes shut when he speaks, surprising me with his thick voice. "I remem-ber this ear . . ." He tugs it a little.

I open my eyes to find him staring at me.

I melt.

"When you tease me, it hurts."

"No, this hurts." He curls his hand around my arm and I respond a little, moaning in my throat. "If I put my hand on you, you arch to my touch. You push closer so every inch of my hand is on you. You look at me like I'm a bastard, like I gave you your every dream and then took them all away. But you still want my hands on you?"

"Yes. But I want you to trust me."

"Trust you? Rachel, I don't trust *myself* with you."

I wipe a stray tear. "I want dibs on you," I whisper, broken.

Our eyes meet for the slightest second and the moonlight hits his face so that he's so beautiful it's otherworldly. He grabs my face and inches his head closer, tilting his mouth to my ear.

"I miss you," I blurt out, reddening when I hear myself say that.

"Do you? Miss me?"

"I miss you so much. I can't forget you, and I don't want you to forget me either." I swallow.

He grabs my face and inches his head closer, and when I open my mouth to say more, he says, "Shh." Careful like I'm fragile, he draws my face to his.

I shudder as his lips ghost over the corner of my mouth.

His voice is so textured, it's hardly understandable. Warmth from his big hand seeps into my cheeks as he edges back and strokes his thumb over my lips. "We're going to start back up slow and easy." The forests in his eyes are deep with intensity. "And when I'm ready, I'm going to ask you to be my girlfriend, and it's going to be the last time I ask, Rachel. If you say no, that'll be the last no you say to me about anything."

God, I want him to ask me now. I turn my face and press a kiss on his thumb and he uses my action to rub his thumb along my lips a little, like he did when he fed me wine.

Longing unfurls inside me like a ribbon, soft and warm. I can't even describe the way I want him to kiss me again.

"Don't tease me," I whisper.

"I'm not teasing you."

My eyes well up. "I want you to be greedy, to want all of me, like before, Saint."

He grabs my face firmly in both hands. "Go out Friday with me."

"Yes," I gasp, "I'd love to."

"It's black tie. Do you have something to wear?"

I look at the violent tenderness on his expression, my lungs like rocks in my chest as I keep on nodding and nodding. "I . . . I'm sure I have something here to wear."

"Go buy a dress, it's on me."

"No!" I laugh. "Sin."

"Yes," he insists. "There's no more saying no, remember."

My breathless voice is barely audible. "At what time should I be ready on Friday?" I ask.

"Quarter to nine? Starts earlier but I've got a long week ahead too."

I know why, Saint. I know it's because you need more and more and always more and I want you to want me like that, all of me.

And I know why you want me at M4, Saint.

Even when you were mad at me, you were trying to protect me. You still are.

"Still getting the moon?" I ask.

He's quiet. Then, "Something like that."

And silence again.

I step out his door, peering inside. "Thank you for my lifetime collection of wine," I add with a little smile.

His smirk is back. "You're welcome."

We stare for a minute. From the shadows, his eyes gleam a pure male gleam as he looks at me. I hurt thinking this isn't real, it can't be real.

"I'm a challenge to you, Saint. You'll finally get me and then you'll be done with me."

Before I can turn around to walk away, he grabs my hand in

his. He pulls me closer to the door. Reaching out with his free arm, he snaps open the glove compartment, and brings out a pen.

My heart stutters when I recognize the pen.

It's the pen from the hotel room.

I'm singed by his fingertips on mine as he brings my palm to his lap. His eyes blaze between his lashes when he notices me tremble, and his gaze never leaves my face as he scrawls something on my palm. Then he curls my fingers closed.

"Don't underestimate me," he whispers.

I savor the possessive way he looks at me as he speaks, so thickly it's almost inaudible, as he slowly—torturously slowly—lets go of my hand. "Good night, Rachel."

I feel his eyes on my retreating back as I head toward my building.

When I turn by the door, my sexy parts tingle as I see him one last time; he's lounging back with an arm draped on the passenger seat, predatorily, with deceptive relaxation, but I've never seen eyes look at me so intensely as he stares at me through the open car window.

Helpless to free myself from his gaze, I feel for the door handle, manage to open it, and then exhale when I'm inside.

Shutting the door, I put my fingers on the glass. I can feel Saint through it and the rumble of his car as he starts it back up. I feel his chest under my fingertips and the energy of his being, like a bolt of white-hot liquid lightning flowing through my veins.

I force myself to go upstairs, then walk into my apartment and then lean on the shut door, breathless and I open my hand to read what he wrote.

DIBS.

BLACK TIE

"I say the baby blue."

"I vote the light pink."

"Baby blue. The perfect event deserves the perfect dress, just like the perfect man deserves the perfect girl," Gina argues with Wynn.

"I'm not perfect, but I want to look perfect tonight," I tell them both.

"Your billionaire just struck gold with you tonight, you look like a million bucks—well invested and soon to yield."

"Wynn!" I laugh.

"I still don't get why you didn't just bring him up to your room yesterday and let him stake a physical claim on you."

"Because . . . we haven't been together in a month."

"Exactly why you shouldn't have talked at all! What's there to talk about? He wants you, you want him."

I rummage through my earrings for a pair of small silver

studs that bring out the gray in my eyes. "He . . . well, we've gone over it, I've told you two."

"No, you haven't. You get red and that's it. You can't talk about him without spacing out . . ."

I groan. My friends, Gina and Wynn, they want to know that I'm going to be all right.

"He read my article," I say.

They're looking impatient, their faces alive with anticipation. And I'm remembering. I feel his hands cup my face again. I feel his eyes on me again. His lips so close, and so far away. And suddenly . . . on the very edge of my lips. I look down at the palm of my hand, the invisible *Dibs* that unfortunately washed off after a week of showers.

"He asked me to go out with him tonight."

Gina opened one of my wines and when she comes back with three foam cups, I tell myself—please don't ever let Sin see we're drinking this wine in foam cups. "Publicly?" she asks, handing a cup to each of us.

"Finally?" Wynn asks, taking a sip.

Setting mine aside, I nod as the butterflies fly fly fly in me. *Still* hidden in my closet is *his* shirt. I pulled it out of hiding last night—a shirt that brings back every memory—then I quickly stripped and slipped my arms into the sleeves, buttoning it up.

And that's how I slept.

It felt like hot, sheet-clawing sex on my skin. I lay in bed, my hormones all crazed, telling myself that I'm not going to do anything sexy until *he* does it to me.

"And I said yes. And he told me to get a dress."

He'd said it low but casual, as if it were the most natural thing for him to do for me, in his voice that never fails to get to me. Then I refrain from telling them the rest; that he marked my hand with a pen . . . and I went to my bed, and called my mother in the darkness, and told her . . . and unexpectedly, burst out crying from the happiness when I heard her voice.

"We're doing this black tie thing and if it's the last thing I do, I want to look incredible tonight," I admit, looking at myself in the mirror above my vanity.

I haven't looked this happy in a while—but I haven't felt this happy in my life.

"This dress does the trick. The side slit is perfect, the strapless bare shoulders, the way it goes all the way down to your toes. You want to say: *you know I'm naughty deep down but it's only for you*," Wynn says.

"Oh please, like he's not naughtier than anything we've ever known," Gina groans.

I laugh. My cheeks flare red as I think about him and wonder if he's as desperate to be with me as I am with him.

"But did he read your article? Something in it must've done something to him."

Wynn brings out the copy of the magazine I have hidden under my bed, mainly because it has a picture of him, and taps on the last sentence. "This part: *I'd leap blindly into the air if only there were even a 0.01 percent chance that he'd still be there, waiting to catch me.*"

"Wynn. You two. Help me get ready!"

They turn on the music and with "Sugar" by Maroon 5 playing, I keep prettying up for him, repeatedly brushing my hair until it falls down my back, as lustrous as glass.

For weeks, I've been alone, staring at my laptop, hearing its low hum. It's quiet for the night, the reporter tucked away. Now, the one humming is me. I'm wearing a dress fit for a princess. Now my friends are fussing around me, pulling out matching bags and shoes.

Gina is being especially helpful. Gina, who's been concerned about me getting my heart broken. "Now you're all eager for me to hook up with the same guy you wanted me to stay away from? You're Team Saint now?" I tease her.

She pauses. "I'm Team what makes you happy. And . . . well, from what Tahoe told me, yes."

I roll my eyes. "You believe that man?"

"He loves Saint as much as I love you!" she says. "He didn't enjoy your breakup any more than I enjoyed watching you mope. He said . . ."

"What?" I ask, my full attention on her.

"He thinks Saint is really into you because usually people only fuck up with him once," she specifies.

Wynn scowls. "What else did he say? If you're going to be talking to him then you must tell us when you talk about Rache."

"I only talked to him yesterday, and he said, and I quote, 'Saint's really into your best friend. Never seen him like this—ever.' "

I never thought my sexy parts could blush but they've been blushing every time I think of him.

"What does Momma Rachel say? Does she know?" asks Wynn.

"Mother?" I laugh. Her name is Kelly, not Rachel, but the girls call her Mom or Momma Rachel.

"She wants to meet him. She's excited that he came over. But I don't want to pressure him right now, my momma will have to wait until we see where this is going."

"Okay, let's get real here though. Are you planning to sleep with him?"

"YES! Dude, YES, I PLAN TO SLEEP WITH HIM. I'M DYING TO!" I say, laughing with pure giddy anticipation.

"The car's downstairs!" calls Wynn from the window, then she goes to the kitchen to ring him up, and peers into my room. "He's coming up."

"Okay." Inhaling sharply at the news, I hurry to finish strapping up my shoes and get a sheer blue shawl from a closet.

"Hey, Rache," Gina says, grabbing my hand. She looks at me and squeezes. "I'm happy for you, it's been breaking my heart. Because I do have one, you know? Paul didn't take it all, only the men's part. But the girl's part is yours and Wynn's." She looks a little emotional, her eyes glistening a little. "You know I don't believe in love. But I believe in second chances, and this is yours, Rache. And you know, I kind of admire his persistence. He really seems set on getting you."

I squeeze her hand, breathless at the thought. "You have no idea how he is when he's after what he wants. Patient but so, so ruthless."

She smiles at me, and I smile back. Dropping my hand, she heads to peer out the door. "Don't open it yet, Wynn, she has to look perfect," Gina orders, but seconds later, Wynn is the one we hear speaking.

"Saint, come in! She's just about ready!"

I hear his low voice as he greets her and I'm not immune to the sound.

I'm in my bedroom, but through the parted door, I see a glimpse of a long arm in a black jacket, silver cuff link and white cuff—his hand at his side. Tanned and square, his long fingers idle. I feel a visceral reaction seeing that hand, those strong, knowing fingers, my body flushing in remembrance of how it feels when he touches me.

I take one last look at myself in a strapless blue dress that falls to my feet, with a long, sexy slit on the left side, the color bringing out the bluish shades in my gray eyes. My hair is loose and, because my shoulders are bare and I could get cold, I draw the matching shawl a little higher.

The nerves tangle up inside me as I step out and take in the full image of Malcolm. His back is to me, but I take a tiny pleasure in seeing the back of his head, his confident stance, the incredible amount of energy he seems to suck from his surroundings.

"Oh, there she is!" Wynn happily tells him, signaling past his shoulder.

He turns, one hand in his pocket, the other at his side, and I can't help but notice how he makes a fist when he sees me. "Rachel," he says.

A massacre of emotions sweeps over me.

I can't fight the nature of my body, and though I want to look cool, I'm blushing bright red as I smile shyly. "Hey, Sin."

I walk over, tentatively set my hand on his chest and, seeing the admiring way he's looking at me, press up on my toes to kiss his jaw.

He touches my bare back and holds me in place, prolonging the time that my lips are on his skin.

"You ready?" he asks quietly into my earlobe, so only I can hear.

I nod and we say goodbye to the girls. He slips his large, square hand into my smaller one, and as he leads me out of the apartment, I turn and see Gina mouthing, "Ohmigod!" and Wynn, a big wide "AAAAAAA!"

When we reach the sidewalk, Otis opens the door of the Rolls as Malcolm gives him instructions. I've barely slid into the center of the seat when the door on the other side opens, and Sin slides onto the bench opposite mine.

I don't know if he likes my little strapless blue dress, the pink-painted toes displayed by my pumps, or the long slit on the side of said long dress. All I know is that my skin has broken out in goose bumps because of his nearness. And as he settles down across from me and his eyes take a slow, delicious trek up my body, there's a little bonfire in my stomach.

I check him out too, because his tuxedo loves him so thoroughly it's an instant aphrodisiac to watch them together. God, I'm this living, wanting, throbbing ache now.

"Hey," he says, his eyes just a little bit liquid. "You look beautiful." His eyebrows pull low then, shaping a perfect frown. "Though I was supposed to buy you a dress."

"No," I deny, smiling and shaking my head firmly.

"Yes," he grins. "Stop saying no to me."

Jesus. He looks at me with his green, green sparkling eyes, and I'm gone, gone, totally gone.

"I said yes to this black tie," I counter.

I'm not supposed to feel shy right now. If there is a man who knows me, it's *this* man. But he's so masculine and looking at me as if I'm so female, he has the ability to make me feel so young and so terribly fragile.

"I bribed you with wine, I've come to know your vices," he gruffs out teasingly. Then, he reaches out to take my hand and draws me across the car, to his bench. He chucks my chin when I'm settled down. "Your *every* vice," he adds, deathly sober now.

"Do you?" I playfully say. "You don't know them all. If you did, you'd be kissing me."

He steals a heavy-lidded look at my mouth and I get a delicious little squeeze in my lower body when I realize he *is* going to kiss me. "But if you kiss me, you're going to mess up my lip-stick," I say, but he's already curling his strong arm around my waist and slowly, surely, dragging me flush to his side.

"Your lipstick will look great on me."

"Sin!" I throw my head back and laugh.

He trails his thumb along the curve of my neck. "That laugh of yours," he tells me quietly.

He says it as if it's his greatest discovery.

A hairsbreadth from my ear, he whispers, "I can think of over five feet of you that I can kiss without messing your lip-stick."

Suddenly trembling in anticipation when I recognize the look in his eyes, I let him brush the shawl off my shoulders, laughing faintly and chiding "Malcolm" as he eases my hair aside to reveal the curve of my neck and shoulder.

He rubs his thumb along my collarbone and looks into my eyes as he continues to gently fondle my skin. He kisses the roundest part of my shoulder, his lips caressing up and down, side to side, before he sets a second kiss upward, heading toward my neck.

"Rachel," he whispers, so thick and raw, trailing his fingers to the R necklace resting at the base of my throat.

I'm acutely aware of his fingers shifting the small, gold let-ter aside. Then his warm fingertips are lifting the metal so he can press his lips into the delicate nook where my pulse is flut-tering wildly. I'm mad with lust under his moist breath on my skin, the space between his thigh and mine, the deliriously slow path of ghost kisses he drops on his way up my neck, toward my jaw.

"I lose," he says when he reaches my mouth.

I'm confused. I'm bewildered by his meaning. He's defi-nitely not falling asleep—his stare is as alert as ever. But he said

I lose and I can *see* that he's really determined to lose somehow. Determined to lose against whatever it is he's fighting. He looks completely unapologetic too.

"I lose," he repeats.

My eyes widen when he reaches out and brings me over to his lap and every bit of Malcolm is surrounding me, enveloping me, maddening me. The dark gleam in his eyes is completely serious, completely unlike the times he teases me. Jaw set, he curls a hand around my nape and pulls me to the wall of his chest, so close that all that's between us is my dress and his shirt.

His eyes are fastened to my mouth now and OMG, I'm so breathless when he brushes his lips across mine.

"Do you think it's this intense between us because of what happened?" I whisper.

His lips feather across mine again. "I don't know . . . but I'm pursuing it. I'll take this fire any day over the ice I live in."

His chest is rising slowly, and I'm starting to pant. I'm trembling all over. My heart is beating madly and I'm holding my breath, waiting for what he'll do next. His warm hands, his strong chest, his soft mouth suddenly pressing to the corner of mine. I catch a sob as he sets the ghost kiss right there, right where I need it, where I love it, where it branded me from the first time.

The lipstick doesn't matter anymore, nothing matters.

I open my lips, but he drags his mouth up the side of my face and exhales slowly, fisting a hand in my hair as he holds me to his chest. I don't move a muscle. If he's giving me time to protest, I can't. I just can't. I missed him so much, a ball of emotion is forming in my stomach and my throat and my heart.

His delicious scent is killing me. So familiar I'm high.

His hair tickles the side of my face as he goes to the other corner, and I can smell his soap, and when he sets his lips fully on mine, I quiver. He slips his tongue lightly into my mouth, as if testing my resistance.

I open easily and when his tongue strokes over the side of mine, I rub back languorously, a low, dull throb building between my legs.

He eases back and then he's staring down at me with smoldering heat that's almost frightening. He's looking at me like I'm something else, something extraordinary, something perfect, like he can't believe I'm trembling in his arms.

His hands frame my face, his palms swallowing it as his lips start to crush over mine harder. Groaning, he starts kissing me a little bit faster, and I can't get enough, can't work my mouth fast enough to get all of him that I want. I push my fingers into his hair—his hair! And let him use the small of my back to press my breasts against his chest as he sucks on my tongue, slow and greedy. Saint is kissing me like he wants me more than the world he likes to conquer and more than the moon he's never been able to get.

We kiss a little more.

I pour all my love into the kiss. My walls are crumbled at my feet when the kiss stops, but I have no energy to pull them up right now. My lids are heavy, but so are his. I'm struggling to breathe, but his chest is pushing against his shirt as he breathes deeper too.

"I missed you," I whisper.

He murmurs into the top of my head, "I missed you too."

We fall silent then, simply in each other's arms, until we reach our destination.

I've never been both so relaxed and at the same time buzzing all over.

When the car halts, Saint wipes my lipstick off his face, strokes his thumbs over my lips while I fix my hair, then he steps out first to a few audible gasps outside. He stretches his hand into the car for me, I slip my hand into his and then let him pull me out, immediately stunned by the dozens of heads in line at the entrance of the party already fixed in our direction. They spot Saint and immediately their curiosities are piqued as to who he's with, so they glance at me and can't seem to hide their surprised faces.

I'm shaking inside but his hand, oh, it feels so steady as we head over to the bouncer to be admitted inside.

He squeezes my fingers to catch my attention. "The look in your eyes. What are you afraid of?" he asks as the bouncer swiftly recognizes him and tugs open the door for us.

"The world."

He grins down at me, so tall and powerful. "Relax," he says. "The world's in my pocket."

And I feel relief flood me as I let myself believe it.

The ballroom is glistening when we arrive. It seems like all of the rich in the city are present. I force myself to hold my head high.

Modern glass chandeliers hang like tangled wires from the ceiling, while a wall of shimmering waterfalls greets us to the right. There's a live orchestra, chocolate fountains, and perfect round tables covered in white linens and silverware, complete with Tiffany chairs to match. We venture deep into the crowd, walking amidst an impressive amount of glittering dresses, men in black ties, women in exotic perfumes. I'm aware of how those women watch Saint, and the men watch me. God, it's incredible, the eyes he draws. Even if people don't know who he is, Malcolm's presence is so magnetic you instantly know he's *someone*.

"Don't let them own you, Rachel."

"I won't," I say.

"You're with me."

I look into his eyes. "I know."

"Then let's make a round and I'll take you away . . . if you're good," he warns. And there, suddenly, is the spark of mischief in his eyes that I've missed so much.

With a brief look at my mouth that reminds me of the kisses he just gave me, he leads me to our table and introduces me to our table companions. I keep expecting to be sneered at, shunned. But soon I realize, no. These people respect Malcolm too much for that.

And they steal him away every second they can too.

I engage in a brief conversation with a couple he introduced me to, shaking my head when three different women come to flirt with Saint.

When we finally come back together, I can't help but tease him. "Can't you be alone for a minute? Without anyone catering to you?"

He smiles at me and turns me to a spectacular-looking older woman. "Rachel Livingston, this is Norma Dean. She's our host."

"Oh, I'm familiar with your work! I read your piece on *this* thing right here." She smacks Malcolm's chest. "And I was hooked by your voice. Such a lovely, smart, passionate girl. What took you so long to snatch her up?" she chides.

"Traffic."

When I look up, Malcolm's lips are curled slightly and his eyes are twinkling and a ribbon of heat unfurls in my stomach.

And then I realize after her comment that maybe, incredibly, some of these people also respect me.

He soon leads me back to our table and introduces me to a few CEOs and their wives, philanthropists and entrepreneurs. They're all older than us and very friendly.

I feel like I belong, even though I've never belonged here before, and I realize as we sit here discussing everything from ponies that they bought for their daughters, to business merger news, to the best hairstylists in town, that Malcolm wouldn't have brought me somewhere if he thought I'd be shunned or laughed at. He respects these people too, and expects them to respect me. Every time one of them says his name and leans forward a bit in their seat to talk to him, they do so with such admiration that I realize he knows that my just being in this space of his will protect me. And I do feel safe.

A man has taken up a conversation with Malcolm on one side, while a woman is completely telling me the story of her marriage to the man sitting beside *her*. She's at the part about how the ex-wife and her actually became good friends, when Malcolm whispers, "Let's get away for a bit, Rachel." He looks at me as though it's not even a question. "If I can borrow her for a bit, Julie," he apologizes.

I'm aware of us drawing a few glances when we stand, his friends raising their eyebrows as he takes me by the arm and helps me to my feet.

He puts his hand on the small of my back and I feel it rush through me until I feel it in the tips of my breasts, between my toes, as we head out of the room to a set of elevators.

I notice that a couple of groups of young ladies in the room pause what they're doing to watch us head to the elevators. They clearly don't like him leaving with me.

"Your girlfriends weren't too happy about you stealing away with me."

His lips curve in amusement. "They're not my girlfriends."

"So what do you call all those girls who strip for you and cater to your whims for a day or two . . . or four?"

He stares at me, laughing, his smile like a bolt of light. "They're just girls."

We reach the top of the building, and he leads me out onto the roof terrace. "Come look at this."

I turn with him and head to the very edge of the building's roof, by the railing, with a breathtaking view of the lake. A sliver of moonlight dances in the middle of the water tonight. As he looks at it, I watch him in my peripheral. I have a thousand pictures of him but none like this. Pensive. Raw. The face I see right now isn't for any camera, it's for nobody to see.

"Won't your friends miss you downstairs?" I ask, my voice whispery.

"They know I'm a busy man. They also know I enjoy my privacy when I feel like being private." He studies me with the moonlight gleaming in his eyes. "I have a date with that blue dress of yours."

"No you don't." But my stomach dips in excited contradiction. "I have no intention of letting it get acquainted with your tuxedo."

"Yes, you do."

He takes my hand, his warm fingers closing around mine. "I feel like being private right now."

There's a swooping pull in my insides as he reels me closer.

He's the first to move, his hand lifting only a fraction to rest on my face as he curls me in his arm so we both face the lake.

I hadn't ever grown accustomed to being held like this, the few months we were together. I stand here and just absorb the feeling of being close to someone who's so much bigger and harder than I am.

MANWHORE +1 129

We stay like that. The very air over the water seems electrified. He runs his hand through my hair and the sensation is so sweet and so intoxicating, I couldn't move if I wanted to.

He obviously knows he affects me. But he looks affected too, his body stone-like and buzzing with tension. "I wanted to show you this. You see that lake?"

The wind brings his scent toward me and I swallow and almost taste it.

"I don't ever want to leave Chicago simply because I love being near that lake. My mother used to take me out there— the *Pearl* was her yacht," he says. "She'd never let me get in the water. After I was sick, she became paranoid. So I had to test my limits in private."

"She took you out there just to look at what you couldn't touch?" He shrugs. "And now you test your limits all the time."

"I do. Sometimes to feel immortal, and sometimes to remind myself that I'm not."

His eyes are mesmerizing right now.

"She was a good mother?"

"She was a good mother; I was a bad kid." He smirks.

"No," I say, instantly.

He smiles.

God, my stomach moves every time he smiles at me.

"I'm telling you, Rachel."

"No. I don't believe you were a bad boy."

He laughs. "I'm still a bad boy, only I'm a man, with the ambitions of a man. The desires of a man."

As he investigates my reaction with a quiet but penetrating look at my face, I remember his father. The things I've seen and read online. In every video of them together I've seen, Saint is chill and controlled, admirably diplomatic even when the father is aggressive and full of venom. If Saint had been a "good" boy, though, he'd never have become who he is. His father would have kept his "good" boy under control, but instead, he became Malcolm Saint, and now the shadow Saint casts is so much grander than his father's ever was.

"You know," I hear myself offer, my voice showing my admiration for him, "my mother worked too much. Day and night. Maybe that's why my imagination flourished, it was sometimes the only company I had. We didn't really get to spend a lot of time together. Which makes me always want to give back, but it never seems like I can make it up to her."

"I know what you mean. I can never say goodbye to mine."

I've never been more aware of him as a human being.

Malcolm stands with his legs spread apart, staring out at the city, his profile mysterious and unreadable. I can tell by the sound of his deep breath he's trying to remain unaffected. By the conversation. Maybe by me. But when I brush my body against his and he looks at me, his eyes turn to fire.

"Come home tonight, with me."

One second I'm opening my mouth, trying to come up with an explanation why maybe we should take it slow, the next he brushes his mouth to mine.

"What are you doing?" I laugh nervously. "I'm going to end up with no lipstick at all."

My skin breaks out in goose bumps when his reply is merely a curve of his lips. "Tell me you want to talk about Interface," he whispers in my ear. That used to be our code for kissing . . . making out. "Tell me you left something at my place." He rubs his nose against my ear. "Tell me you want me tonight."

"I . . . I want to talk about Interface," I say, not able to hold back a small laugh.

He strokes a finger up my arm, watching me. "My goal is complete domination of the market . . ." he murmurs as he lowers his dark head, his lips soft and warm as they press on my throat. "Elimination of all competition . . ."

He ducks his head and I feel his mouth brushing, almost like air, over the tip of one breast. I can't breathe.

He lifts his head and frames my face in his hands, warm, strong hands, and then he smoothes a hand back, pulling me closer, his long fingers encompassing so much of me I feel it like a collar around the back of my neck. A collar that's remarkably welcome, that makes me feel safe and controlled while the rest of my body's in chaos.

His voice is low and gruff and his breath is too close to my face, my ear. "I'm taking over," he continues in a husky voice. "Until there's absolutely nothing left. Nothing before it. Nothing after it. Only what's mine, what I claimed and what I make of it." He kisses me then, and we kiss for a long time.

"Maybe I'll invest in this Interface," I whisper.

"Come down with me. One walk across the room to meet a few of my business partners. And then we leave."

"I haven't said yes yet."

"I'm not asking on this."

When we head back downstairs, he places a hand on my waist. He caresses it as we go down—and oh, I definitely feel like his date.

"You're a devil." I laugh as I check my reflection in the shiny elevator wall.

"And you want me."

I mock-gasp. "You're a deluded devil."

"I'm one who won't stop until I get what I want."

When we step off the elevator, he guides me into the ball-room with his hand on my nape. The touch is light enough to remind me I'm free to choose, but with just the right amount of pressure that says—*I'm here. I desire you. Turn yourself over to me for a night and I'll make every inch of you remember you're my woman.*

He lowers his hand to the small of my back, even when he's stopped at a table to chat with a few businessmen. I let him introduce me and talk mostly to the men.

Only a few of the younger women at the table make me a little uncomfortable.

They're draped in the most beautiful jewels, and looking at my tiny, simple R. Their dresses glitter and sparkle as they take in my plain silk one. Their hairdos are styled and swept and elegant as they stare at my straight locks. And judging by those looks, they just can't seem to believe that the one standing next to *him* is *me*.

And still Malcolm's hand remains on the small of my back.

I'm surprised that, for the first time since I've known Malcolm, I don't care about these women, if they read my article or not, if they're jealous, if they think I'm pretty enough for Malcolm Saint.

I'm human and flawed and hopeful and afraid and strong and weak and independent—and in love with him in a way I'm *sure* they are not.

I'm proud to be who I am.

I'm proud of where I stand.

REBOOTING US

Once we're in the car and the partition between us and Otis is fully up, Malcolm presses me up against his side and his lips come down on mine. He parts my lips and his taste fills me, going like a shot of crack to my heart. A soft noise leaves me as I kiss him back with all I've got.

My fingers flutter over his shoulders and then I curl my hands around the back of his neck as we slow down and start kissing more leisurely, savoringly, getting reacquainted again.

"Are you okay with this?" he asks as he sets my mouth free. His eyes are so dark, I can hardly see the green in his pupils.

Nodding and breathless, I slide my fingers into his hair and pull his delicious mouth back to me. He fits his lips to mine, to the way he knows just how to.

He plays with my tongue a little, sucks gently on my lower lip.

The fingers of one hand trail under the fall of my hair and then he slides them upward to cradle the back of my head in his palm, and with that motion alone, he's got me pinned in place. I'm helplessly subjected to his hungry mouth, and the way he's kissing and sucking on me is so downright hot I've never been so turned on.

I end up lying down on the bench seat with his body above mine, my hands anxiously gripping fistfuls of his collar.

His tongue sweeps and sweeps into my mouth and when he retreats to give me a smoldering look, I notice the way his green, green eyes have darkened like a night forest.

"I miss you," he rasps, looking at me so fiercely it's as though he's commanding me to understand what this means.

"I miss you too," I croak feelingly.

"I miss the taste of you, the feel of you, the sounds you make." Clenching his jaw as if he's remembering what it was like to miss me, he strokes his curled index finger down the line of my jaw, watching what he does. I watch the emotions play across his features as he opens his hand and caresses my face and neck. Determination. Hunger. Control.

I'm panting, aching, wanting, *waiting*. Holding me by the back of the neck, he pulls me up to a sitting position and in for another wet kiss. Leisurely, his mouth slants from one side to the other as he tastes me from all angles. I feel delicious, juicy, luscious. Wanting to taste him just as thoroughly too, I draw his tongue into my mouth and suck, surprised by how the sucking motion causes every centimeter of my body to squeeze and Saint to reflexively tighten his hold on me.

He groans and draws me onto his lap and shifts me so that I straddle him, then he lowers the top of my dress with a little tug at the elastic of my strapless.

"Malcolm, what are you doing?" I gasp, covering my chest with my arms as my breasts pop free.

"I'm looking at you." Completely shameless and in control, he takes both my arms and lowers them to my sides.

I squeeze my eyes shut, then open them, embarrassed to realize he's probably noticed I used nipple stickers to keep from having to use a bra tonight. I didn't want my nipples to be poking out, and now my perky breasts are staring up at him with two small, round tan stickers on them.

He runs his thumbs over each. My sex squeezes when I notice his gaze is loving, appraising, possessive. And dark. So very, very dark.

"I meant to take them off before you saw," I whisper.

He kisses the corner of my mouth. "I'll do it." Then he leans close and kisses one tip of my breast over the sticker. Then the other, his lips warm and gentle. He then raises his head as he seizes each sticker between his thumbs and fingers and looks into my eyes as he gently pulls off one, then the other.

A frisson of need runs through me.

The act is strangely intimate. Looking into each other's eyes as he does this to me.

He lifts his thumb to his mouth and my sex tightens when he licks it. He does the same with his other thumb. Then he uses both to rub my nipples clean, and I almost moan out loud.

He speaks to me in a thick voice—my toes curling. I can feel how hard he is between my legs. "They're all mine now," he says.

He centers me on his lap again and drags the skirt of my dress up to my hips, and once it's bunched up where he wants it, he ducks his head to take one nipple into his mouth, and when he covers the hardened little point with heat and wet, I rock my hips against his hardness. "Saint," I beg.

He releases my breast and looks at me. He looks as if he

wants to devour me whole as he leans in to continue kissing my lips.

He just won't stop kissing me, his hands cupping my ass as he draws me up tighter against his erection.

I quiver in need. "Oh god."

Gasping, I rake my nails against his scalp as I drag my mouth across any part of him that I can: the crown of his head that smells of shampoo, his shadowed, raspy jaw. Then I bite his earlobe. My body's acting of its own will, pressing closer, a moan leaving me when he rubs my nipples with his thumbs in the most delicious, heart-stoppingly slow way.

I want to make out forever, and I want to let go when he can let go with me. But he's hard between my legs, his mouth is killing me, and I feel the tension in my body tighten and tighten for orgasm.

"We need to stop," I groan apologetically, fisting a handful of his hair. "I'm at the edge already, and I don't want to be there alone."

"I'll be right there with you."

He grabs the back of my neck and only kisses me the rest of the way to his place, and when the car turns into the building's driveway, he stops with one last grazing kiss on the corner of my mouth as he tugs the skirt of my dress down and then pulls the rest of my strapless back up.

I try to pull myself together and fix my hair, a little mortified. "I can't imagine how I look."

He runs his eyes quickly over me. "You look ravishing."

"Ravished by you," I say, shoving his shoulder a little bit with a laugh.

He grins. "Yes."

He smoothes a hand down my back as he leads me into the lobby of his apartment building.

"Mr. Saint," he's greeted by the staff.

He just lifts his hand in greeting.

Once in an elevator, I get a glimpse of us in the mirror and he looks divine, his lips a little pink, his hair a little messed up, and I look kind of sultry, my hair slightly mussed, eyes heavy. As we ride the elevator to the penthouse, a couple rides with us, and I try to behave and keep my hands at my sides. The couple is whispering and I realize they know who he is. And maybe they even know who I am.

"Good night!" they say effusively as they step out.

"Good night," Saint murmurs as I smile and nod at them.

The elevator doors shut and he tugs me back to him, his head sweeping down. We kiss, softly, until the *ting*, and then he pulls away, his eyes as heavy as mine feel.

I'm shaking in anticipation when he takes my hand and draws me into his apartment.

He leaves me to press a wall switch to turn on a few dim lights, tosses his jacket aside, drops his cell phone, and kicks off his shoes.

The city blazes with night lights behind him as he comes back. And the sight of him in those slacks, white shirt, hair rumpled by my fingers, bulldozes through any fear I could have, any tentativeness about doing this. I don't just want to do this. I never want to stop.

He walks toward me, eyes warm and liquid. He lifts his hand when he reaches me, his gorgeously strong and smooth hand, his fingers slowly caressing my neck.

Pheromones: the delicious scent of him. I swear water is the substance my thighs are made of now, and the rest of me is fire—and Malcolm Saint is the gasoline that's lighting me up.

My world feels right again as his fingers drag down the front of my body, over my clothes, down my hips, then up my ass, the small of my back, until they come back up to curl around half of my face.

Green eyes capture mine, and I can see the silent question there. And then, I can hear him asking it, his voice pure dry bark. "Slow and deep? Or fast and hard?"

"Both," I breathe.

He inhales sharply, his jaw clenching at my answer, then he coaxes me closer and, as an affirmative, sets a soft but firm kiss on my lips. "Yeah," he says.

I hear him unzip my dress and a sigh of gratitude leaves me as he gently pulls it down my body.

"Take me," I breathe.

"I'm taking you."

"Use me. Do anything you want to me."

"No," he says chidingly. "You use something you discard. And I'll never be done with you."

My dress falls in a pool of blue at my feet. I stand motionless as a statue, trembling as the air surrounds me, wearing nothing but my panties and my strappy high-heeled sandals and my heart in my eyes.

Saint kisses my eyelids. As if he sees.

He *sees*.

Then, he presses his lips to mine as he eases his fingers into my panties, finding my wet folds and playing gently with me. My knees buckle when he touches me; he catches me with one arm and then draws back to stare down at me—the breaths leaving my lips, my face dewy with lust.

His face is harsh with need as he moves his fingers into my wetness, his eyes the most beautiful shade of all, a kaleidoscope of green. When I gasp as he enters me with a finger, a flash of wild lust appears in his eyes. Then there's the dark black of his pupils growing and growing. And the glimmer of greed—greed for *me*.

No sooner does another gasp leave me than he kisses me harder, deeper, one instant apart, the next he's the owner of my mouth, then he's lifting me up and taking our wet kisses all the way to the bedroom.

"Here you are, Rachel," he says as if he can't believe it, and lowers me down on the bed.

"Don't . . . leave me, just stay," I curl my legs around his hips and my arms around his shoulders.

He reaches between my thighs and parts my legs a few inches, locates the wet little groove in my panties and rubs a little. His thumb slides, up and down, finds the swelling bud of my clit and rubs in a maddening circle.

"Does that feel good?" he asks, his voice raspy on his throat. Rasping on my *skin*.

My answer is one word, "perfect," my own voice textured with my emotions.

He rubs a little harder.

He's stroking me with his fingers over my panties as he leans over and nibbles on my lips—an innocent kiss on my lips, but I'm so raw with need, I'm slowly unraveling beneath him.

He reaches between us and tugs my panties down my legs. I'm still wearing my heels and I think they look sexy but Saint tugs one loose, then the other, dropping them to the floor.

"Saint . . ."

God, this man is going to kill me before he gets to actually *fuck* me.

He shifts above me, caresses one breast, bending to kiss it, wet and fast. His lips stay there, his hand curving around my hips to the curve of my ass, holding me as he sucks hard.

Pleasure slams me so hard I buck.

He murmurs tenderly, "Easy." Then he sucks my other nipple gently into his mouth, rolls his tongue over it, then draws it into his mouth again.

I fist the sheets in my hands as the orgasm builds fast and hard, a tension knotting from the core of my body. "Saint, I can't do foreplay right now." I tremble beneath him.

"God, I missed you," he rasps with a happy light in his eye, sliding his fingers up to cup my face, the look on his face so reverent I feel perfect. "You're like a spark, Rachel, all I need is to breathe on you and you catch fire."

I'm so undone, I'm a heartbeat away from coming. "Malcolm, please don't let me do this alone."

"You're not going anywhere without me," he says, not in the least bit worried as he pulls away to look at me with eyes that have never looked this heavy-lidded. I can't breathe. I'm gasping, my hands trembling at my sides as he starts to undress.

He strips off his shirt and then his slacks, I feel like I'm dreaming. He's shedding his clothes until it's all bare, all for me.

Tan, cut muscles, over six feet of pure testosterone-primed man. His skin feels so smooth and hot and hard when he lowers himself over me.

"Say you want me . . ." he murmurs, and then he dives and sweeps my mouth with his tongue. He twirls and pushes my own tongue with his, showing it where to move, what to taste, where to go . . . with his.

"I want you," I groan.

Reaching over his muscular shoulders as he settles between my thighs, I curl my legs around his hips and lock my ankles together. He takes my hands and draws them over my head, then he laces his fingers through mine, and drives inside.

Body-slammed. Perfection in every way. We groan once he's inside, and our bodies stop moving and stay like this.

"Like that?" He cups my face and looks down at me.

We're both motionless from the pleasure. We stare at each other. We're each taking in the other's face as if we can't believe we're here.

He pulses thickly inside me and it feels like every inch of my body is holding on to him. And I swear at this moment that I never ever want to let go of him, and as long as I can help it, I never will.

"Yes," I finally breathe, squeezing his hands holding mine above my head.

His green eyes flare bright with an emotion so raw, all my muscles tighten with the urge to orgasm to that look alone.

I don't think Saint has ever looked at me so possessively.

He moves out of me and then back in, and I moan as our flesh touches with his motions. Going up on his arms, he withdraws and pumps in again, establishing a rhythm that is deep and savoring and intense, almost as if he can't control it anymore.

He surges inside me and starts kissing my neck, as if he needs to taste me. I'm holding tight to him, clutching his bigger body to mine with my arms and legs, my mouth latching to any hard part it can. The rightness of being consumed like this and taken like this by the only man who's ever owned me is beyond believable. It's Sin inside me, Saint inside me, Malcolm inside me. Tension builds in me fast. He's in me; so in me, it's like we were never apart. We're moving as if we never stopped.

He takes my face in his hand, and his voice textures until it's barely discernible as he deepens his tempo. "Look into my eyes. Don't look away until you come apart for me."

I do.

I bite his neck, and then I do as he says and look into his eyes.

Watching the way his face clenches every time he's fully embedded inside me. With all that gentle strength of his perfectly under control, he pulls my arms up over my head, pins them beneath his as his body weight pins me down too, and feeling physically so helpless—as helpless as I've been, emotionally, all this time—I feel a ball of fire burst from inside me. I gasp and convulse beneath him, his name raw on my lips, his green eyes mercilessly watching me unravel. "Malcolm."

He keeps me in place as I come, driving slower and more deliberately inside me to prolong my orgasm, watching me with burning green eyes and then kissing my mouth the rest of the way through as he pumps faster, deeper, as exquisitely as ever. And then, what most gets me is the way his powerful arms clench all around me and I know he's letting go, coming with me.

We're motionless for a long time after. Saint is breathing deeply, and I'm breathing fast.

I smile against his face, where he set it down against mine as we recover. He smiles too, and slides a hand down my side to squeeze my ass affectionately. He laughs softly. All hot and male against me. I swear I just want to lie here and be super fucked and be super happy.

"Vixen," he murmurs as he rolls to his back and settles me against his bare chest, brushing my hair back. "You feel even better than I remember," he says quietly, looking into my eyes as he curls his hand around the back of my neck and gives it a squeeze, stroking the back of my ear with his thumb. "And I remember every time with you very well, Rachel."

God. These feelings.

"I remember you too," I finally manage.

We smile a little. And I'm so affected by his smile, being with him in bed like this, I feel a flush creep up to my cheeks.

I tug the sheet up to cover myself, and he raises a brow, but says nothing.

He disappears into the bathroom and when he comes back, I sit up uncertainly, gauging him. He drops on the bed and rests his back on a pillow, not even bothering with the sheets, his tan skin contrasting with the whiteness around him.

I remain sitting, hesitant, wondering if I should leave.

Using his palm, he turns my head, locks the angle of my face so he can start to kiss me, holding me firmly but gently against his body. "You'll remember tonight too," he says.

Body melt.

"Is that a promise?" I ask him.

"I break my promises, remember?" He studies my face, then he speaks, his eyes pure devil, "It's a warning."

We're sweaty and relaxed in his bed, the covers tangled around our feet when his hand starts wandering dangerously up my rib cage.

"Saint . . . you're killing me. You're just . . . wicked. I can't keep up with you."

"Come here," he coaxes.

His arm wraps around the back of my neck and pulls me to his side only to embrace me. His voice murmuring close to my ear brings out the goose bumps on my bare arms. "I'm only going to hold you, Rachel."

But just as he finishes speaking, he leans and kisses the corner of my mouth.

I feel the kiss between my legs. In my nipples. In my heart.

Breathless, I steal a touch and cup his square jaw. "You said you were only going to hold me. And you just kissed the corner of my mouth. Do you classify that as only holding? Sin?"

"I do." Although he smiles, the look on his face is intense. "Would you like to pretend I didn't do that?" He rubs the spot and looks down at me with hot eyes. I'll never forget the lust on his face as he looks at me. "Would you?" he presses, his voice gruff.

"No."

He kisses the corner of my mouth again, holding my face in one big hand.

I'm melting.

I'm scared.

I want him so much.

"If you hire me, you can't get away with that," I whisper.

He looks at my lips with the hunger of a panther. "Oh, I can get away with it."

"You've never touched any one of your employees."

"I make the rules." He raises a brow in challenge, and then starts lowering his head again.

I sit here, shivering, as his warm breath fans my face on the other side of my mouth. I swallow back a whimper, sliding my fingers into his hair. He exhales and goes to my ear, kissing the back of it, relaxing a little as I let him draw me back into his arms.

We stay there for a little while. I think I'm going to die tomorrow remembering.

I wrap my arms around his neck.

I want to speak but I don't want to break this. He seems to need to hold me and for me to let him, and I need this connection.

"Malcolm Kyle Preston Logan Saint," I say.

I feel him smile against my hair.

"Why so many names? Hmm?" I peer into his face.

"Because my father's stubborn. He was determined to name the first boy like *his* father. And my mother wanted to have four children, so she gave my father the right to choose first if she got to use the three she wanted next." He inhales and peers down at me. "I wasn't an easy birth. When they told her she might not be able to have any more children . . ."

"She gave all the names to you? Kyle, Logan, Preston . . ." I smile, then breathe, touching my fingers to his chest, "Saint."

"God, Rachel, you don't know what you do to me."

"Tell me."

"One day I'll tell you."

"Good things."

"Yeah. Good things."

His mouth starts trailing and my lungs start overworking as he puts them on my ear. My forehead. My cheek.

"What did you do all this time?" I ask him.

"I worked." His shoulder lifts carelessly. "Bought a new car. Tested a few planes. Got the top four. Three for the M4 directors and one for me."

"I've been watching baseball," I offer, setting my face on his chest with a smirk.

"Since when do you watch baseball?"

I shrug. "You know. I branch out now and then."

"Do you?" He's amused.

God, I love him amused.

"This is the year the Cubbies break the curse. Did you know that?"

"Really now."

"Hmm. Yes. With our star pitcher? And that ERA? It's definitely the year."

"Really now?" He purrs, shifting, interested, amused.

"Are *you* watching? Baseball?" I ask, and peer up into his face.

He peers back down at me with a cocky little grin. "I'm busy watching you talk baseball right now."

I shove him. "Come on. Have you?"

"Yeah."

I sigh and settle in closer, and he hugs me a little tighter. "You're right, it *is* the year the Cubs break the curse." He grins at me, and I grin back, melting so hard.

Melting so hard and wanting him again equally hard.

We haven't slept, aren't aware of time or space or place, only of each other. Holy god. I'm so aware of him it's as if I'm memorizing him all over again. The scent of his soap, his sheets, his shampoo, his warm, toasty skin, all the ways his green eyes change as he makes love to me, and how good it feels, right now, as he holds me.

He eases his forehead down on mine, then his hand turns my face aside so he can kiss me—I reach one arm behind me and caress his hair as I kiss him back, him inside me. "You're insatiable," I tease him. "Are you ready to go already?"

He tugs my ear. "As you know, Rachel, greedy men are insatiable by nature."

I laugh and drop back, pulling the sheet to cover my sweaty body just because I'm suddenly shy. Is this really me?

Am I back in Malcolm's bed?

Fucked to my bones?

My chest feels so full I am grateful, humbled, fearful, joyful. My job situation is a mess and I still worry about my mother and yet if I can slowly fix things with him, I feel like I can do anything.

Malcolm . . .

God, please let him be greedy. Please let him want all of me, not just this.

I watch him get up to get a foil packet and I plump the pillow, rearrange my hair, and pray to god I don't look a mess by the time he comes back. I hear him run the sink water.

I said I loved him before, but shit happened and I haven't had the courage to say it again. What happened after I said "I love you" the first time must have devalued my words so much that I'm not sure he even wants to hear them again. But I think he knows that I still love him.

I think the only reason he forgave me was because he seems to have an intuitive knowledge of me and I think he feels the love I feel for him as much as I feel the hurricane of his energy drawn toward me.

God. This falling in love—it's the subject of so many movies, songs, books, and artworks. It's as common to us as being born and dying and somehow just as mysterious.

There's never a warning.

You think it's lust first.

That the powerful feelings are something else.

Admiration and respect.

Then the feeling becomes stronger, deeper, and when you would do anything for them, when their happiness is your own, when even their flaws are fascinating, and when you want to be better, worthy of them, you know it's love.

What now?

He walks back to bed, flops on his back, and pulls me over him. Seeking closer, I twine my legs around his hips and wrap my arms around his shoulders as we start kissing, and after I mount him, and ride him, letting him take me to places only he's ever taken me to, I end up more exhausted than ever.

When we're done and I fall onto my back, we're both panting. I tentatively reach out and place my hand on top of his, staring at the ceiling in the way he is—kind of waiting to see what his reaction is.

I didn't know that I was holding my breath until he turns his hand and grabs mine in his grip, and holds it like it's the most natural thing in the world.

After our Saturday sex Olympics, we sleep almost all day Sunday.

We wake up slowly, lazily fucking. Then he tosses me one of his shirts as we head to his kitchen. Later he's in his living room as he works a little bit and I finish my coffee.

"I really should get home," I keep saying.

"It's raining out. Just stay here," he keeps saying back.

And by the time he seems to realize I am going to go change to leave, he stops working, scoops me up, and takes me to his bed, and then the only things raining are hot, smoldering Malcolm Saint kisses all over me.

ALL THE COLORS
IN THE WORLD

On Monday morning, I feel as if someone just turned on the light switch. Colors are bright and clear, my awareness of my body is exquisite. I wake up and Malcolm's chest is beneath my ear, his heart beating solid and slow, our bodies tangled along with the sheets.

When the alarm of his phone buzzes, he stretches slightly, exhales, then gets up to shower. I stay in bed, deliciously dead. I text the girls, I feel so delicious today OMG! And sore to my bones. I never want to leave this bed ☺

I'm excited to scream with my friends but that's almost the extent of what I plan to tell them—what I wrote on the text.

Is it strange that when you grow close to a man, you start keeping details from your closest friends? Friends who used to know everything about you? I'd never held things from my friends until I met Malcolm. Now there are things that seem to be private. Worthy of just me and him.

I text my mother, Momma, how are you feeling today?! So much to talk about when I see you! Love you!

Then I send an email to myself reminding me to work on my column when I get home.

I roll over and my sexy places hurt.

He rode me to the crests last night over and over.

It's like the world contains only two people, him and me.

I ease up from the bed, force my sore body into walking mode, and follow him into the huge bathroom. Quietly I brush my teeth with my finger using a little bit of his toothpaste and then I wash my hands, dry them, and run my fingers through my hair.

In the mirror, I see the frosted glass of his shower and I can make out the dark shadow of his tall, muscular figure inside. Then there's the pattering noise of water slapping his hard skin. After all the sex we had I shouldn't be instantly hot and aching but I am.

My phone pings outside, and I run out to check it. *Interview*, it warns. I check the time and notice I only have fifty minutes. Feeling too embarrassed to just leap into the shower with him, I go ahead and dress and then wait for him in the kitchen.

I prop myself up on the massive granite kitchen bar and sip my coffee, light streaming from the floor-to-ceiling windows. It's sunny today, windy of course because the flags and trees are swaying from what I can see, and from here it almost feels possible to hold the entire city if you spread your arms wide enough.

Between that view, and the view of the storm coming out of his bedroom in black slacks and open shirt, his hair wet as he talks on the phone and stares out the window, I feel a sigh work its way up my throat. I think of Gina and suddenly wish she didn't think donuts were the thing to sigh over; this is so much better. Maybe she *should* give Tahoe a chance?

Rachel! You're turning into the girl who wants all girls to see hearts and stars just because you are? That's Wynn! And Tahoe and Gina? Really? The last thing she needs is another broken heart.

Scowling at that, I scan the online news, stopping when I see some comments about Chicago's Darth Vader, aka Noel Saint, on the usual sites I visit.

NOEL SAINT'S LINTON CORP. TO ACQUIRE LOCAL MAGAZINE THAT EXPOSED SON'S SECRET ROMANCE ONLY LAST MONTH

I feel sick to my stomach.

Malcolm's just hung up and is having his own coffee, the *Tribune* spread before him while he's scanning his phone with the other hand. I slide off the bar. "Saint, I have to go. I can't be late today. I have an interview."

Malcolm frowns a little and lifts his head. "Interview? Where?"

I hesitate. "Well . . . I don't want to jinx it. But you know that I made some calls."

"Tell me who's seeing you," he coaxes.

His attention is too intense for that to be a casual question. One beat later under his scrutiny, I add, with a reluctant smile, "Please don't pull strings."

He cocks an arrogant brow. "Strings are there to be pulled."

I laugh. "Saint! Promise me."

"Tell me where," he says, setting everything aside.

"Not M4," I assure. I search his unreadable expression, then sigh. "I can't be at *Edge* anymore. I don't feel safe there."

He looks at me in silence as if waiting for me to say more.

"I can't go with you either, so don't suggest it. It would complicate things and I have a hard time with all the attention you get. This would only put your business sense into question."

"I disagree. I've got perfect business sense. We'd be lucky to have you." He cocks his head, and his eyes suddenly bathe me with admiration and concern. "You did everything for that magazine. You bared your soul for that magazine."

"It wasn't for *Edge*. I ended up baring my soul for *you*. I can get another job. *Edge* is not going to survive . . . you know that. Not without someone very savvy behind the wheel and with large pockets too. And if your father succeeds in purchasing it, I don't want to be there."

His glance becomes opaque as it always does when his father is mentioned.

"I know truth and loyalty are important to you, Saint," I continue. "And I won't work for a man who's constantly butting heads with you."

"Come work with me, Rachel." His voice is full of its usual depth and authority but it's silky with entreaty.

Hating to deny him, I still manage to shake my head. "I couldn't have you as a boss and then come to your bed, a girl has to draw a line somewhere, Sin." And then, when I realize what I just said—and wonder if I'm jumping into fourth gear too fast—I backtrack. "I mean . . . IF you want to sleep with me again."

Fuuuuck. I turn around and take my plate to the sink to quickly wash it.

God, did I say that?

He approaches. "What's so wrong about working for me?"

I set it aside to dry and then towel my hands before turning to meet his gaze. I take his face in my hands, boost up on my toes, and set a soft, dry kiss on his lips. "We said we'd take this slow, but wherever this goes, I don't want you to be my boss. Promise me."

He looks at me carefully as I drop down to my toes. His jaw starts to flex in frustration. "Don't make me promise, Rachel." He shakes his head and heads back to fold the newspaper.

"If you promise me, I'll believe it," I say.

"We'll discuss this later. I can't make that promise."

Urgh. Impossible man. But because he said we'll discuss this later, I let it go with a little tingle of joy at the prospect. "You won't sway me, I'm sorry to say, but you can try with sex and kisses of course. God, I'm so late." I hurry to get my bag from his bedroom and when I come back, he's also getting ready, knotting his tie and then pulling out one of his many identical jackets.

I pause and take a moment to drink him in and think, incredulously, *Dibs on that, bitches.*

"I'm late too." He shoves his arms into the sleeves and steps into his ruthless Saint persona the moment the suit is fully on him. "Otis called in sick. Claude's picking up my eight o'clock, who flew in from Dubai."

As I finish strapping my shoes, I grab my phone to call a cab service when he stops my hand and tucks something into the palm of the other.

"Here," he tells me.

I'm super confused as I investigate the shiny leather and steel key ring, suspicious by the twinkle in his eye. "What is it?"

"Your ride."

SOMETHING
BORROWED

I feel suddenly so spoiled and decadent when I slide into the front passenger seat of the shiny chrome-and-black BUG I Malcolm gave me the keys to. It smells divine, looks divine, and I'm horny just thinking about driving the fucker.

I exhale as I close the door, and click the ignition button.

The motor rumbles and scares a little laugh out of me. Holy crap.

The wheel slides under my fingers, the seat hugs me, vibrating with the rumble of the motor. This car isn't a bug, it's a *beast.*

A beast that should be driven at breakneck speed and I'm cautiously driving at half the speed limit to a thousand envious stares of those passing.

An old man passes by with a grin and I'm glad he got to feel superior today.

After a quick pit stop at home for a fresh set of clothes, I walk into *Bluekin*'s kick-ass downtown offices in Chicago. I'm running on adrenaline.

The thing I most love about this place is . . . well, hell. Everything. Their covers are usually hand-drawn sketches, and somehow this allows for a very ample diversity to the content inside. If anyone colors outside the lines, it's *Bluekin*.

Their pieces on human interests are always real, sober, and very heartwarming—but that's not all they feature. They have everything from funny articles to the most somber articles, covering every topic under an umbrella that they keep making wider and wider.

I'm rather blessed to be interviewed by Mr. Charles Harkin today, a very well-respected member of the company who used to work at a big New York magazine.

"The CEO is an acquaintance of Saint's. He was impressed by how thoroughly you seemed to grasp him, and especially how brave you were in your honesty. You should be very proud of that piece."

Fuck *me*. Does everyone have to mention that or know Malcolm? I hear him say "Saint" and I can't stop the reaction: visceral. Like an elephant—*Rosie*—just kicked me in the heart.

Sleep deprivation weighs on me, but I feel as relaxed as if I were buzzing with alcohol. What swims in my veins is better than alcohol. Intoxicating. It's pure beautiful torture to remember last night. He told me I wouldn't forget spending the night and he's right. I feel . . . possessed.

I exhale. Forcing myself to get out of his penthouse and come back here, to the HR department and the interview I never thought I'd want until the sacrifices I made for a career I loved brought too many complexities to rein back under control.

"Sometimes the good pieces are the ones that take the most from us," I finally tell the man on the other side of the desk, admitting to myself that, well, that piece took so much from me I'm still not fully recovered.

He's a nice, unassuming man, but behind the glasses, his gaze is shrewd and admiring. "In a way, I can relate. The hardest things to do are sometimes the ones that prove most meaningful, but not necessarily the ones we remember most fondly."

We share a smile and then he reviews the pages before him. "It says here you're interested in covering serious topics." He nods approvingly. "We're definitely looking to bring someone like you on board, who's not afraid of taking risks."

I wait and try to settle down my nerves as he reviews the paper again.

"Sorry for going into territory which might seem personal but . . ." he adds, "we'd like our reporters to gain their reputations for their pieces, rather than who they're involved with. And dating such a figure in this city, well, it's got to be tough. Saint is a man known to overpower what he wants and we're surprised you'd be interviewing here . . ." he admits.

I smile a little. "He respects my career choices, I assure you."

"Hmmm . . ." he says.

I start getting the feeling they're somehow concerned that *hiring* me will piss off Malcolm.

"So you're not interested in even partly writing on your previous subjects?" He looks down. "Your column usually discusses the trends around the city, though lately you've seemed to be steering onto dating advice for women."

"Yes. But I'd like these new pieces to involve me a bit more with the community—helping share the stories of people who don't have a voice yet."

He jots down notes. "You have vision and ambition." He taps his pen to the paper where he's writing stuff. "And your output *is* impressive in your amount of time at *Edge*." He nods, then seems to drop the mask as he takes off the glasses.

"Look," he folds his hands on the desk and looks me in the eye, "I'm going to level with you here. The bosses, they're friends of Saint's. You're brave, which they love, edgy, but they'd need to be very sure you are here for the long term."

"I am."

"Are you really?" He leans back then, a challenge as he crosses his arms. "Malcolm Saint . . . he knows about this interview?"

"Yes."

"But isn't Interface starting a news department . . ." he trails off meaningfully, because of course the implications are *where Saint could hire you?*

"Yes, but I want to work my way up."

Something akin to admiration appears on his face. "Okay then. Well." He claps his hands and rubs them, as if that's that. "I'll put in a good word for you."

"Thank you. Thank you so much for your time." Feeling a little sinking sensation in my gut, I sense this is goodbye. I pump his hand effusively and smile anyway.

It's a smile that leaves me the moment I exit the building. Sighing, I lean against the exterior. I groan and shake my head because I don't think it went well at all. I sense they believe that I'll start here and then be lured into the Interface news arm.

Will they all be afraid of Malcolm reaching out to scoop me up under his wing?

Crossing the street, I go buy a copy of the *Chicago Tribune* from the nearby newsstand and carry it back into the underground parking lot, tuck it into the front passenger seat of

Saint's Bug, and when I slide into the front seat, I set my fore-head on the wheel and sigh.

Okay, Rachel, it's just one interview. One. And not the only one.

I absently run my hand over the dashboard, enjoying the smooth luxury of all the sleek black leather and chrome.

The next interview will go better.

It has to.

I turn on the engine, the loud, rumbling roar scaring an-other little laugh out of me as the seat starts vibrating. God, if Sin's car doesn't look good, smell good, and *feel* great. And isn't it great the man upstairs didn't see me in this, or he'd never even given me a chance to walk in the door.

I don't have the same luck in keeping the Bug out of sight at *Edge*, though. Our underground parking lot is minuscule and limited to purchased spots, and since I don't find any parking, I have to call Valentine. "Val, I brought a car."

"You don't have a car."

"Well, I brought one. Please, please let me borrow your space? I can't leave this car out there at the mercy of the ele-ments, it's . . . you'll understand, I promise."

"You, woman, are in debt to me," he declares, and hangs up.

He comes out, grumbling as he gets into his car and pulls it out of the garage, and I park with care—triple-checking all my mirrors. Then do the same when I open the car doors and slide outside.

Valentine comes running back into the parking garage. He gapes. "WHA—!" He cuts himself off with a breath.

"I didn't mean to bring this," I promise, lifting my hands when he levels accusing eyes at me. "Otis is sick, I planned to take a cab to my interview, he said, 'Here.' And when I left he said, 'Drive it like you stole it—but don't get caught.' I'm nervous driving it. If someone scratches it I'll die."

"What—I cannot—" He's shaking his head and having a combustion. "Dude, it's a fucking BUGATTI! It's worth like two-point-three million dollars!"

"Hush, it's hard enough to drive it carefully without knowing that. It's responsive and energetic. You touch the pedal and the bastard just goes."

"'Cause it's a V-sixteen engine and like twelve hundred horsepower. *You* . . . Bugattis shouldn't even be driven by women, dude, this is rude!"

"Bug off, you're gay, Val, you're like half woman."

"Holy shit, let's see it inside!"

My excitement from holding Malcolm Saint's key in my hand comes back when I let Valentine open the car and peer inside. "Dude, holy shit! This sends a message—he's so pussy-whipped, man. Did people see you take this out?"

My lips curl. "A tiger doesn't lose sleep over the opinion of sheep. He doesn't care what people think."

Valentine drools and moans and rubs it for a while. Then, "Where did you interview?"

"*Bluekin*." My face crumples a little as I lock Malcolm's baby and we head to the elevators. "I can't stay here, Valentine. Saint's father is taking over, and my loyalty is elsewhere now."

"I *know*, Rache, I can't sleep, I tell you. I don't even know what I'm going to do either, but I should probably start looking too. Everyone says Noel Saint's a fucking asshole. The only one who can take him on is his son and they say Saint is done with him—rightly so. A man's got to move forward, not stay with those who want to bring him to the pits."

Completely unlike Valentine, he suddenly looks crestfallen.

He sighs. "When new owners take over it's like everyone will be canned, they like to start fresh, bring in their new blood, take care of any little mafias inside, purge it all. If you hear of anything where you're going . . ."

"I will," I promise as we hit our floor. "Good luck, Valentine."

In the newsroom—well, let's just say it's not called newsroom for nothing. It seems the little white Bug in the parking garage caused quite a stir.

Helen summons me to her office a few hours after I start jotting down my new piece, which I think will be called "What does your car say about him and/or you?"

"I'm kind of jealous of your position right now," Helen tells me when I walk in.

"What?"

"You look radiant. Look at you! Everyone is talking about you and your Saint. His car downstairs. I'm becoming a bit of a Saint fan."

"Because we're being bought by the dad?"

She zips her mouth. She grins. "Tell me all the rumors are true. The three S's."

"What?"

"Size, stamina, and seduction."

"Who said that?" I roll my eyes. "Stop talking about him."

"Sex symbols are objectified."

"Off-limits to discuss here from now on, Helen. That piece should be enough. Permission to go work now?"

She waves me off with a chuckle, then calls, "Rachel . . ."

"Yes?"

"Is it true? You're looking?"

I realize she was joking with me, acting my friend and teasing, because she wants to know.

I look at her, suddenly feeling a like a complete deserter because I'm leaving *Edge*. Like those rats who instantly jump and leave the sinking ship, rather than staying there and manning it. But I'm so determined to work things out with Malcolm and staying here under his father's thumb wouldn't help my cause in the least.

"I won't work for Malcolm's father," I say.

"Does your boyfriend know?"

"He's not my boyfriend. We're just . . ." I inhale. "*Edge* won't be hurting my relationship this time around. I love it here but . . . my relationship with him now comes first. I really want to make it work, Helen. In my gut it just feels so right, if I let him go without a fight I'll regret it for the rest of my life."

Her eyes soften, then she shakes her head as if angry at herself. "Enough about this speculating! Get to work." She snaps her fingers. "But Rachel . . . I don't think the owners are going to let you go that easy. Noel Saint wants you at *Edge*."

"Well, then that's even more of a reason to leave. He can go BLEEP himself for all I care."

I go back to my desk and then text, People are dying at the office over my ride

I love it, he writes back. But paying for their funerals is going to consume so much of my time that I'd rather spend it doing something else. ☺

So when can I take your Bug back? You could play a little with me too if you'd like

OMG! I'm such a slut. I did not text him that.

But I did.

I did and he answers, I'm feeling rather playful. Sadly, 9:00 is the best?

SOCIAL MEDIA WHIRL

Before I leave *Edge* for the day, Valentine updates me on the latest social media whirl after our club sighting.

Latest blog entry from *chicagogal243*—
Malcolm Saint, our favorite bad boy, in a relationship? So, readers, do you believe that our sexiest bachelor could ever be monogamous? I sure don't . . .

Twitter:
Spotted this weekend @MalcolmSaint back on with the lying reporter!
She's SO wrong for you @MalcolmSaint SO WRONG!!!!
YOU'RE A PRINCE AND SHE'S A FROG!

On his Interface page:
Saint, my darling! Jeremiah and I sent you an invite to our 1st anniversary—you can bring your friend along.

On Facebook:
Just PM'ed you, S. We're planning the yearly group trip to
Monte Carlo. RSVP soon?

His Instagram:
Your new girl is luscious and lovely! Call me if you want me to
meet her and kiss her, give you a little show. CALL ME!

"You've hired a team of bodyguards, I hope?" Valentine asks
me when he closes the internet search.

"No, but I have a Saint protecting me," I say, tongue in
cheek.

"So it's a *no* to that threesome that woman's offering?" he
baits.

"Really, that lady has no clue how full Saint's hands are
going to be with me."

Valentine laughs, and I shake my head and head to the elevators, smiling to myself. Sin, oh *Sin*, should I learn to wrestle
so I can properly deal with these chicks?

Can't we just tell them all I'm the one who has dibs on you?

THAT NIGHT

It's 9 p.m. And I've already called Mom, and told Gina I won't be sleeping in, and am heading to his place. I find him striding out of his bedroom, recently showered and in a pair of jeans and slipping into a soft navy blue T-shirt.

God, I *tremble* at the sight of this man.

"How was it?" he asks.

"What? The car? The interview? My day?" I set his keys down on the coffee table along with the *Tribune* I brought.

"Let's start with the interview. I already know the car's good stuff." He smiles, then cocks his head when he drops down beside me and I curl up against his side.

He kisses my jaw and gives a little cup to the swells of my breasts rising enticingly to press into my top. I kiss the tendon in his throat that I bit the night before, noticing a slight pink mark at the bottom of his neck, hidden under his shirt.

"Do you realize someone recently left you a hickey?"

I moan when he ducks his head, seizes a piece of skin, suckles and does the same.

"Now she's wearing one to match," he says wickedly.

I moan again as he sucks one more time. It feels so good I don't want to talk, to eat, to do anything but fuck with him.

He nuzzles my ear. "You make the best sounds when I've got my hands all over you."

"Sin, you're making me self-conscious now . . ." I groan, and he smiles against me.

I drag my hands up his chest to his face. "I thought about you all day."

His eyes darken. He brings me close, until I'm sitting over his thigh. "This is getting in my way," he says in mischief, fingering the top button of my blouse but not removing it yet. I think he knows—we both know—if he takes it off, our talk is over. "So how was it?"

"Good."

"Good?" he repeats, clearly not convinced.

"Not spectacular or anything. I don't want to get my hopes up."

When he keeps giving me a that's-just-bullshit look, I sigh.

"Not really good," I finally admit. "But I love *Bluekin*. I love how they do things, how they don't box themselves into a certain market, they're read by young people, by old people, women, men . . . they're open."

"Who did you see there? Harkin?"

"Yes." I narrow my eyes. "He said you're friends with his boss."

He nods and eases away, pours us drinks and comes back to pass me a glass.

"Where do you think I should go?" I ask him, taking a soft sip.

"You know where." He smirks as he lowers back down on the couch next to me, his eyes twinkling but serious.

"Come on, I value your opinion."

"*Bluekin's* good," he says, furrowing his brow in thought. "*Buzz*, *Lokus*, the *Sun-Times*, the *Tribune*, the *Reader*. I can get you into any of those. Maybe even *RedEye* too."

"*No*. No string pulling. I need to do this on my own. What would you do if you were given something just that easily, hmm?" I dare.

"I'd take it and use it to go higher." He lifts his eyebrows, challenging me. "You pull yourself up by your bootstraps or by whoever's are closest, Rachel."

"*You* say that because you have the biggest bootstraps and don't need anyone to help you up." I add, "I'm not even considering the mag where Victoria is."

"Was." He shrugs. "I can get you in there too."

"Was? What's she doing now?"

"Not messing with you."

I gape at him, perplexed and amazed. "How do you even *know* all these people?"

"Fund-raisers. Benefits. Business. They like my wallet." He winks at me and smirks a little. "Some even like me." He lifts his wine to drink. "Still, don't take me off your list," he murmurs.

"Why?" I groan, then jokingly frown. "You want to keep tabs on me every hour of the day?"

Thoughtfully but intensely, he runs the back of a finger down my jaw. "M4 is the only place I know without a doubt you'll work on what you want."

Before I even know what I'm doing, I cup his hard jaw.

"I can't believe I'm leaving *Edge*." I think of my friends for a moment, especially Valentine and Sandy. "Maybe this purchase will be good for them?"

He laughs softly, then stands to refill his glass. As though he needs some space on his own, he remains staring out the window, cradling it in his palm, the stem between two fingers.

"Do you want to talk about it?" I ask softly.

"Not really."

A gazillion city lights flicker outside, and there's this space that is as dark and serene as the sky, which is the lake. Will he ever take me there again? To our little spot where nothing else matters—nothing?

He turns to look at me after a moment, his eyebrows slanting low over his eyes. "What's so awful about working for me, Rachel?"

"Nothing. I just don't want to." I scowl.

He scowls back.

This is what I've wanted. To write what I want. He's giving me that. He's giving me all that. And I'm afraid to take it. That taking it would mean, eventually, that I'd lose what I most want: the possibility of having a long-term relationship with him.

I can't. I don't even want to be *tempted.*

"Malcolm, I promise you, I won't be there when your father takes over. I won't be there."

He clenches his jaw. His silence is heavy, thoughtful.

My frown deepens. "I'm promising I won't be there. Malcolm, I won't be there." I look at him. "Don't you believe my promise? Is it because you don't think promises are worth a damn or because you don't believe in me?"

He narrows his eyes. "Can you blame me for not jumping to believe in your promises?"

That strikes me, and it hurts.

"Are we in a relationship beyond working each other out of our systems, or am I just along for some kind of four? Four weeks? Four months?"

I remember what has been said about him and maybe it's haunting me. Maybe Saint's reputation is still haunting me, and my own feelings of not being up to such a powerhouse like him.

"We're taking it one step at a time," he says measuredly.

I chew on my lip.

When I don't look ecstatic about it, he narrows his eyes. "Is that not enough for you, Rachel?"

No. Because I love you, I think brokenly.

"You've taught me to be greedy. I don't know anymore," I say. "Do you expect me to go work for you knowing that in five months you could be parading around with dozens of women, none of them me?" I challenge, slowly coming to my feet. "I have pride too. I can't compartmentalize with you, I just can't. I know you want to protect me. But I needed to believe that I can find something on my own. I want your respect, like I respect you. I need . . ."

I pause when a little bit of my emotions start getting too riled up.

"I guess I just need *you* to believe I can find something on my own too."

Eerily silent, Saint seems to be trying to figure out how to tread into this, and I realize this conversation is going to go nowhere fast.

Fuck, I'm tired. He's temperamental about this job issue.

We're fighting already? On day two?

"You know what? This is a topic we're not seeing eye to eye on, and I'm tired. I'm just going home."

"Fuck," I hear him say, smashing a palm into the wall, but I just ride down the elevator and hail a cab home, proud and misty-eyed and needing time to think about what I'll do to make a living while still fighting to try to have a relationship with Sin.

NIGHT VISIT

I've been morosely sitting in my bed pondering my life situation for the better part of an hour when Gina knocks on my door. "Rache? Someone's here to see you."

She peers inside to see if I'm decent, and then she steps back and widens the door.

Saint stands on the threshold, his hands at his side, his jaw set thoughtfully . . . and my heart turns over in my chest.

"Hey!"

I rise to my feet in shock, battling to conceal the excitement spreading over me at the sight of him in my apartment.

He shuts the door slowly behind him as he looks at me, in his shirt. I feel weak in the knees. "Nice shirt," he says.

"It's yours."

I swear my room feels smaller and so much more feminine whenever he's in here.

He starts forward, his gaze shining appraisingly on me. "I like you in it."

I nervously bite the inside of my cheek. "I didn't think you'd want me to wear it while you were hating me."

"I wasn't hating you." He keeps walking forward and for some reason I find myself backing away. Maybe because I feel vulnerable that he sees me so at home in his shirt. Maybe because I just poured my heart out to him in an email he might never read.

"I don't respect a lot of people, Rachel, it's hard for me." His gaze searches mine. "I respect *you*." He reaches out to stop me from walking and cups my face in one hand to force me in place. "I get you, Rachel. I may not say it, words are your turf, not mine, but I get you. You're the only woman I've ever gone this far with. Ever even wanted to. Promise me now that if you don't find anything by the time my father takes over, you'll come with me—and I'll believe you."

His eyes are so green right now, heavy like anchors holding me down. We stare at each other as if we're both trying to understand what the other needs. Him, calmly, and me with so much longing inside me, I feel soft like a noodle.

I know that he's never done this before, being with someone like he is with me, and I haven't either. I close my eyes when his thumb starts to caress the skin on my neck where he holds me. "I do. I promise."

He smiles then—a slow, male, grateful smile—then he pulls me close to his chest. "Was that hard now?" he chides.

"No. But you are." I smile against his neck.

He laughs softly as he reaches between us and chucks my chin. "It happens when you're around."

"Does it? I hadn't noticed." I smile.

His smile flashes back at me. "It's pretty much permanent."

Ohgod, he's making me so wet. I shove him away and back

away a little with a mock-frown. "Rumor has it it's like that all the time when any lady's around."

He starts after me. "I'm a hungry man. I won't apologize for my appetite."

"And you used to like a buffet?" I hop on my bed and avoid him when he reaches out to grab me.

His eyes twinkle, his teeth white against his tan. "Why not? If I'm hungry."

"Do you still crave it?" I hop back down and keep backing around my room, while Saint, Saint continues calmly coming after me.

"That hunger of yours is so big maybe nothing will ever satisfy it," I continue taunting.

"Maybe." He catches me in a swift move, pulls me close, and he leans to my ear, voice dropping, "I still think you wear my shirt better than I do," he says huskily.

I moan and press closer. "Saint." *Fuck me right now. On the bed, the floor, and against the wall.*

He playfully, and oh-so-wickedly, pops open one button and runs the knuckles of his fist inside to caress the skin between my collarbones.

"I want you," I whisper, giddy and gooey inside. "See, I'm ambitious too."

His voice is pure husky. "Good, aim high. Always. I like my girls greedy."

"Plural! You're such a piece of work." I shove at his hard chest playfully and back away again with a mock frown.

"And you like me anyway." He keeps coming forward, and I swear the smile he's wearing right now is about as hormone-wrecking as his hard-on is.

"I'm aiming . . . high . . . it's just that I'm trying to put a name to us and it frustrates me not to have one."

What am I, exactly, to you? I want to ask, but Saint pops open another button, and whispers, "Only you would want a word. But there's no word for this."

He grabs a little bit of loose hair from my nape as he tilts my head up so he can kiss me. And . . . *kiss me.*

Our lips collide, his firming over mine, making me soften as his tongue dips into my mouth and a spiral of heat swirls in my stomach. I start pulling him by the shoulders as we kiss, backing us eagerly to the bed.

The backs of my knees hit the mattress and I end up sitting there, then lying there, and he leans over me, his mouth still slowly, powerfully moving over mine. The heat of his slow and thorough kiss burns me to ash.

I trap back a moan and look up at him dazedly as he sits down next to me and holds me to his chest with one arm. I start kissing his neck and jaw and sit here in a pile of lust, feeling his hand run down my side to stroke up the side of my bare leg.

"So we're clear then," he murmurs against my mouth, delivering one of his most demanding looks.

I lick my lips and nod.

He shoves his tongue into my mouth again. Leaning over me, he's all raw manpower. Dominant and possessive, unapologetic, he circles my tongue with his. Pressing, circling, stroking, stoking my fire, the space between our upper bodies nonexistent. He caresses my side with his hand, moving it up to the little triangle of skin he revealed under my throat.

I grab his jaw to speed up the kiss. But he won't have it.

"Easy. Let me savor you," he quietly coaxes as he slows down, prolonging it for us as he sips from me like a wineglass.

The fabric of his shirt I've been wearing is so flimsy compared to the hard substance of Saint's chest against mine.

I hear the air-conditioning, the noises of the city. Feel my soft bed beneath me as his mouth roams over my neck. The weight of his upper body on mine makes me sigh. The smooth skin of our chests rubbing. The wet warmth of his mouth on my skin. My fingertips digging into the back of his head. The hard wall of his chest to my breasts. Smell the scent of his neck. Hear our breathing. I'm breathless and still, he caresses me with his fingers between my collarbones.

We lie there quietly, looking at each other before he sweeps in for another kiss.

He turns his head then and gives me another pile of long lazy kisses. "Are you going to keep your promise to me, Rachel?" *Kiss.*

"Hmm . . ." Lazy kissing from me to him. "Yes, Sin."

"Good girl . . ." More lazy kissing, then he rolls around and gets up from the bed.

"Where are you going?" I sit up in confusion, pushing my hair out of my face.

"I have to go. I have something important pending at my place." He heads to the door.

"You mean you're not spending the night?"

He stops to turn, then lifts one dark eyebrow. Then the other.

And then, I see the twinkle appear in his eyes.

He comes back to me.

Leaning down, he buttons up the button he unbuttoned, his handsome face sober now.

He cups my breast over his shirt as he opens up his mouth and dips his head for one last taste of me. He sucks my bottom lip gently, then does the same with the top lip, then he dives into my mouth, which gets a delicious little tongue fuck before he sets one soft kiss at the corner of my mouth. He touches my body like it's his and I'm starting to worry. God, I'm addicted.

But then he whispers, "Not here, little one."

"Why?"

"Your friend's here. And I want you to make *noise*." He looks at me meaningfully.

"I'll see you soon?" he husks out, easing back and once again heading for the door.

He's leaving.

I watch him grab my doorknob.

"I planned to hit the Cubs game next weekend. I have a mind to take you there."

"Cubs game?" I nearly leap off the bed. "*Yes!*"

His eyes glimmer. Those naughty lips of his tug upward.

I blush when I wonder if it's because he *knows* how I feel about him. "I'm excited because I've never been to a live game."

His eyes glint. "Of course."

I know *he* knows I'm excited to go with him.

I want to say *I love you* but before I get the courage, he's gone. And I lie in bed, wondering about us.

The next morning, I tell Gina a little bit about the fight and how he said some bone-melting things to me and I ask her if she thinks Saint loves me.

She gives me a you're-shitting-me look.

I reply with a no-I'm-not-shitting-you look.

"You're kidding?"

"I never kid about Saint, Gina."

She shoves her spoon back into her plate. "I wouldn't know, Rache. What I do know is that he makes you vulnerable and you're putting up walls."

"No I'm not."

"You don't want to expect anything. You're still scared."

"Okay, maybe I am scared."

"Scared of what?"

My shoulder hikes up. "Everything," I laugh pitifully. "I'm always scared."

"About it not being reciprocated?"

I nod.

"Of his fame and his groupies? How ready they are for him to tire of you to welcome him with open legs and arms?"

"Gina!" I scowl. "He's not like that."

But in a way, I *am* scared of his groupies. I'm scared of being in love. With . . . him.

"They're all like that, Tahoe and Callan too." She pauses. "Dude. I'd be scared too. But . . . Look at his actions, Rachel. Those should be worth more than sweet-talking words. Paul used to tell me . . . I don't even want to remember. But he didn't mean it, his actions said otherwise. God, I could've killed him for being such a cheating liar if I hadn't been so . . . devastated."

She eyes me somberly.

"What Saint has done for you, Rachel. Offering the job. Canning Victoria's article but not yours. That safety thing he did with End the Violence. Coming here last night to talk it out . . . I know you're a words girl, but he's more of a doer than a teller. He's doing things to be close to you. Maybe you should start 'fessing up and *telling*."

I open my hands in a helpless gesture. "I told him I loved him, on the phone. Once."

A stab pricks my chest when I again wonder how he took it?

"Before the shit happened. Maybe he wants you to take the leap again. In that article, you wrote that you'd leap if you thought he'd catch you. Don't you think he will?"

A warm glow fills me as I imagine leaping *knowing* that he

would catch me, and my lips curve a little. "Since when are you so perceptive?" I ball a paper napkin and toss it over the table at her.

She tosses it back. "Since, hell, I don't know." She shrugs and shoots me a wistful glance. "Maybe I just want my faith in men restored."

She laughs and shrugs as if this admission is no big deal. But it's a huge deal.

It's been so long since Paul, and Gina's been so determined never to go through that again.

"Our first time falling in love . . ." I trail off as I bring a box of Lucky Charms and a cereal bowl for myself. "It hasn't been a walk in the park for either of us," I tell her.

She grabs the pink marshmallows in my bowl before I can add the milk. "More like a roller coaster." She pops some into her mouth. "But like Tahoe says . . . 'cause he and I are like buddies now. Are you impressed?" Then she chuckles a little. "Anyway . . . walks in the park can get boring."

CUBS GAME

It's Cubs game day, and I'm running around in matching black panties and black bra. My stomach is a big jumble of nerves. I feel like I'm watching a horror movie, and it's at that part where some stupid girl is about to open the closet, which contains some kind of serial killer/psychopath, and I can't do anything about it. I'm that girl. And I'm about to open the closet door, except it's Malcolm waiting on the other side of it, and I don't know what scares me more.

Sin, on the other side of the door. My addiction. My *love*.

I smell like vanilla perfume and my hair is freshly ironed, feeling warm against my back, silky straight, hitting me just below my shoulder blades. I'm so excited, I feel like a teenager. I check my phone, and his last text is still glowing on the screen:

I'm on my way.

Four stupid little words and I feel like I can't breathe. But I want to squeal like a little girl too. I haven't seen him all week; work getting in the way, save for a few texts. As I contemplate what to wear, I'm thinking about what will happen. How I'll be in his car with him soon, surrounded by leather in a confined space . . . and then I start thinking about whether he'll come back to my place or not, and I find myself thinking—no, hoping—that he will.

So I pause to make sure that my bed is made, my room sparkly clean.

I finally put on an emerald-green silky blouse and a pair of white shorts that make my butt look good. I slip on some flats, spray more perfume on my neck, swipe mascara on my lashes, a little blush on my cheeks, and a smack of cherry lip stain on my lips. I'm looking in the mirror, deciding I look okay, when I hear a knock on the door.

I focus on my breathing, hearing my ballet flats tap on the floor. No one else is home. The apartment only has a couple lamps on, and I'm just now realizing that somewhere between my getting-ready routine and obsessing, the sun has gone down.

I open the door, and he's standing there with his hands in his pockets, wearing dark jeans and a long-sleeve black T-shirt that defines his huge shoulders and is pulled tightly against his biceps. Weirdly, the nerves in my stomach subside. He's looking at me with his green eyes. His square jaw clamped tight. His eyes are roaming from the tips of my toes to the blush on my cheeks.

He clears his throat, and when he finally speaks, I swear to god I almost start crying from how much I like the sound of it. Incredible, how much I've missed this voice. How his chest seems to vibrate with the power of it. How I can basically *feel* his warmth, emanating from his body as he stands there, and all I want to do is get sucked into his force field.

He steps closer to me, so I'm staring up at him and he's staring down at me, and he says simply, "You look amazing."

I can't say anything back. My nerves won't allow me to. It's our second official date—after that one night I spent over.

"Mmm . . ." he says, lowering his head slightly so his lips brush the side of my neck. "Smell good too."

I swear I'm melting right here, and as if he doesn't even know, the bastard straightens up again and shoots me one of his trademark smiles. "Ready to go? We'll be late."

"Yeah." I take a good breath. Then I look back at my apartment, turn off the lights and take my purse from the stand next to my front door.

"Talking Body" by Tove Lo is blaring on the speakers. The skybox overlooks the field, with several rows of exterior seats to get in on the action connected to the private suite—which is where we are. The moment we walk in, warm golden light fills my vision. Black leather couches, plasma TVs, and a pool table are the first things I see. Then I see a huge window looking out on the baseball field, the lights shining down. I can practically smell the peanuts and the beer. We're on top of the whole stadium, in a glass box.

We grab drinks and then sit down on one of the couches looking directly out the huge window. We're immediately loving the game.

"Damn right, run, Rizzo!!" Malcolm's voice sounds deep as he bellows and shouts. "Fuuuck." He throws his head back and groans, then returns his gaze to the field. He takes a swig of pinot noir.

I try to suppress a giggle with a sip of my little cocktail.

It's a tight game and we're all going crazy wanting to secure the win. I should've been paying more attention but I do love the sportgasms Sin gets when he's watching games. I love how serene he sits, calm and controlled, then yells from deep in his belly and pumps his fist when things go his way. And I love how he makes a piece of my brain take a walk when he puts his arm around me, and rubs his hand slowly down my arm.

He looks perfectly content now, sipping his wine, his arm around me, sitting in his majestic glass box overlooking the stadium. Might as well be his stadium, the way he sits here, as if he owns the place. Meanwhile, I'm sucking in the experience of a live game, which I've never, ever been to before. Gina says it's because there were no men in my life—no father, brothers, boyfriends. Maybe she's right. I love how the air crackles in the stadium, and how it crackles where Saint is right now.

"It's in the bag, I can fucking feel it," I hear Malcolm mumble next to me. He has a look of concentration on his face.

I'm terribly amused. "If you say so."

He stares at me for a moment before tightening his jaw and closing his eyes for a split second. If I hadn't been looking at him, I would've missed it. He leans over. "I *do* say so. We're going to run them into the ground."

At one point some friends below the box start yelling his name, and we head outside to the line of seats adjoining the box. "Saint! You fucking all-star!" one of the guys shouts, then asks if his crew can come up, eyeing me rakishly.

Saint simply says, "No," and flips them the finger. He takes my arm and leads me to an outside seat, then sits beside me and leans forward as we continue to watch the game.

Between those gaps in the plays, we watch the Jumbotron. I'm laughing, watching the couples smack kisses on each other as soon as they appear on-screen. A young dark-haired man flashes on the screen. My body jolts with pure feminine awareness. He's alone on-screen as I—and the rest of the spectators—register *who* he is, and then the camera shifts a little to include . . . *me* . . . just as I feel fingers sliding underneath my hair, tugging me around, and his lips take mine.

I hear the cheers and, stunned, I can't look back at the screen. Only at Sin's yummy mouth, which I just felt kiss me.

His eyes twinkle as he draws me closer for another kiss, this one just for him, for his eyes only. His very hot male eyes.

He seems very calm and at peace with himself once the Jumbotron moves on to its next victims.

Three innings later, I'm still feeling shy and girly. But Sin's recovered and is fully in the game. It's the bottom of the ninth and the game is almost over. One strike and the Cubs lose against the Cardinals. Our Cubbies. Up to bat is Sweency, who's had a few home runs this year. We still have a shot and our guys could win.

"Now we're talking. Bases loaded," he says, clapping, then lifting his brows at me as he gestures toward the three bases forming a perfect arrow in front of us.

My lips ripple as I try to tame a smile. I'd forgotten how he loves anything competitive. It gives me a secret little tingle when I see his passion right out there, flashing in his eyes.

I suddenly ache to play with him. "I bet you were an expert at the *bases*, juvenile as that sounds." I raise an eyebrow. I wonder when it all began, and I'm fishing for it. That little sliver of knowledge of how he became the most wanted man in Chicago. I wouldn't be surprised if it started during elementary school. He *did* get a headline when he was born—and the headlines have never stopped following him.

"*Were?*" he jokes. "*Am.*" He lowers his head to mine and runs the tip of his nose against my temple. "I still got game." He places a small kiss where his nose used to be.

"I would know. You're such a big-time player, the umpire should be up *here* calling the plays."

He doesn't laugh like I thought he would. His eyes look darker, as if he doesn't like me calling him a player, and I can tell his energy changed just now.

I peer at him, and he's studying my hand as he draws his thumb up from the base to my fingertips. Tingles race through my skin, bubbles through my veins. He has a look of concentration, like he's just discovered something he's never seen before. Like he's definitely *playing* with a toy he never expected to play with. He lifts his lashes to look at me. The momentary glimpse of the fiery heat in his gaze makes me drop my eyes back down to stare at our hands, my stomach gripping nervously.

He lifts our hands and slowly kisses my knuckles. When he lowers them, I'm panting little breaths. He smiles at me and I smile at him as he lets go, his touch lingering on my skin.

"You turn me on like nothing else," he whispers.

He kisses me softly but briefly. Then he snaps out of it and turns back to watch the player on home base. The ball is hurtling through the air, and with a smack, I realize the batter made contact and the ball is heading somewhere out in midfield.

Malcolm is ecstatic. The whole stadium is screaming. If the Cubs get two men in, they'll win the game . . .

One hit.

The crowds stand.

Malcolm stands.

I stand.

A roar outside, and suddenly I'm crushed in his arms and flung in the air so hard my breath leaves me.

"Malcolm!" I cry. He catches me, kisses me, squeezes me and twirls me around, grinning down at me. And when he sets me down, his eyes go from fiery celebration to something stormy and uncontrollable.

He slides his arms around me and pulls me into his chest, and this hug is different. "I just want to make you smile," he says, gazing back at me and I guess I'm still smiling.

"I like your smile too," I admit.

We hug again, and stay there, watching the stadium. We're starting to feel like a couple, like Wynn and her boyfriend are, like Saint was *made* to hold me just like this. His huge hands just cradle me to him as the stadium empties and we wait to leave.

He's rubbing his hands against my back slowly, moving his head until his lips are rubbing against my neck. It feels amazing. Beautiful. Warm. Soft. And I can feel my breaths coming faster, but a tightness is here. He's holding me, and just when I think I can't possibly like it more, he keeps embracing me and doesn't let go as we finally walk out. He leads me out of the stadium.

It feels cold outside in the parking lot, I can see the trees folding, swaying, bending with the force of the cold Chicago wind. The Windy City—the name came about because of the hot airs some city politicians and braggarts put on in earlier centuries, though many people think it's because of the wind. And *this* is exactly why.

As we wait for Claude to bring the car, some people are approaching to greet him. A man with two girls, one on each arm, who smiles and exclaims, "Saint!"

"Hillz," he says tonelessly, taking my hand before they can reach us and leading me to his car.

"Why don't you want me to meet them?" I ask once we get in the backseat.

"You're too good for some of my crowd," he says in my ear.

My stomach starts churning. God, these butterflies just don't cease. It's like someone's tickling your stomach and you feel like you might burst out giggling at no particular time for no particular reason, except I know I'm about to get kissed to death. The black leather seats feel cool on the bottoms of my legs. The partition is closed between us and Claude, and as the car drives away, Saint takes my face in both of his hands and gives me a light, soft kiss. "Thanks for coming with me."

"Thanks for inviting—" Before I can finish speaking, he starts kissing me. And I let him deepen the kiss.

Instantly it's like we're molded into one, our movements are in sync. I can feel his hands on my body but my head is somewhere out in space, dancing next to Jupiter and counting Saturn's rings. It's like a high. A hot, burning, needy high. I lose it a little bit and straddle him and run my fingers through his soft hair. His mouth is on my neck, hot and wet, sucking and kissing.

I feel like a teenager, making out with him in the back of his car. I can't breathe. I just let him do whatever he's doing because it feels like heaven. His fingers play with the waist of my shorts, tracing circles and gently rubbing my skin. I kiss him again and start to rub against him. He groans and grabs me by the ass, using one hand to grind me closer, harder.

His other hand reaches between my legs and unbuttons my shorts. My heart beats so loud it seems to be the only thing I can hear. I feel him smile against my lips.

"Want me to stop?"

His lips latch on to my skin and his tongue traces slow, lazy circles on my neck.

"Never. Kiss me," I plead.

He kisses a perfectly delicious path back up to my mouth.

"I've been thinking about this all day." He licks my lips and keeps kissing me, hungrier than before. His hands are dangerously close to touching my panties, but he keeps running circles along my navel, his mouth moving deliciously against mine.

He tears his mouth from mine and drags his lips back down the column of my neck, sucking, nipping, tasting, nibbling.

"God, I've been wanting to do this since I saw you at your apartment."

I'm panting crazy hard by now, tearing myself free so I can breathe. I'm at the point where the merest touch in any sensitive part could set me off. I'm glad his phone starts ringing.

"Work?" I ask.

Well, not work, I find out when he hangs up.

"The boys are blowing up my phone. They want to come over, celebrate. T wants to see if your friend Gina wants to come." He lifts his brows at me, waiting.

I reach down to pat my swollen lips. I swear Saint just helped me invent the female equivalent of blue balls. "He'd better keep his hands off Gina. But I'll text her." I pull out my phone and shoot her a message.

Saint is breathing hard too. His hair is rumpled by me. He looks *sexxxy* with triple Xs.

"You don't like T and Carmichael?"

"I didn't say that."

"Your friends hate me too."

"They don't. They've misjudged you. They never knew what to make of you."

He thinks about that, then leans back and spreads his arms out as he thinks about it some more. "All right. Let's talk about how this affects us."

I blink.

"If it makes you feel any better, I've already talked to my friends, Rachel."

"What do you mean, talked to them?"

"I told the two bozos that I like this girl, I like this girl very much, and I expect them to respect my choices."

"I didn't know there *was* a choice."

"I chose to get serious with you—and I wanted it to be clear I won't be taking any shit from them. They fuck with you, they fuck with me."

This conversation is . . . I cannot. I look at him. "Saint, you're a player the likes of which this city has never seen."

"That's what the world sees. Is that what you see?" He looks at me curiously, starting to frown. "Tahoe threw a thousand and one parties for me. I had fun. That's what people saw. I got drunk. I was surrounded by girls."

I'm frowning now too. "Tahoe just cares about getting laid and he thinks that's all *you* care about."

"But it's not. Is it?" He looks at me intently. "There were a hundred women for the taking, every weekend. I could have. It was all there, no strings and available. I wanted to take them. Over and over."

I inhale sharply, and suddenly, I want to puke at the thought of his hands on anyone.

"But I kissed one right here," he touches the corner of my mouth with a pained look, "and I starved even more."

My throat hurts as if I swallowed arsenic. I have no right to feel this jealous. But the jealousy is here, like a knot of bitters in my gut. "I bet they know all kinds of sexy moves, your groupies."

His answer is feather soft. "They do." He strokes his pad across the corner of my lips again, and then leans back in his seat, and looks at me quietly and almost reverently. "But not one of them talks to me the way you do. They want money or fame but not one of them has asked me to save the world. Not one wanted my comfort. They look at me with lust but never like I'm the spot where their sun rises and sets. I see a girl who didn't know what she was getting into with me. I see a girl I can't forget. What do you see when you look at me?"

"I see you. I have no words for you."

"My friends see a guy who got fucked up over a girl." He leans forward and tips my head back with his knuckles, angling it so his gaze can grab on to mine. "They play when I want to play, but they know me far beyond the shit we do. We've known each other since we were ten. They know me . . . like I thought you did."

His eyes grow shadowed.

"But you didn't know me at all, Rachel. You thought I deserved for you to play me? You saw me like everyone did and all that time I was standing there being real with you."

I drop my gaze as the regret sits heavily on me again. "I was scared of believing it to be true. If you get tired of me and want something new . . . or a foursome again . . . there will be no power on earth that will be able to draw your eyes back to me."

He laughs softly. "I don't want to look away." His expression mellows as he looks at me between his lashes. "I'm hooked on you," he says. "My friends know I'm serious."

"So do mine," I whisper, then look at him. "Saint, I don't hate your friends. I *like* your friends. I just don't want *your* friends messing with *my* friends."

"If you mean Tahoe and Gina—"

"That's exactly who I mean," I say as I start to get off him, waving my hands in the air, but he catches them, locks them by my sides as he pulls me down flush with his lap.

"It doesn't concern you and me."

"Tahoe is a player. Jetting across the world with champagne and naked flight attendants. He's used to getting it all, whenever he wants."

"Is that so?"

"Yes, that's so. He's used to several women catering to him at once, giving him all kinds of sexy treats like blow jobs together. How can Gina compete?"

"How can she? Against several at once?" He clucks, but he looks amused.

"See. It's impossible. And she's . . . a good girl. She doesn't stand a chance with a guy like him."

"But it's guys like us who maybe don't stand a chance with a smart, good girl who actually wants us for more than a quick . . . fuck . . ." He lifts his brows devilishly.

"You stand every chance. You sweep us off our feet with just one sexy corner kiss."

He leans in. And grazes his lips across the fringes of mine. Every corner of my body feels this most perfect kiss. Squeezing my eyes shut against the onslaught of emotion, I breathe, "I'll kick his ass if he hurts Gina."

When I open my eyes, Saint's eyes are fixed on me, his voice low with conviction: "I'll kick his ass for you, Rachel."

CELEBRATING

We're on Sin's terrace, celebrating the win, talking, the drinks flowing. Gina and Wynn and I are lounging in the outside sitting area by a pristine blue pool while Saint and his guys stand by the bar, discussing the plays. Soon, Tahoe is bitching about his dumb hedge fund manager, and how they've sliced his net worth by over half.

"Seriously," Gina calls from where we sit, "I invite you to come and work at my posh department store one day, and I'll be the oil tycooness shopping there for a day, even at half your wealth." She adds snarkily, "You're still worthless anyway. You act like you're still in kindergarten."

"I'm a Princeton grad," he counters.

"Then you shouldn't have trouble finding a good job if your oil wells dry up."

"Ha. *You'll* be a dried-up old lady by the time that happens," Tahoe assures.

"Seriously, men." Gina scowls when she turns back to us.

"We're royalty when they want to fuck. Thrilled to have as much sex as their anatomy allows, and then we're nothing." She shakes her head. "Women need a reason to have sex, men just need a place."

"Between your legs," Wynn mumbles.

I burst out laughing, but Gina keeps scowling, and tells the two of us, "I swear, boobs are probably the only thing a guy like Tahoe can multitask on. Two may be one too many for him."

"Well, why don't you find out?" Wynn nudges her cheekily.

I find Malcolm watching me while his friends keep talking to him, and a fierce ache in my chest starts to grow. Saint is momentum. Movement. He's a man who's always moving forward, pushing for more. Where is he taking us? Where does he see *us* going?

"You fucking sly dog!" Tahoe calls over on their side. "Stop eyeing your juicy little steak over there like you haven't been slobbering over her all day!"

Saint lifts his glass to me in toast. "To my classy friends." A curl hikes the corner of his lips while that same smile touches his eyes.

Tahoe shoots me a look that's like a mix between admiration and annoyance. "I swear you're like his favorite damn poison, woman."

"*We* swear," Gina points at Wynn, "He's her favorite crack!"

While our friends laugh, I feel myself go hot, and Malcolm only looks at me, neither smiling nor laughing, simply those green eyes of his looking straight at me from his chiseled face.

Callan clears his throat when he notices our silent communication. "Well, fuck, Saint, you liking your new leash?"

Tahoe chuckles.

"Shut the fuck up," Malcolm growls.

That voice probably sends groups of elite businessmen out

of boardrooms having just peed their pants. But having been friends since childhood, Tahoe and Callan just laugh harder.

"What's so funny?" Gina asks, as if she didn't hear.

Tahoe wanders over and answers her in his slight Southern accent, his deep voice a lazy drawl that I have to admit is pretty damn sexy. "We're mourning over having lost our dear brother to the most powerful thing on this earth."

"What's that?" Gina counters, sounding curious, leaning over to him flirtatiously.

Tahoe murmurs something in her ear.

I hear a sharp sound of skin hitting skin, which I don't have to see to know Gina just playfully whacked Tahoe on the arm.

The boys laugh, all except Malcolm, who's not laughing but whose perfect lips are forming his perfectly lopsided smirk.

"Sorry, ladies," Tahoe apologizes. "To be fair, you did ask."

"Of course we know it's just about sex, with men," Gina says. Her trademark realism, what others call sarcasm, is heavy in her words.

"Why do you say that?" Tahoe asks, sounding somewhat serious now.

"Men don't love like women do. It's different for them."

"Well, I object," Tahoe says. "I love my mother," he finishes proudly.

Gina chuckles a little. "That's different. We love our mommas too. In fact, Rachel's momma is anxious to meet Saint."

Saint looks at me.

Then Callan says something about going on the yacht tomorrow, and Gina and Wynn start debating about bathing suits and weather predictions. Slowly, Saint wades his way through the terrace and drops down beside me. He stretches his arm behind me and looks down at me soberly.

"Your mother wants to meet me?" he asks.

I chew the inside of my cheek. "Everybody wants to meet you," I hedge. And when he just stares at me, I admit, "She'd love to. She's been asking."

"Then I'll meet her," he whispers.

"Serious stuff, that," Tahoe whistles, sitting down nearby. "Just don't take her to your dad, Saint. Unless you want her to quit you."

I look at Malcolm, and he's as calm as usual, though I'm all tense now at the mention of Noel Saint.

"Why?" Gina asks.

"His dad's a real piece of work!" Tahoe declares.

"He couldn't even stand us stopping by the house," Callan growls angrily.

I smile wanly at Malcolm and although he returns my smile, he promptly steers Tahoe back to the topic of his portfolio and ends the subject. Easy as that.

"So T," he begins, and everyone follows his direction into that.

I know Saint's dad is an ass. He's called an ass by most everyone who knows him. Blunt, rude, presumptuous. I read it and saw it online, countless times, how he tries to pretend he's so much bigger and grander than his son. Though Saint seems to reject even the thought of the bastard, he's made it clear he doesn't want me within the same zip code as his father. Still, the thought of Noel Saint setting a foot on *Edge*, a place I have come to love and sacrifice so much for, haunts me a little.

It doesn't last long.

Five minutes later, Otis comes up to the penthouse. Saint greets him for a minute by the elevator, then comes back to head to the guys. On his way there, he says, "Livingston?"

I perk up from my chat with the girls and turn to see him ball a piece of fabric into his hand.

"Got you something," he says.

He tosses it into the air, and it lands softly on my lap.

"What is it?" Curious, I spread the cotton fabric open and make out the Cubs T-shirt, size small. *Signed by every fucking player who played tonight.*

"You didn't!" I look up at him, balling it up and tossing it back at him as if it burned.

Holy shit!

Holy, holy shit!

He catches the shirt easily, then frowns and looks down at it. "Yeah, I did." Frowning harder even as his eyes start glimmering with pure amusement, he brings it over and presses it into my hands. "It's yours," he chastises me.

When he bends to kiss my cheek, I burst out with glee, "I'll frame it!"

My friends manhandle my present so much, I hide it in Saint's closet next to his perfect designer clothes, occupying a hanger of honor right in the middle. When I return to the living room, the girls inform me they're leaving. Sin's friends are still going strong and seem cranked up for more, as if it's not 2 a.m. already.

I waver on what to do.

This staying-over, not-staying-over thing is new territory for me.

For . . . us.

"Saint?" I draw him out of the group for a moment. "I think I should maybe go with Gina," I tell him.

He glances at the girls for a second, then peers down at me with a little smile. "I think you should stay."

"I . . ." God, I'm blushing? "I don't have fresh clothes. And don't even mention my T-shirt 'cause that's getting framed."

"All right. Then Claude or Otis can drive your friends home, and if your roommate will pack some things for you, he'll bring a bag back." He waits for a reply, and I can tell by the vibe he's putting out that he very much wants to be with me tonight.

"It's okay," Gina says, shrugging. "I'll happily be driven home in Saint's car." She smirks.

Sin watches me, his green eyes reeling me in, pulling me under. He looks expectant and . . . adorable and . . . irresistible. Ohgod. Is this going too fast for us having just started back up?

No way.

Or . . . yes.

Maybe.

"Rachel." He steps closer, and I can see he understands my hesitation—we're supposed to be taking it slow—and his voice low as his lips brush my ear. "You don't want to leave any more than I want you to leave."

"You're asking me to sleep over again?" I put an inch between us to search his face. "Your friends are still here—"

"You want my bed more than yours right now, and I want you in there."

God, I'm in so deep. So very deep I'm almost frightened but he makes me reckless enough to want to go even *deeper.*

"Okay," I say, smiling at him a little.

"Okay?" His eyes lighten at that, and he tips my chin up and firmly kisses my mouth.

It's so warm, so absolutely perfect, his mouth, that I smile against it and tell him, only so *he* hears, "I'll be in your bed."

And him, only to me, lips grazing my earlobe: "You won't be alone there for long."

I head to his room, first check on my present, then drop down on the side of the bed that I always end up on, taking a minute to think about today.

When he smiled?

I think the jerk tapped a vein and injected me with pure happiness.

I think of me and him, and sports, and how his passion flared, and how we as people go crazy over the stuff we love.

Which reminds me . . .

I need to start a new article. As I try to stay awake and wait for him, I pull out my cell phone and write down notes and ideas in an email to myself.

I write about the stuff we get crazy over. Obsessed. Like our favorite sports teams. The Cubs can lose a thousand times and we still love them. They can fuck up, and we still believe in them.

I take down a lot of ideas while absently listening to the men laugh in the living room, somehow specially attuned to Malcolm's laugh. I like his laugh more than any other. It's deep and it resonates in his chest, but it's never too loud or obnoxious. Another obsession.

Smiling while I reread the email with ideas, I send it to myself and text my mom, who usually paints until very late during the weekends.

Are you up? I try.

Just finished cleaning up the studio, she replies. Off to bed! Everything all right??

More than all right. Mom! You're going to get to meet him!! I don't need to tell her who "him" is; she knows exactly who's got her daughter hooked.

Almost instantaneously she writes back, WHEN? Are you bringing him over for dinner?

Don't worry about that, I can order something for us and bring it over.

My phone rings. I pick up to hear her immediately chiding me. "Rachel, absolutely not. You're not gonna bring anything. It's gonna be homemade and delicious! He's your first boyfriend!"

"Well, he's not . . . kinda, I hope so." I exhale and shake my head. "Don't call him my boyfriend yet, I don't want to jinx it. We're still working things out. Make your yummy peppermint chocolate pie for me."

"What does he like? Fancy things?"

I laugh just as the men outside release a round of simultaneous laughter. "No, Mom, he enjoys normal things. He likes . . . me." And I'm *so* vanilla to a physical man like Sin. "Don't worry, whatever you make is fine."

"When are you coming?"

"*You* tell us when," I counter.

"Fine, give me a week or two to prepare."

"Okay. Love you, Momma."

"Rachel." She stops me from hanging up. After a deep, excited breath, "I look forward to meeting this man I've heard about."

God, the things my mother must have heard. Probably that he's a manwhore.

"He's not a saint, Momma," I quietly tell her. "But I like him very much."

After a couple minutes of hearing the men banter, I start to get sleepy, but the anticipation of knowing Saint is coming to bed soon keeps me from fully relaxing. I study his big bed underneath me. I consider pulling back the comforter and stripping to my undies. Would that be too slutty? Yeah. Yeah it would be.

And maybe he'd like it?

I start to take off my shoes and quietly strip to my bra and panties when I realize the guys are protesting.

"Ah man, we're having a good time."

"Fuck, Saint. Seriously?"

Ohmigod, he's kicking them out.

I'm so excited and suddenly panicked, I'm scrambling to get naked as I hear the guys shuffle out.

I'm standing in the middle of his room wondering if I'm going to be a slut, shouldn't I go all the way and just get naked? *All* naked?

I hear silence next and the sound of familiar footsteps make their way to me. Feeling a kick of adrenaline, I yank my bra off over my head and nearly stumble as I pull off my panties and toss them aside and scramble into bed.

I pull the sheets up to my chest when I hear him answer some sort of message, speaking in another language. I comb a hand through my hair then spread it out behind me on the pillow, hearing his voice growl some business instruction.

He seems mad about something.

I try tying the sheet around my body and letting it drop a little so he can get a peek of a shoulder. Then I decide to let him look at both shoulders. Then I lie back and fan out my hair a little again, kind of annoyed at my body for being so . . . well, so ready so soon. But my skin feels the delicious touch of his super-soft high-count sheets, and I can't suppress the chaos in my body as I wait for him.

I hear silence again. Footsteps. And the door opens. A sliver of light from outside appears and his silhouette at the door. The air starts crackling. I can hear my heart. *Thump. Thump.* Strong. Resonating though my ears as I look at his shape—his awe-inspiring shape in the door. His hair a little standing up as if he pulled it in frustration, maybe. Our eyes lock. My Saint hormones go crazy.

I sit up and pull the sheets to my chest, pushing my hair out of my face. "Hey," I say.

He reaches behind him to shut the door. "Fuck me, I like you so much in my bed I need to figure out how to permanently keep you in it."

"Just put yourself in it. I'll stay."

He cracks out a slow smile, looking genuinely pleased as he looks at me. "I'm here."

Um, yes he is. The energy in the room shifts with him here with all the power he projects, attracting anything weaker than him.

"Like I wouldn't notice."

He walks into the room and picks up my panties and bra, and I flush like crazy. "Nice," he murmurs, his eyes sparking appreciatively. He keeps his eyes on me as he reaches behind him, fists his polo in one hand, and pulls it over his head.

He's mouthwatering.

So beautiful I can't wait.

I go up to my knees and knee-walk to the end of the bed, the sheet to my chest with one hand as I reach out and stroke my fingers up his chest. I don't know how many times it'll take to see him naked and not feel absolutely buttery, but his every hard plane is perfection and my every soft part tingles. Before I know it I'm setting my lips over one small brown nipple, lightly sucking. God, his taste is addictive.

He fists my hair, pulls me back, and takes my lips, deep and hungry. I'm tingling with happiness as our mouths search, find, and fuse together. I keep trailing my fingers up his chest and when he eases back to look at me, his breathing is ragged, his fist still in my hair.

"Where to even start with you," he says as if to himself.

He tightens his hold on my hair and pulls me up for another mind-numbing kiss.

"That's a good start," I admit into his mouth. "I wanted to stay and thank you properly for my shirt and for today."

"I wasn't letting you get away." His voice is husky and sure. He tugs the sheet down to look at me. My throat closes as he drags a hand over my upper body, to cup the globe of one breast in one strong hand. "That's not exactly true. You could've left," he tells me, tugging my ear playfully with his free hand, "but I'd have chased you."

"Maybe I'd have let you catch me."

He smiles as he gently fondles my breast, as if I'm deluded, thinking I could escape him. Resist him. He knows what he does to me. He found me naked like one of his groupies in his bed. "What do you say we turn a light on in here?"

"Why?" I pant as he eases off me.

He sends me a thousand-volt greedy look. "I want to look at you."

"But . . . there's light coming from outside," I protest.

He walks around. "I want to see you."

I clutch the sheet back up as he stands to flick on the lamp by the bed.

It bathes him in light as he comes back to me. He grips the sheet in one hand and starts tugging and I feel my resolve melt and melt as his gaze starts sliding down my neck, soft as a caress. I force my fingers to release it.

"Saint . . ." I protest.

"God, come on. Don't be shy with me, Rachel. Not with me."

I stop tugging at that, and he looks at me with such a look of tenderness, I melt.

He lowers it to my waist and my pulse quickens as his eyes take in my breasts in the lamplight, my abdomen, the lower half of my body hidden still by the sheet that dropped there. As he lowers it down my hips and it slides down my legs, my body starts to ache horribly for his touch. My senses coming to life before he even touches me.

He tosses the sheet at my feet now.

"What do you want from me?" I croak.

His hand coasts down my rib cage, his thumb slowly stroking my hipbone as he leans over and nibbles my ear. "Everything." I sigh. His lips slide across my jaw and back to latch on mine. He doesn't seem to want to talk now.

I can't speak now either. I'm too busy tasting him back. Fingers wandering into his thick hair. Breasts pressing to his flat chest. And his warm tongue and strong lips leaving mine to wander . . . wander . . . down my throat. He moves the little R necklace aside and sets a kiss on the nook below as his hand caresses down my flat abdomen.

I start closing my thighs—this always makes me vulnerable. Thinking he'll kiss me there. He stops my thighs from fully closing and urges one open to the side.

His breath coasts over my nipple before his mouth crosses the peak. On the inside of my leg, his thumb travels up my thigh.

"Saint," I whimper anxiously.

He tastes my mouth again, harder. He rolls me to my back and comes over me in his jeans, his bare chest hot against mine.

And that sexy smiling mouth of his kisses me, and I'm dragging my hands up the grooves of his back, undulating as I try to get him to give me what I need—him, all of him—right now.

He's running his hands up and down my sides as he samples the skin of my neck, the tips of my breasts, my navel, like he truly doesn't know where to start. He's savoring, but at the same time, hungry. His lips nip and bite and his tongue swipes out to taste, his hands kneading as they go, his muscles taut with tension, his energy intense, I wonder if I'm enough to appease him.

He licks his tongue into my belly button and parts my legs with one wandering hand. I stare up at the ceiling and groan as I try to calm my body down, rolling my head to the side as pleasure rocks me.

He teases his thumb over my folds first, and then brings his two longest fingers to stroke over the outside. I fist his hair and pull him away from my breast, pulling him up hungrily to my mouth. He gives me the kiss I want, but then tears free and edges back. His eyes miss no detail of me splayed on his bed. My wet folds slick under his two fingers. My breasts rising and falling. My face, which feels soft and weak with desire.

One nipple disappears into his mouth again. His hair gleams in the lamplight, shadows cast across his muscles. He's still in jeans. And I'm so very naked, so very caressed, so very turned on and vulnerable as he inches his head down. I sense him look at me down there as he uses his two hands to spread my legs open.

"Oh, Malcolm." I'm red all over.

He leans down and sucks my clit. I arch up and groan.

He rubs me under his tongue and as I rock my hips instinctively, taken over, his fingers are there, ready to penetrate me. He watches me arch. I should've known he'd want everything. Take everything. He warned me he would. My instinct of self-preservation wars against the pleasure arrowing through me and the need to be taken by him.

I sigh his name and let my legs skew open. He whispers my name reverently and sucks and kisses me a little more.

"Saint, I'm going to—"

He doesn't stop until I come. I'm still shuddering when he stands to undress; I'm too weak to cover myself. To pretend I have control over this kind of want. It's like he knows my walls are up and he's determined to crumble them.

I didn't know desire like this existed. I see him stand there, rolling on a condom, ready to take me and I lie here, spread open and aching for him to. I relax in anticipatory relief when his naked body covers mine, and he opens me up to receive him.

I groan as he wraps my arms around his neck and my legs around his hips, my head falling back . . . ready, eager, wanting. He kisses my breasts, grabbing my ass and tilting my hips upward as he drives inside. Our bodies tighten in pleasure as we connect.

I feel him stretch me . . . take me.

Then we begin to move. Quiet. Only our breathing audible.

My every sense is sensitized to a million.

I stare, in hazy ecstasy, up into his face, lit by the lamplight and golden and perfect, and ohmigod, his eyes look so hot for me. So violent and fiercely tender for me as he stares down at me. I knot up inside.

My chest flutters as I wonder if he can see it right in my eyes in every wild beat of my heart, I love you I love you *Iloveyou* . . .

I stay staring as we move, my hands caressing his chest, his body hoisted up by one arm while his free hand makes love to my skin. And then we start kissing, and we don't stop, the connection of our bodies too delicious, our mouths tasting, savoring, hot, wet, mine eager and soft, his more demanding and thirsty, our bodies moving together.

We lie there after he goes clean up, silent and sweaty and I've lost all modesty at the moment. I feel raw and open and unable to pull myself together right now.

I let him kiss my mouth for a while; my lips are red and I like it. I like his bed, I like our bodies tangled, I like that he broke me down and I get to stay and sleep here as I pull myself together again. I realize his breathing is deeper and shift a little, and he's asleep. I reach up and touch his lips and quietly set a kiss on them.

I know Saint usually has trouble sleeping and I wonder how many nights he's lain here, in this bed, without shutting his eyes. Enough that he's fast asleep now, as if he too feels at peace having me back in his arms. I take his arm and curl it around me. And kiss the corner of his lips.

"Good night, Sin," I whisper.

I never thought I could love a guy this freaking hard.

SOMETHING NEW

Helen loved my "Things That Obsess Us" piece inspired by the Cubs game, and I'm excited to be writing again. I'm hopeful these newest pieces will help me open the door to one of my job prospects.

I was already at *Lokus* this week, and I've already queried every one of the places Saint mentioned. But my phone is silent.

Sometimes at night, when Saint leaves bed to work, or sometimes even when he's holding me, I quietly worry about my options.

Or lack of them.

Valentine tells me that sometimes it takes time. That I may have to freelance, but I'm scared to lose the security of a full-time job, especially with my mother and our lack of health insurance for her.

Helen hasn't mentioned Noel Saint again. But . . . can the deal please fall apart?

I know Helen doesn't want me to leave. She's trying her

damnedest to act as if *Edge* isn't in the midst of an acquisition, but I can tell by her shut office door and the flurry of meetings with her bosses that it's happening.

There's a long-standing war of wills going on between Noel and Malcolm. I mean, why else would his father, whose business mostly involves real estate, just *happen* to be interested in journalism, just as his son is being seen with me?

And I know how ruthless Saint can be. Saint is not a guy who'd let his father win, especially where *I'm* concerned.

The week goes by in a blizzard of texts, and anticipation of seeing him on Friday.

He warned me he was working late, but that he wanted to see me. I'm already in bed when he finally texts, I'm coming up.

I tiptoe out to open the door in nothing but a tiny pair of lace bottoms, and when I swing the door open, he lifts me up.

I crawl higher up the trunk of his body and bite his neck. We're both ravenous when he takes us to my room. He shoves his hands into the sides of my panties and gives a hard pull and when I hear them give with a spectacular tear and snap, I gasp his name, raw on my lips. Another breathy gasp escapes me as he throws me on the bed and jerks off his clothes. Then he covers me, and my nails sink into his shoulder blades, ankles lock at the base of his spine.

"Inside," I beg.

He tortures me for a little while. "No. I want you like this. Wild and hot." He's not very obedient. The arousal and lust in my body triples. I ache for it, need it.

"Inside . . . get in me. Oh Sin, give it to me."

By the time he rolls on a condom and lets me have it, I'm a mass of delicious contractions and heat.

He holds the back of my head in one hand, kisses me. "The way you squeeze me, Rachel. The way you just don't want to let go of me even when you know I'm coming back, hard and deep . . ."

The next morning, I awake to an empty bed and a shiny black credit card lying next to the cell phone on my nightstand. And a text: Get some new ones.

I roll to my side and see the torn panties, and smile so hard my face hurts.

Then he texts again: Get some swimwear while you're at it. Let's hit *The Toy* later.

The Toy.

I've been combusting all week, and have been churning out dating pieces and how-to-tell-what-kisses-mean pieces and how-to-seduce-the-man-of-your-dream pieces like crazy for Helen.

I have the best memories of being on *The Toy* with Saint. Memories of nothing but the lake around us. I love going out on his yacht because all the social media doesn't exist; all my fears fade away. The times Malcolm and I have been alone there together are some of the best of my life.

Saint and I are leaving later. So now Gina and I are in the swimwear section of her department store. There's a very simple, well-cut black bikini that sits snug and lovely on my butt and tits. I feel beautiful, the material smooth, the cut making my legs look sleek and long.

It's a little bit expensive and I just don't know if I can let this big spender of a man buy it for me. On the other hand, letting him buy it for me makes me feel so sexy I can't stand it.

And Gina says a guy has to feel like a provider sometimes and I have to let him.

"He needs to feel like a man," she says.

Groan. Like Sin needs to feel any manlier.

After a while of turning and checking my appearance from all angles, I take a selfie in the mirror and then examine it closely. Do I look good? I want to look *awesome*. Not just good. Send it or not, send it or not, send it or not—

Shit! Clicked "send."

This one? I force myself to casually add after the stupid photo just flew over to his phone. Dammit.

YES is the only reply.

I feel bees in my stomach. OK. I'll be done and ready to sail as soon as I figure out how to use this black card I got.

Don't worry, it works just fine, he writes back. Then adds, Where are you? I'll pick you up in 20.

I tell him I'm at the department store where Gina works. Then I tell Gina I think I can buy this one.

She peers at my bikini through the curtain, and snaps, "That is *terribly* sexy. Why are you hesitating? GET THEM ALL! Paul never bought me shit. It shouldn't be difficult to let Saint do it."

"Well, because it's from him. I want it to be . . . perfect."

I come out with the swimsuit and head over to pay.

It's ridiculous how excited I am.

I've never let a man do this for me.

I'd never even realized how easy it would be to agree when that man . . . well, when that man is the one you want to be with. And when that man seems to delight—seriously, get high!—in getting you things.

Ohgod.

Is this me being spoiled rotten by him?

"You sure you only want one?" Gina asks as she inspects my selection. "You know, those black Centurion credit cards are so costly to own, you might as well use them or you're throwing money away."

"Gina," I groan as I watch the lady swipe the card and package my swimsuit as they do in the expensive stores like this one. "I'm not going to throw his money away! I only need *one*," I scold her.

We head toward the stairs and she gets distracted by a shoe display. Shuddering after she checks a price, she sets the shoe aside while I check out a pair of sleek Louboutins, the designer shoes with the red soles.

"Has there been any news of his dick father?" she asks as I stare in shock at the price and quickly return the shoe to the display.

"No."

"And the job interviews . . ."

I shake my head.

"So maybe you'll work with Saint?"

"I couldn't be his employee, Gina, I feel consumed as it is."

Dibs . . .

Oh, shit. *Dear brain, can we please try to forget that?*

But every time Saint touches me, I feel his fingers and his tongue are saying dibs and dibs and dibs . . .

The word is no longer visible on my hand, but I feel branded by it.

Gina leads me downstairs to the Chanel department, where I stock up on eye shadow and eyeliner. When we walk out of the store, we see some people across the street all staring in the same direction—a few more even stop walking to gape. I follow their gazes and stop in my tracks, my heart in my throat.

A silver Bentley's parked at the curb. Something buzzes over my skin as Malcolm heads toward me. He is absolute sin in fucking jeans and a polo that makes love to him.

A few paces behind him is Otis, walking with Saint's same long stride. Malcolm signals at his driver to get my tiny bag and then he looks down at me.

"She's ready for your yacht, Saint. She's got the perfect bikini. But unfortunately she's not ready for anything else," Gina says.

"That's not true!" I groan.

Gina chuckles and waves at us dismissively as she heads off to where she was meeting Wynn for brunch.

When I turn back to my green-eyed devil, I see he's just looking at me. "You didn't buy what I told you to."

I scowl in confusion when I realize he's walking me back toward the store.

The salespeople seem startled enough that I deduce Saint doesn't come here often, but they seem to know him or about him. Oh yes, they do. The level of chatter around this man starts to spread in hushed tones across the store.

He leads me into the women's department and then into . . .

The lingerie department.

My heart stops as he winds through the racks, his big, muscular body contrasting with the flimsy bits of nothing hanging all around him. He brushes his lips over my ear. "Let's get you some things."

"Malcolm," I say, as his voice in my ear leaves a lingering earthquake in my tummy. I shake my head. "I already bought the bathing suit, I'm not comfortable buying anything else."

He's already scanning the articles on a panty table, his brow furrowed as he hunts down the perfect pieces for me. "You won't be buying it. I will."

God.

He doesn't waste time.

"How about this?" He's dangling a red lace thong between his fingers.

I shake my head and feel myself flush.

"This?" His eyes begin to light up when he notices I'm beet red, and I bite down on the inside of my cheek. *Play his game, Livingston!*

"Too mainstream." I dismiss it with a flick of my fingers. He lifts his brows.

"Well, in that case." He hunts around the tables for another pair of lingerie. He picks up a yellow thong with a bow on the back, which I assume would be perched right between the tops of my butt cheeks.

I take it between my fingers. It's made of lace, and the bow is soft silk.

"You want me to look like a present or what?" I playfully tease, gesturing to the bow.

He teases right back, his adorable smile part devil and part saint. "If I get to unwrap you? Yes."

My body temperature is suddenly too high for what I assume is healthy so I step away toward the bra area, finding the matching one to the yellow thong he seems to like so much.

I walk around the store, picking up other stuff. I'm playing along, a little excited and more than a little reckless. Some black lace stockings with a matching garter, a white silk cami set, and Malcolm brings three more thongs (dark blue, white, and purple), and a tiny-looking corset, oh god.

"This has to go on you." Now he's being just wicked.

"If you want a corpse in your bed. Saint, these don't let you *breathe*."

He discards that and goes to find a pearl thong. "All right. So this." He looks at me coaxingly.

"That's sooo uncomfortable. I like my pearls on my neck

and soft things between my . . ." I go up on my toes and add, "Cheeks."

He catches me by the hips and pulls me close. "Try it on for me."

"Nobody tries on underwear before they buy." I walk around when he follows me and wraps his arms around me.

"Then let's buy it. Try something on for me. A nightie. Sheer and pretty where I can see your blush just beneath."

I scan the store quickly. "I don't see any nightie here with that description . . ."

He produces a flimsy-looking gauzy thing from behind his back, eyes glinting.

"Malcolm." I groan, and though I keep rummaging through the offerings, now I'm just looking for things to tease him. I grab a pair of huge granny panties. The kind that cover you up to your breasts and cut unattractively down on your leg. "This looks comfortable."

"Like hell."

"And this." I pull out the plainest, biggest bra I can find. "Would you let me buy these?"

"Yeah minx. And we'll use them for a bonfire."

His eyes turn devilish and he grabs the big panties, the big bra, and the little nightie, and then tugs me to the dressing rooms, and I'm acutely aware of the salesladies possibly watching us. He yanks open a velvet dressing-room curtain, and when I go in, he follows me inside.

"Sin! What if they see you in here?"

"Trust me, they know I'm here."

I stand there, dumbly holding the panties and nightie to my chest. Dressing-room lights are always so *bad*. Though Saint looks glorious as usual. He's leaning back against the wall with his legs spread and his hands in his pockets. The top three buttons of his polo are unbuttoned and he's looking at me with laughter in his eyes.

"Can you at least close your eyes?" I plead.

He shakes his head no.

When I just stand there, shy like I *shouldn't* still be feeling with him, he lowers himself to the only seat available and crooks his index finger at me. "Come here."

I walk toward him, entranced by the gleam in his eyes right now. I hold my breath when he puts his warm, strong hands on my hips and places me between his legs, the top of his head reaching just below my breasts.

He eases my blouse off first, then he unbuttons my jeans slowly.

My throat starts to close at the utter sensuality of the moment. I focus on a spot on the wall behind him, trying to calm myself down. He slowly pushes my jeans down until they're a puddle on the floor. I step out of them automatically then toe off my shoes, and he runs his hands slowly up my legs until they're resting on my hips again.

I'm standing in my top and light-blue panties. He looks up at me with his green eyes and I know in this moment that he could do whatever he wanted to me and I would let him. Wholeheartedly, I would let him.

I'm scared of how reckless he makes me. I can feel my breathing get faster as he hooks his thumbs in the edge of my panties and slowly starts to pull them down. His eyes stay on mine the whole time, until my panties are on the floor. I step out of them and he reaches for the nightie, taking my arms and sliding them into the flimsy, fluttery sleeves. I fasten the bow at the center as he watches. By now, I am a horny mess.

He leans over, and parts the already-wide parting of the nightie and places a kiss on the top of my navel. Edging the bow up and kissing my stomach softly before turning me around in his hands so I can see myself in the mirror.

The nightie feels weightless and soft as a cloud wrapped around me; I can feel the silk molding to my body, hugging my waist, fluttering to my bottom, where it just—ends. Exposing my ass. I can tell he's having fun because he's looking at the back, smiling. Then his eyes hold mine in the mirror. He looks dark, manly, and powerful, with his hands on the sides of my thighs while he sits back on the bench, looking at me in the mirror.

My body's gone haywire but I can't help my reactions to him and I think Sin very well knows it. Oy, me.

He pats my ass after he stands in that deliberately slow way of his. "I'd say this one for sure," he murmurs close to my ear, brushing a hand up my side in a caress that hums through me like his whisper.

We can't seem to take our eyes off each other as he slowly undoes the ribbon and lets it unfurl open. I'm shaking head to toe, ready to make out or even do more, when I look for the first thing to cover myself. I hop quickly into my panties as he sits down again and pulls out the huge panties.

"Go on. Turn me on."

I hike one brow. "The only way I can try it is over my jeans." I slip on my jeans and then slide on the humongous panties. And I'm laughing so hard at his face. Then his eyes darken and he pulls me down on his lap, and says, "These look like a dress on you."

"A very ugly dress?"

He shakes his head, smiling.

"A very big dress?"

He shakes his head.

"Should I take a thousand of these?"

"I dig you in these, Rachel. I dig you in everything." He looks at me with hot tenderness, stroking his hand down my back as he looks down at the ridiculous view. "The more you get, the more I get to rip off you. So yes. Take them off." He pats my ass. "We're getting you everything," he says, almost to himself.

I'm laughing and tossing the huge panties at him along with the nightie and everything else.

But inwardly, I'm blushing.

Is he blind?

I looked ridiculous.

He looked at me like I was so . . . perfect.

When he brushes past me to pay, I swear that this simple intimate act of shopping together has taken my arousal to a whole other level.

When I slip on my clothes and step out, the saleslady is gushing at him and handing Malcolm her card. "Anything, you can absolutely call or email and we will be happy to help."

"Thank you," he absently murmurs, his gaze on me as if I'm the most beautiful thing he's ever seen, and that's where it stays as he swings the bags behind his shoulder and we head out of there.

"Saint," I chide. "Don't spend this kind of money on me. You're already like the man of my dreams."

I laugh and duck my head after the admission, blushing when I see the hot look in his eyes.

Outside, I shoot him a sidelong glance. "Do you give your black credit card to all your lady friends?"

"No, I give them the gold."

"Malcolm!" I hit him playfully. He grabs the back of my

head and leads me down the street, where a guy approaches us quite frantically.

"Saint, any comments on your father's acquisition of *Edge*?"

Malcolm puts himself between me and the guy and continues walking me toward the car, silent, leaving the guy behind.

"I admire you." I shoot him an awed glance and shake my head. "How you so easily dismiss the attention."

Then I loosen the elastic band on my hair and pull it to my sides to use it as a curtain to hide my face. He watches me in confusion. I can feel people staring at us now, and uncomfortably, I grab the aviators he just pulled out and slip them on my face.

He looks down at me with a half smile and eyes narrowed in speculation. "Want a fake mustache with that?"

"I'm good." I grin.

I follow him to the car and we don't bother to set the bag in the trunk. The car is super spacious anyway. He opens the door before Otis can fully make it and we ease inside.

"Rachel . . ." He falls sober, plucking off the aviators.

I'm smiling, but I also feel ashamed. "Sin, I'm sorry." I drop my face. "It's going to take me a while to get used to the attention you get."

"Don't notice it. Don't give it even a moment's thought. I never do."

"Hmm." My mouth twists wryly. "It's not only the attention, but wondering what lies they'll put out . . . having no control over that." I feel my heart squeeze a little as our eyes meet, him sitting across from me, broad and muscular and drop-dead gorgeous. And I admit the closest thing I can say to *I love you*. "It's hard when everyone stares at the man you want, and you want him to want nobody but you."

He simply says two words that melt me.

"He does."

THE TOY

When I come out in my bikini, Malcolm is leaning on the railing. He seems to be talking to some guys out on the lake. He's in swim trunks and a polo, his wide torso stretching his shirt in a way that I can see the muscled grooves on his back as he leans forward.

I hear the guys down on the lake daring him to take out his Jet Ski and race them. They're boasting quite loudly that they're going to kick his ass this time. "It's long due, you fucking bastard!"

In reply to that, Saint lets go a low, throaty laugh, and he yells down at them, "Nah, I'm with a friend today!"

"Lady friend or lady friends?" they bait. But Saint doesn't bite, and I hear the zoom of Jet Ski motors as they leave.

Barefoot, I kind of stand a few feet away, not knowing what to say. Every muscle on his back and shoulders is visible through the stretch of his shirt as Malcolm jerks a hand over his hair and then he pulls out his phone, starts dabbling.

"Do you know everyone on the lake?"

When he hears my voice, he turns, and the smile he's wearing fades. There's a breeze and I hate that my nipples are quick to scream, *We're cold!*

I rub my arm and he says, lowering his body sideways onto a nearby chaise, "Come sit."

He pats the space beside him, and though he looks in control, I see him inhale, very slowly and very deeply. I take the chaise next to his instead, smiling and feeling shy.

"This is . . . well, I guess you bought me this. Thank you."

He doesn't look at the bikini; he's looking at my face, almost as if he's seeing me for the first time. "You're welcome." He leans forward, elbows on his knees, and his voice drops a decibel. "You're making my mouth water."

I stare at his sparkling green eyes, at his seductive smile, not knowing what to say.

A nervous laugh leaves me.

But he just stares, his extremely intense attention homed in on me. Water laps against the boat as the Chicago wind does its thing.

"Do you believe your father's interest in *Edge* is purely business?" I ask him, remembering the reporter we just encountered.

"He's competitive. I'm like him in that respect." His lips curl in a sneer as he turns to contemplate the lake water.

"He's competing against . . ."

"Me."

"Goading you?"

"Using you." He levels his stare on me. "He sees you as my weakness. He's right. He's waiting to see if I rise to the challenge. He's been wanting to show me he still has power over me for years."

Silence.

The heavy kind that weighs on your heart.

"After Mother died, I broke free of him. Moved out, left the family business. I was old enough to take my stock. I sold my shares to his worst enemy, forced him into bed with the last man he wanted there." He snarls and laughs, his eyes gleaming ruthlessly now. "Payback for all the times he cheated on my mother."

I wait with bated breath for him to tell me more, and it doesn't take him long. It sounds as if he's speaking about someone else, he's that distanced from his father.

My father died; his father is alive, but somehow it feels as if we both grew up without one.

"With that money, I started my empire. I supposed he thought I'd lose it all on whores and Vegas. I don't need to pay women to be with me. And I have better sense than Vegas." He smirks proudly at that. "No one has ever underestimated me like my father."

"What happened to the family business?"

"Weakened. He lost control of his own board. Had to buy back his own stock to recoup the majority of his business. By then he'd formed a bad reputation. Not paying suppliers. He couldn't stand growing weaker while his weak kid grew better and stronger."

His smile is brief and regretful.

"I'm over it, but he's never backed off from trying to step on my heels. For years I've been weeding out his hired snoops, who are rabid to know what I'm after next." He looks fondly at me and winks. "I move too fast for him. But damn me if I shouldn't have seen *this* coming after . . ." He trails off.

I ache in my ribs, my chest, my stomach. "I'm sorry, Malcolm."

"*Edge* is worthless to him without you. He's testing me out to see how much I care."

"But we're not formally together. After what happened, why would he think you cared?"

"Because I do." His green eyes flash almost violently, hot and fast. "I just do." And then, a low, amused laugh follows when I just stare at him stupidly. "Rachel, it's obvious."

He drags a hand through his hair, looking away thoughtfully while shocking me. No. Stunning me.

"Cathy and the girls would share looks when I scheduled an appointment with you. Otis would get a look on his face when I'd ask him to pick you up. Roth and Carmichael still won't let me hear the end of it. People who don't know me at all speculated about you and me. It's very obvious."

"What's obvious?"

He shoots me a look, then his lips curl a little and he runs his knuckles down my jawline. "That I'm into you."

He touches his thumb to my chin and there are dozens of hot, tangled sensations all over me.

"I swear, those looks you give me, Rachel," he murmurs under his breath.

"What looks?" I laugh, flustered. We're so relaxed, bantering; I missed this so much. The way his eyes look at me, openly amused. There's something unguarded and warm in his humor. It's enchanting because he's always so in control at work.

"This one." His thumbs brush over the outside corners of my eyes. "This one." He uses his thumbs to shape a smile on my lips, his green eyes both humorous and tender. "This one," he adds huskily, brushing his thumb over a frown on my forehead. "And the one that tells me you want me *here*." He cups my sex, then brings his dark head close to my ear. "The one that says you're scared and want to be saved. And the one when you're happy, as if I gave you the world, like when I bought you lingerie."

"Oh, I bet you loved that last one, hmm? You like the ones that cater to your ego best?" I bring my hand up to stifle my laugh. "The ones that go straight to here." I then give a tap to his head, and he's just smiling.

"Do you know," I stroke a hand aimlessly up and down his abs, his pecs, "the story of Psyche and Cupid?"

He cocks an amused eyebrow.

"Psyche's beauty compelled men to worship her, incurring Venus's wrath, and Venus commissioned Cupid to enact her revenge. But upon seeing her, Cupid accidentally pricked himself with his own arrow and fell in love with Psyche, so he hatched a plan to make her his wife. Now, Psyche believed she was fated to marry a monster, and when Cupid himself told her not to look at him, she was pretty worried about who he was. She didn't trust what she couldn't see, and one day, encouraged by her jealous sisters to kill him, she dared to look upon him. And he was so beautiful . . . her Cupid . . ." I blush. "So just when she realized he wasn't the monster she thought he was, she lost him. Cupid told her that love couldn't dwell with suspicion, and he left her." I blush more.

"Go on." He leans back, paying the kind of attention to me that only he does, intense and a little bit nerve-racking.

"Then Psyche realized she had to return to serve Venus, who put her through terrible trials. But Cupid started interfering— he rescued Psyche from a deep sleep and finally made her his wife."

His laugh is slow and marvelous, catching.

"Little one, I can't possibly be Cupid in that story."

When he lifts his brows in a dare, I realize, he *is* Cupid to me, mischievous and conniving, but demanding loyalty when he unexpectedly falls for Psyche.

But Saint doesn't want to be Cupid. He shoots me a look that warns me what will happen if he is. Delicious sex torture?

Oh god.

I wonder how stupid I might have sounded, basically assuming that he loved me. *Stupid Rachel.*

"Well, your true form, Hades," I improvise, "stole Persephone and took her to the underworld, where he abused her sexually before they ended up falling in love. You know what always puzzles me?" I add.

"What?" His eyes gleam like glassy volcanic rock.

"Zeus, the most powerful 'good' god, was always having affairs on his wife. The 'bad' god, Hades, was pretty much obsessed with Persephone, and seemed far more in love with her than Zeus was with his wife. For all his sins, Hades was so much more devoted. I think . . . there's always something beautiful breeding in the darkness and pain."

"Is there?" he asks quietly.

I nod soberly. "So no, you're not Cupid in that story, I guess." Then I tease, "You're Zeus *and* Hades. A saint here," I touch his heart, "and a sinner here," I touch his thickening erection.

He laughs softly and pulls me to his chaise, and we lie there, soaking up the sun in silence.

The lake is mostly calm, save for a few Jet Skis passing by, an occasional boat. I think about his father, how calm and rational Malcolm has been throughout this.

"You won't let him goad you into doing anything reckless . . . will you?"

He laughs. "I'm over reckless." He shifts his shoulders so

he can look at me. "But on my word, he won't be hurting you. Slowly, deliberately, very subtly, I'll crush him if he comes near you."

"He won't come near me. I'll leave before then."

He cups my face in a gesture of male gratitude, and asks, "How are you going to introduce me to your mother?"

I smile. "She already knows you're not saintly at all," I tease.

He looks at me quietly, the silence stretching.

"She's worried," I admit.

"Is she?"

"She thinks you're too worldly."

"That's a negative against me?"

"And too rich."

"Really now?" His brows slant thoughtfully.

"She's worried you're a player and that you won't be able to help yourself and play with *me*."

His eyebrows furrow even more. "Well, it won't be the first time I'm underestimated."

"But she likes you! It's just that . . . she's been a victim of what she's heard. She was rooting for us but it was hard to hide from her that I was so . . . sad."

He tips my head back; his eyes darken. "You put yourself there. Not me."

I drop my eyes. "I know. Are you sure you want to? Go?" I ask hesitantly.

"Yeah, I want to." He moves his hand up to play with a little tendril of hair by my ear, his voice dropping an octave. "I'm not a saint. But you, Rachel . . ." He trails off as though searching for words.

"I'm not a saint either." I'm laughing at that. "I'm a sinner," I assure him; then I smirk a little and playfully push at his shoulder with the heel of my palm. "And you're my Sin."

He catches my wrist in his grip, and my laugh fades as he pulls me closer.

The glow of lust in his eyes as he studies me opens up a painful ache in my midsection. I am rabid for him. He's my Achilles' heel, the greatest pleasures in my life somehow now tied to his smiles. And right now, I quiver with the knowledge that he wants *me*.

So many years of being practical, and now I feel my romantic side taking over. I've spent every night for almost the past month reliving the ways he's spoken to me, looked at me. He is unattainable, and yet he's all my fantasies, all my dreams, put into one single human being, with warm flesh and a thudding heart and a beautiful face with a mouthwateringly muscled body.

His expression is fully relaxed now, his lips wearing just the hint of a smile as he asks, "Are you hungry?"

For you, I think, but I shake my head no.

He gets to his feet, pours us some wine and pops a cherry into his mouth. He knots the stem and shows me his perfect knot. "You ever do that?" His deep voice as he sits near me warms me up.

"It means you're good with your tongue."

His gentle laugh ripples through the air, and oh, I feel his smile between my ribs, between my legs.

He heads back to the table. Joining him by the little fruit buffet, I eat a cherry, put aside the seed, and try to knot the stem. He eats another while he watches. After a minute, I give up and shake my head, taking the straight stem out of my mouth and showing him.

"Nope," I confirm, laughing.

He just smiles down at me, his voice low and husky. "Nobody ever gets it right the first time."

He grabs another one and knots it again, moving his tongue

slowly inside his mouth in a way that causes all kinds of lusty thoughts to run through me. There's a curious swooping pull to my insides as I watch him do it, and when his lips curl upward as he gazes at me, the swooping is followed by a shock wave that rocks me.

Before I can take another one, he grabs my wrist, his other hand lifting to rest on my face. He brushes my lips with the pad of his thumb. I shiver involuntarily.

I'm entranced by the thoughtfulness on his face as he draws my cheek to his chest and caresses my hair. We stay like that. The very air over the water seems electrified. He runs his hand through my hair and the sensation is so sweet and so intoxicating, I can't move.

He obviously knows he affects me. But he seems affected too, his body stone-like and buzzing with tension.

As if getting control of himself, he peers down at me. "Do you want me to teach you how to knot one up? Or want a dip in the water?"

I glance at the cherries, and his lips curl. My toes curl in response. Reaching out, he raises a cherry, dangling it from the stem.

I ease down onto the chaise near the buffet table and start to feel warm from his body heat, suddenly so very near.

He leans over, holding the cherry by the stem, and I part my lips and pluck it off. I bite into it with my molars and feel the cool juice slide down my throat. I've never been more aware of him watching me eat as I take the little seed out of my mouth and I set it on a small plate on the table.

He sits beside me, his shoulder touching mine, his face looking down at me, and I swear the sun looks better on his face than in the sky.

My lips part when he offers the stem, and I pull it into

my mouth and give it a try. He bends his head closer to speak through the noise of the wind. "Curl it around your tongue." His voice is absolutely low. "Like this."

He dips his head and before I know it, his lips connect with mine and his tongue is moving, guiding the cherry stem around mine sinuously, expertly knotting it in my mouth.

When we separate, our eyes hold for the longest second as he pulls out the knotted stem from his mouth. *Which he just took from mine.* His lips curl as he sets it aside, his eyes smiling too when, gently, I feel the brush of his thumbs on my cheeks as he cups my face.

"I know what else you twist around so easily," I breathe.

He stares deeply into me as he waits for more.

"Me."

And then he's not smiling anymore. And neither am I. A tremor runs through me as he ducks his head. And then, ohhhh. Ghost kiss. Against my mouth, he speaks, deep and gruff, "Do you want another cherry stem? Or do you want my tongue inside your mouth?"

Immediately, I close my eyes and tip my head back.

Another corner kiss.

He's breathing slowly but so deeply his chest expands, clearly fighting for control. And I want him to lose it. I want him to snap and kiss me, fuck me, *love* me.

He caresses my cheek with the knuckle of his forefinger as he ducks his head again and this next kiss is so close to the center of my mouth, I can taste cherries on his lips.

"Come here." He reaches out and pulls me off the seat. He does it in one fluid move until I'm sitting on his hard lap, my legs draped to the side, and I struggle with a nervous laugh but ultimately fall still. Oh boy. It actually feels better every time. His arms around me. It makes me feel small in the best ways.

I'm adjusting to the sensation of safety—a sensation I'd kill to feel for the rest of my life—when I see Saint look at me as if I'm the juiciest thing he's ever seen.

"Put your arms around my neck," he says quietly in my ear.

He rubs a hand up and down my back. I do what he says, my arms trembling. Though we're in the end of summer, it's so cool today, the wind, but then he takes hold of both my hands at the back of his neck and moves them up and into his hair.

My fingers bunch warm fistfuls instinctively as he curls a hand around my nape and pulls me finally to his mouth. When our lips connect, they're already parted, and our tongues meet halfway as they search for each other.

He caresses my back and then settles one strong hand on my hip, his fingers spreading out, toward my butt, while his thumb caresses the jutting hardness of my hipbone. And as his warm tongue keeps knotting me up tighter than the cherry stems, I forget everything else.

That my name is Rachel Livingston and my career is in a jumble and I want my world to stand still.

Right now I just want Saint's tongue and I want the world to spin and spin and spin the way only he makes it do so.

His hand slides down my thigh and grabs behind my knee and he slowly folds my leg, bringing it up and curling it around his hip.

I shift my other leg to straddle him and his hand trails down the small of my back, then his fingers start sliding into my bikini. He cups my ass, pressing me to him as he kisses me. And all the time his tongue is grazing, playing, rubbing, *tasting* as his mouth moves on mine, devouring, taking—*taking*.

The heat of our bodies could melt a glacier. His other hand slides into my hair, into my ponytail. He holds it in one big fist and leaves my mouth burning with fire when he edges away from my lips and plants kisses on my shoulders, neck, face.

My hands chart their own journey, massaging down to his shoulders, but his fist keeps me from moving my head, so that he can come back to devour my mouth whenever he wants to. I'm gasping, breathless, as he raises his mouth from my neck and for three long heartbeats, looks heatedly into my eyes. I feel raw, vulnerable, and his eyes are stormy with lust but so clear, I'm afraid he *sees* me; sees he's my one true weakness. And so I close my eyes and offer my lips.

When his lips latch on to mine, his mouth is wetter and hotter, slower and firmer. I taste him back, feeling greedy and desperate as I slide my hands under his shirt, aching to feel his bare skin.

He jerks it over his head, and I tremble when his warm flesh presses against my skin.

He reaches between us and slips his fingers under the triangles of my bikini top, moving his fingertips over the peaks of my breasts—which feel so tight and achy, a jolt goes through me as he strokes up and down, around and around.

I press a little closer to his hands, a barrage of sensations fluttering in me as I kiss near his ear. "I like the things you do to me," I quietly confess.

"I get high on you," he gruffly whispers before he goes back to kissing my mouth, caressing my lips with also a little bit of teeth.

He slides a line of kisses down my neck, my chest. "Right here. Where it's pink and pretty for me. I'm going to kiss you right here tonight." He bumps his nose against the tip of my nipple under the fabric.

An exquisite shiver of wanting runs along my spine as his

thumbs stroke my nipples again. I feel the electricity of his touch in my core, my toes, my very being.

"If you want to," I agree.

"I do want to."

He cups my breast and suckles through my top. His head lifts a fraction when I gasp, and he brushes my lips with another kiss. Gently, leaving me gasping.

"Saint," I breathe.

"Malcolm," I hear him murmur into my mouth.

"Mmm . . . I get to call you Malcolm now?"

"You get a lot more."

He unclips my hair and watches it fall to my shoulders, and the lustful glow in the depths of his green gaze sends a shiver through my being.

"What did I do to deserve this absolute . . . privilege?"

A smile shines bright in his green eyes. "Malcolm, Rachel. Say it," he coaxes.

I frown a little. "It's such a respectable name. Why do you make it sound so dirty and naughty? Malcolm?"

He both laughs, low in his throat, and groans at the same time; then he ghosts a kiss over the corner of my mouth as though to let me know he appreciates it. We hear the noise of an incoming boat and I separate a little, self-conscious of it approaching even though he doesn't seem to mind.

It's a speedboat with eight individuals and blaring rock music. I notice they're taking out their phones to take pictures of Saint's yacht. No. I hear the shrill women's voices in the yacht and realize they're taking pictures of *Saint*. And . . . me.

I roll my eyes. "Oh great. They're going to have a field day with this."

"SAINT! OHMIGOD, MALCOLM SAINT! Can we

come on board?!" someone shouts. "It's Tasha! TASHA! My friends and I met you once at Decan's club, the Orion!"

They could be talking to the air.

While I stare at them, I notice Saint surveys my reddened mouth a little bit, and then takes in the rest of my face.

"Come here," he says, stretching out his hand.

"What—"

"SAINT!!!" one yells, then loudly whispers to the friend who's hovering at the edge of the boat, "Take pictures, bitch . . . *are you taking?*" Then to us, hands cupped at her mouth, "CAN WE HANG WITH YOU GUYS FOR A WHILE?"

I hear a splash and turn to stare, wide-eyed at the other boat. "Did she just throw herself in the water?"

"My guys will take care of it." He takes my hand and leads me down to the cabin area, stopping one of the crew and making a hand signal.

"Right on it, Mr. Saint."

I'm laughing my ass off as we reach the cabin, peering through the window. "Is she for real? Oh no, *all three* are swimming this way!"

"Come here," he whispers, tugging me back to him. I close my eyes when I feel his lips.

"Malcolm . . ."

I squirm a little but he quiets me down, pressing his lips to mine.

"Let's just see if your crew . . ." I turn in his arms and take a few steps to try to peer out.

"They're handling it."

His low voice ripples like a feather between my legs. I feel his gaze on my backside, and I turn, and he's watching me, his eyes roaming *all* of me.

"Sin . . ."

He stands there, tall and glorious, as I still hear splashing outside.

He takes a step and runs a finger up my arm, and then over my shoulder, his thumb stroking under my bikini string. I'm panting already.

"Malcolm."

He takes a step closer and sets a soft kiss on my mouth. God. The overwhelming experience of just his strong, soft lips.

His tongue flashes out and sweeps inside. The world goes dim. Hazy. He pulls me to his chest while he teases my lips with his.

I clutch his shoulders, hard.

"*Why?*" I hear a whine out in the lake. "But I know him . . . *we partied once . . .* "

And their male friends from the boat. "Come on, man, it's just hanging for a little while . . ."

"Oh wow, they're super insistent," I say, trying to turn. He stops me with his hands on my hips.

"They can insist all they want, they're not coming on board," he murmurs in my ear.

Before I can escape to watch the spectacle, he boosts me up and carries me to the bed.

"They were also your friends . . . ?" I tease.

He tosses me onto the bed and kneels on it as he tugs on the drawstring of his swim trunks. "Take it off," he says, nodding to my bikini.

I do, quickly, and I part my legs so he can settle between them. He curls his hand around the side of my face, and I tuck my cheek into his palm, the way he holds me so exquisitely gentle.

"Hook-ups. Easy. Simple," he says. And adds, "Nothing like you."

His attention heads south, to my breasts as he strokes his hands appreciatively over my lean frame. The last of the day's sunlight streams through the window; he can see every bit of me. I'm flushing but I wouldn't stop him for the world; instead I let my fingers slip into his thick hair. His breath coasts along the top swell of one breast as he ducks his head. Then he locks around the peak, rocking my world as arrows of pleasure shoot through me.

Oh god.

I hear the speedboat leave. Then a knock.

"Taken care of, Mr. Saint!"

"Thank you," he says in a lust-roughened voice, taking his lips off me for a second.

He smiles at me. He takes my wrists in his hands, and I shudder as a hot flick of his tongue wetly laps up my neck, to my lips. He draws my arms up, over my head, and then secures them in one hand while he lets the other wander over my body.

I arch helplessly. "Malcolm."

"That's right, Rachel."

"Malcolm *Saint*, you're an absolute devil . . ."

"And you're embarrassed to be seen with me."

"Am not."

"Because I've had many women?" Probing green eyes challenge me as he coasts his hand down my side. "Because I like to take what I want?"

"Like . . ." I lick my lips. "What do you want . . ."

He edges back and stands and tugs the rest of the drawstring open until his trunks slide down his powerful legs.

He reaches over to the drawer, pulls out a condom, tears it open, and hands it to me with a challenging spark in his eyes and an adorable curl to his lips. "Put this on me."

I edge up on my knees and stroke him lovingly even though I chide with a scowl, "You're kind of a dictator in bed. Which is why you'll never be my boss—"

He ducks his head and kisses me. I go breathless and let him ease me down on the bed. His hands slide up my arms and he laces his fingers through mine, smiling down at me.

"You like that?" he grins a little as he keeps my hands secured under his.

"No," I lie.

"Yeah, you do." Between searing kisses and slow, drugging kisses, he looks down at me. He stares at me as my body moves like a bow as he takes me. I pant. I beg. And I hold his gaze, memorizing him, powerful and smooth as he eases inside me.

Malcolm.

He wants me to call him Malcolm again.

He holds my gaze, watching me with violently tender eyes, as if he's been living for this moment.

Holding my wrists in one hand, he cups my face and starts to move. It's so hot, this powerlessness, the way he holds me down, and I want him to; the way one hand engulfs my face and his thumb rubs my lips as I open them and gasp. I start coming apart when he drives fully inside me. He slows down his motions as I climax. Twisting in his grip, I tremble and feel broken open even as my hips rock up so he can break and take some more, his hold on my wrists firm and wickedly exciting.

"That's right," he heatedly kisses my mouth, wetly tasting me with the same violent tenderness I see in his eyes. "Give me all of it . . . that's right . . . don't stop coming for me . . ."

"You . . ." I bite his lip as I circle my hips as seductively as

I can. "Come . . . with me . . . *Malcolm,* come with me . . ." A helpless groan leaves me as his hips keep pounding into mine.

He drags his hands down my arms and then flips me around unexpectedly, pulls me up on all fours, and drives inside me again. "I'm here," he husks out, taking me by the hair as he sinks in deeper, groaning my name in my ear.

My orgasm, which had been receding, seems to start up again. He's reveling in me, his thrusts deep, fast, powerful, and oh so good. His mouth is everywhere at once. Wet. Hot. Out of control. His grip tighter. His body desperate for me. No. He is desperate for me.

He hisses near the back of my ear and stiffens inside me, and I come. I come and twist beneath him, aware of how he's clutching me closer, his arms vises and his lips hungrily tugging my ear—the ear I know he loves that matches my "other" one.

Minutes later, we're both limp, I'm draped over his side, and his chest starts rumbling.

I frown a little. Is he . . . chuckling?

I lift my head, confused. His voice is husky as he holds me a little closer to his chest, his lids halfway over his eyes. "You're a little devil too." He rubs his thumb over my lip, and then he grins at me like he loves it.

We spend the next day on *The Toy* again. We eat, sunbathe, drink a little wine, and splash into the water. I can also officially tell the girls that without setting a single finger on it, I can now knot a cherry stem.

CHERRY BLUES

I wake up in my bed Sunday, very late at night—or, rather, too early on Monday.

Confused, I pad out to the living room to find it empty. I head to Gina's room. "Remind me not to drink on a boat," I tell Gina, grabbing my head as I lean heavily on the door frame.

She groans in the bed.

"Saint?"

Gina stirs a little. "You were knocked *out*, he carried you in."

"Why didn't he stay?"

"He stayed in your room a bit, and then he left. You looked like the dead would wake up sooner than you."

"When did he leave?"

"An hour ago."

"I'm sorry I woke you, I think I'm still a little intoxicated." I lean on her door a bit and sigh. "Gina, we had such a great time. We talked . . . we swam . . . we ate cherries . . . we had dinner. I had only two glasses of wine. Two! And I can't remember the rest."

"It's the damn wind and the rocking motion, it knocks me out every time."

I groan and deeply, deeply regret those drinks I had.

"Close the door," she mumbles as I go out.

Back in the room, I turn on the lamp and get my phone, writing, Thanks for bringing me home.

But instead of sending the text, I try calling to see if he answers. When I hear his voice, my veins start buzzing with something even more powerful than alcohol.

"Thank you for bringing me home. I enjoyed spending time with you very much," I whisper.

"Me too."

I glance at the time; it's past 3 a.m. My voice is awkward with drink and sleep. "I wanted you to spend the night."

"There's no way to describe what I'm going to do to you when I do."

"Please do," I beg.

Silence.

"I want you so much, Sin . . ."

Silence.

"You can do anything you want with me as long as you promise to do it again."

"Now that's a promise I'd like to keep," he whispers huskily.

"I know you don't like to make promises but your word is gold, and if you'd stayed over, I would've let you *devour* me. But not all of me, you know. You need to leave enough . . . just so that tomorrow when I'm sober, you can tell me what you did to me."

"So I get everything but your ears?" His voice sounds close to the speaker again and absolutely amused.

"Yes!" I say happily.

"While I devour every part of you with my mouth?"

Every part! Ohgod, yes.

"I'm not sure I can resist your ears," he says in a tragic tone. Desire building and building.

"Okay," I breathe. "Take my ears too."

"You're certain? I'd own all of your senses now."

I breathe out, "I'm certain."

"Rachel, I want you undone for me—absolutely wrecked."

"Okay, Saint."

I am!

"Okay?" he coaxes. Still amused.

"Hmm. I'm game, Saint. Bases loaded."

"Spend the weekend with me after your mother's?"

"I'd love to. I'll be on all five senses. Very attuned to your naughty plans."

"I'll hide the wine," he teases.

"Malcolm!" I laugh, then, worriedly, "Did I say something?"

"Nothing you haven't said before."

"Malcolm! What did I say, you dick?"

He chuckles. "Nothing I wouldn't mind hearing again, Rachel."

When we hang up, I stare at my ceiling. Oh god, did I tell him *I loved him*? Drunk? Why can't I say it like a normal, courageous person when I'm sober, looking into his eyes?

I try to remember and I *can't*, I just can't remember if I said it.

But if I did . . . he wants to hear it again?

I could've just talked dirty, which would be *sooo* unlike me and something Saint would probably love to hear too.

I sigh, plump my pillow, and turn off my lamp, getting haunted and aroused by the simple thought of a knotted cherry stem.

A SAINT IN MY HOME

Tonight is the night Saint meets my mother, and I don't know who's more excited, my mother or I.

Before I go to my mom's, I stop by the pharmacy to stock her up on her medicines, then I buy her three bags of fresh, organic groceries and have neatly stored everything in her medicine cabinet and fridge. Then it's off to help her with preparations for tonight's dinner. I've made sure that the house is sparkly clean, the table set with our prettiest plates and topped with a pretty white rose centerpiece. Mom, apron and all, buzzes busily through the kitchen, stacking things in the hot drawer.

The excitement in our home is palpable.

Since my early teens, my mother has seen me focused exclusively on my career. I'd never really daydreamed about boys before. She's as unprepared for me to bring a man home as I am—even though I'm sure she's been hoping that I'd one day find "someone."

Well.

I *have*.

Holy crap, I have! And my mother wants to meet him, and most shocking of all, *he* wants to meet my mother too.

Exhaling in satisfaction, I give one last look at our home. It looks spotless and homey. Though, a little bit self-consciously, I realize my mother's house is kind of a shrine to me and the accomplishments I've earned so far: framed newspaper articles I wrote for my high school paper. My first piece for *Edge*. Letters from some readers I'd touched that I had stored away.

"I was reading up on him just this morning . . ." Mom says as she comes out to give one satisfied look at the house. "He looks very powerful. Very beautiful."

"He is. He's both. Also smart. Motivated."

I pat her hand and kiss her cheek, and she asks, "He's really coming?"

"No, Momma. I just wanted to put us to work for fun."

She smiles one of her tender mother smiles and this time, she's the one who pats my hand. "It's good that he's coming, Rachel," she assures.

My stomach squeezes at that, and I grin and nod.

I'm both nervous and excited for him to be here. "Remember you promised not to drill him with questions, okay, Mother?"

"Of course!" my mother says as she heads back to the kitchen.

Oh god. Please let them *like* each other.

Pulling back the gauze curtain, I peer out the window to see his Pagani Huayra slide to a screeching halt before our home.

Oh, Sin. Speeding. *Really?*

I'm smiling, but I pretend that I'm not as I swing open the door and shake my head in disapproval while I watch him get out of the car. He's wearing a black cashmere sweater and a pair of dark-wash jeans, a bottle of wine firm in his hand, and he's making my heart race as he eats up the distance between us.

Sin is absolutely at home in the night, though it feels like every streetlight nearby is fawning on him, casting attractive shadows on his face and body.

He looks irresistible.

Dangerous.

Delicious.

"Hey," I greet him as I step outside and impulsively press my lips to his rock-like jaw. "You get a kiss for coming."

He draws me close to his body and speaks in my ear. "I have one for you too but it's not fit for public." His eyes shine devilishly as he watches me go red.

He follows me with one step, and then he's inside. And he looks so very dark in my doorway. Darker than his hair, than the air he emanates. Bigger, somehow, as he takes another step inside, where my mother waits with a beaming smile.

"Malcolm, this is my mother—"

"Kelly," she eagerly interrupts. She seems to want to give him a hug but she stops herself; Saint seems too larger-than-life for that.

He reaches out and gently squeezes her shoulder as he hands her the wine. I watch Mother make a desperate attempt to resist that captivating smile. And I notice his deep voice doesn't help matters. "A pleasure to be in your home, Kelly. With your daughter."

Gushing with gratitude over the bottle of wine, my mother heads over to set it in ice.

He touches my cheek for only a second, that one second enough to fluster me even more.

Damn him.

"You're the first man Rachel ever brought home," my mother tells him.

"This is the first time I've actually gone."

He winks at me and my mother and I both kind of smile. We both mooned over him just seconds ago as he opened the wine in a way only a man who's uncorked dozens of wine bottles can.

Now we're all enjoying dinner, wine, and conversation.

"I always thought she'd have had more friends if she hadn't had an imaginary friend. Monica," my mother says.

"*Matilda*," I correct my mother.

My poor mom, she's so excited and so flustered she can't even keep her facts straight.

"Matilda. Right. She'd blame everything on Matilda. Rachel doesn't like screwing up in any way, you see," she says. "She's a bit of a perfectionist and it makes her mad at herself, so she used to blame Matilda when things didn't go the way she wanted."

I groan and roll my eyes. "This would be so *so* much easier to bear if Matilda were sitting here now."

Saint leans over. "I wouldn't have come here for Matilda. Only for you."

His lips quirk when I redden.

"Rachel tells me you paint?" he asks my mother.

"I do. I like color on everything," she says and proudly signals to her strawberry spinach salad. "Rachel used to paint too—that one's hers." She points at a small frame with my handprint on it.

"I did not paint that. I just set my hand there. Saint has one of those, Mother. A big one."

"Oh, he does?" Her eyes widen in awe. "Those are sold, but in this case, it was a gift from End the Violence for her support."

As we head into the main course, my mother tells Saint all about my involvement with End the Violence—nothing Saint doesn't really know except perhaps that I've been doing it for a decade—while Saint listens attentively as he cleans his plate.

He listens to her tell him about the stories I used to tell as a kid . . .

Me and how End the Violence really made an impact on helping my mother and me cope . . .

Me and my dreams of having a career where I could both love what I do and earn a living at it . . .

Me and how I've wished to make her dream come true of working at what she loves . . .

"Her life has been full of other people's stories," she adds.

"Even mine," he whispers with a sharp gleam in his eye aimed in my direction. He is not mad, just calm as he finishes his wine. Calm, and something else. He seems . . . illuminated. As if my mother's stories have shed light on something that had been eluding him for a while.

I kind of think he looks even more comfortable than he did seconds ago, his attention unwavering as he crosses his utensils over his empty plate, leans back in his chair and cups his hands behind his head, laughing at my mother's stories about young Rachel's antics.

He looks . . . at home, here with my mother and me.

It does something to me. I suddenly feel very vulnerable.

I wonder about *his* mother as he talks with mine. As he talks with mine and occasionally ends her anecdotes with, "Did she really?" in amusement.

And my mom won't shut up about me!

I feel extremely, intimately bared to Malcolm right now.

Malcolm already knows so much about me. What I like and fear and want. That I hope to do good things, but I sometimes do bad. He knows how I *taste*.

And now, having the man of my dreams know me through my mother's stories, I feel completely exposed. As if I have no more secrets from him, while he, somehow, is a box of them that I might never fully open.

Gina's right: maybe I do have a few walls up to protect myself. But I feel them all about to topple.

"Now, Rachel had very few friends when she was younger," she says as she brings over my favorite dessert from the kitchen, a chocolate peppermint pie. "She was reserved and of course it was a concern of mine, as you can imagine. The only people Rachel allowed to know that she didn't have a father were those we met through End the Violence. People like her, who've known loss. She just didn't feel comfortable sharing that loss with anyone else, whom she thought wouldn't understand."

I try to laugh it off, but my laugh wavers. It's only after Saint reaches for my hand under the table and squeezes it that I exhale.

Because he's not judging me.

I'm into you, I remember him saying. I steal a look at his profile. He senses it and turns, and when our gazes meet, I feel like he kisses me with his eyes.

This evening in my home feels so monumental all of a sudden. Like he too is giving me something he's given no one else.

Now my mother is saying I read during the weekends throughout my teens.

"She wasn't a party girl?"

He asked my mother this, but he's teasing me. I can tell by the look—and smile—he sends my way.

A smile that no woman on earth could withstand with dry panties.

"Oh, no, though she enjoys having fun," Mother assures. "Rachel was back from prom at twelve. Her date couldn't interest her long enough to make her stay, a nice young man one of her friends suggested. She wasn't really interested in anyone. I used to think she'd need a man so compelling, her stories couldn't live up to him; he'd make her reality so much more compelling than anything else."

I feel privately caressed when his gaze intensifies.

"So there was no one," he says, sounding perfectly greedy.

I hold my breath.

"No one," mother confirms.

But you, I tell him with my eyes when he smiles at me.

It's better than sex, the way he's staring at me now, the clenching of his jaw as if some unnamable emotion has touched him.

"Sin, we really need to find someone able to tell me embarrassing stories about you, so I can get even," I tease him with a husky, shy voice.

Under the table, he gives my hand another squeeze, his voice dropping an octave just for me. "Give it a Goog. We'll be more than even."

"She'd come up with stories about families," Mom tells him. "Usually very sweet ones. I worried she was a bit too hopeful for the real world, but I'm sure it was the way she coped after we lost Michael."

After a nod of understanding directed at my mother, Saint's eyes seek me out again. Caress me again. But the caress doesn't feel sexual. It feels like so much more. Male eyes, as deep as eternity, seem to simply say, *I understand.*

"I'm sorry to hear that, for both of you," he finally murmurs to my mother, and I notice that it takes him an effort to pull his gaze away from me.

The cold flecks that are so common in Malcolm Saint's eyes . . .

There's not a single cold fleck in them now.

He's living, breathing and human and sitting like a calm storm at our dinner table, still so strong and alive and normal despite him being abnormally beautiful, abnormally powerful.

I see my mother blush a little when his full attention is on her. "I know you've lost your mother as well. I'm sorry."

"I'm sorry too," he says quietly.

"This is your home too, Malcolm. Anytime."

When my mother walks us to the door shortly thereafter and Malcolm asks me if I'm coming back with him, I blush and nod. I'm not even going to pretend I don't want to be with him right now.

He says goodbye to my mother, and then he speaks again, without hesitation or apology. "I'm not good at making promises. But I would like you to know I've never been serious about a girl until I met your daughter, and now that I know I'm the first man she's brought home, I'm aiming to be the last."

I'm red to the roots of my hair.

Oh. *My.*

Did Saint just say this to my mother?

"No promise needed. Just be good to her," she whispers, heartfelt to him. Then— "Please. Take dessert with you. I won't eat it and you two can share it later. It's Rachel's favorite," she adds, bringing over the pie, tightly covered in aluminum foil.

After I hug and thank her and she gives me this huge, huge smile that screams at me how much she likes him, how appeased she is about us having—possibly—a relationship, my heart feels content.

Saint walks me over to his car, opens the door, and when I settle in, he leans over to latch my seat belt. As his fingers graze me, my sexy parts start aching. How can Saint make something as simple as a homey dinner feel like foreplay?

I think he knows I'm burning.

Because the next second, he grabs the back of my head and kisses me.

The kiss is slow and so yummy that my thighs clench. I hazily wonder if I'll ever grow used to his kisses. Strong and sure, he tongue-fucks my mouth. When he adds gentle sucking motions on my tongue, I tighten my hold on his shoulders.

"What was that for?"

"For me." He smiles as his thumb strokes the corner of my lips.

He shuts the door, goes around the car with a hot and satisfied look on his face, and then settles behind the wheel. As we head out of the neighborhood, I notice he drives slower than he usually does—probably because of the pie riding at my feet—and I mull out loud, "I wonder what my father would have thought of you. Would he have hated or admired that you're so powerful?"

He lifts one brow. "Let's put it this way. My own father can't stand me. I don't expect anyone else's to."

"Weak men don't like strong men, they remind them of what they failed to be."

Now both brows go up, and he shoots me such an admiring look, I almost swell inside. He cups my face and touches his thumb to the corner of my mouth. "My father's not weak, but he's stubborn and selfish." He shifts gears, his thumb ring glinting as he does.

"My dad *definitely* would have warned me off you, for sure . . . but I don't know, Sin." Turning my head dreamily in the seat so I can get a good eyeful of the candy that Saint driving his car is, I sigh. "I think he'd admire you very much."

"My mother would've loved you, baby." With a tender curving of his lips, he reaches out and tips my chin up. "Who could not love you?"

"You," I say, then my hands fly up and I cover my mouth. "Ohmigod, don't say anything."

His eyes are alight with amusement as he opens his mouth. "DON'T SAY ANYTHING! IT DOESN'T COUNT!"

Saint just laughs huskily. "Rach—"

"DON'T! DON'T DENY IT, DON'T ACCEPT IT, JUST DON'T. I'm *so* sorry; I don't know why I said that. I went fishing for it and it's not fair to you."

I start laughing and he pulls over and stops the car, grabs me with both hands and kisses me. Not a peck. A kiss I can feel in my knees and that makes my lungs spread open as I try to breathe.

"Don't," I plead when he's done.

"I'm not saying anything," he says innocently.

"Okay. Please don't."

I'm shaking from wanting him to say it now. Say *something*. Maybe he doesn't feel it. Maybe I should've let him speak. Maybe I couldn't take what he'd have said. *Urgh.* I can't even look at him right now. I stare out the window as he pulls us back into traffic and feel my stomach flip when he takes my hand and gives it a squeeze, and I love him even more for that alone. Whatever his reply might have been, he's still holding my hand. He's still here with me.

But when I remain silent, he slows down the car a little bit and leans over and kisses my mouth softly, one hand on the wheel, the other on the back of my head.

"What was that for?" I lick my lips, look at his mouth.

And he says, "That was me doing whatever I want." He kisses me softly again. "Get used to it."

I wait until he hits a stoplight, then grab him. "Get used to *this*."

We kiss a little wilder, then smile. Then the acceleration is back on.

We ride the elevator to the penthouse where he sleeps, eats, lives.

Where he's made love to me like mad.

My heart is pounding so hard, I can't even hear the "ding" of the elevator, just suddenly, the doors open. Saint didn't even ask me if I was coming over—it was a given. We said we'd spend the weekend together as if it's the most natural thing in the world. And it's starting to feel like it is.

I step out of the elevator, the sight of his beautiful apartment hitting me with painful longing, and my lungs start struggling a little bit. I'm spending the night here again and somehow it feels as though we're slowly evolving into something deeper, stronger, further.

I set the pie down on his shiny kitchen counter as he comes up behind me and takes my hips in one hand.

The butterflies awaken in my stomach.

He uses his hand on my hips to turn me around, and my breath catches on a moan as his lips come down on mine. Our mouths fuse effortlessly, and will I ever get used to the electric jolt of his kisses? I feel the natural high he gives me rise in my body. My pulse skipping. My mind reeling. My world narrowing to the mouth currently making slow, hot love to mine.

When his phone buzzes, interrupting us, I'm not sure what

I see in his eyes but the butterflies keep moving. His gaze is as deep as a night forest.

He pecks my lips before he takes the call and steps aside. "Santori," he says, his voice low but clear. "Yeah, I was busy. Update? Hmm . . ." He starts pacing toward the living room, frowning as he runs his hand through his hair.

I wonder who this Santori is as I remove the aluminum foil from the pie, search for a spoon, then lean over the kitchen counter, up on my toes as I take a little spoonful.

Mmmm. God. Mint and chocolate are so good together.

I'm licking the spoon when I realize Saint is staring at me. Grinning, I dip my spoon and savor it so that he realizes he's missing out on *really* good homemade pie.

I keep watching him as he watches me back, the intensity in his stare starting to knot up my body in places only he manages to reach. I set down the spoon and . . . why is my hand trembling? Self-conscious of his very male, very powerful stare, I lick the corners of my lips, and his voice drops a decibel.

"Yeah, I can't . . . do this now. Give me the night to think over our next move."

He powers off his phone and tosses it aside.

My knees turn to Jell-O as he comes over. He rubs a silver thumb ring over my lips, his eyes gleaming with lights. "I thought I could get some business done, but I'd rather do you."

Holy crap. He looks so decisive. So determined.

One sentence from this man and I'm as hot and ready as if we've spent hours on foreplay.

"Do you . . ." I lick my lips and stare at his mouth, trying to level my breathing. "Do you want pie?"

He tilts my head back so we make eye contact. And he shakes his head . . . very, very slowly.

Malcolm is big on eye contact.

He's a predator, and I'm his most willing prey.

He cradles the back of my skull while his free hand curls around my neck, and still holding my gaze until it's impossible for him to both hold it and kiss me at the same time, he lowers his head. "I want . . . these lips of yours. They're all I want . . ."

First he trails his tongue, hot and wet, across my lips. I moan. His smell enthralls me and the hint of his taste, along with the chocolate and peppermint, lingers on my lips. If that isn't the most delicious form of torture, I don't know what is.

He slides his tongue again, and I shudder and part my lips. He thrusts inside. Fierce desire pools between my thighs. He keeps me there, where he wants me, and nips my lower lip, pulling it away from the top.

I mew softly and he brings me closer so that his hard body is aligned with mine. God help me, he owns me. "Sin . . ."

"And I want . . . these." My breasts feel sensitive and aching when his hands cover them over my top.

My heart skips a beat.

God, those lips are wearing the most devilish smile he's ever sent my way.

With one hand, he expertly tugs my top over my head, then lowers the lace of my bra until only one nipple pops free. He takes a moment to look at it with complete appreciation. He frees my other nipple and leaves them there, exposed, with the fabric of my bra bunched up beneath them.

"I definitely want these beauties." When he bends his head, he sucks super hard, making the tip of my nipple swell and my sex ache, needing to be filled. He turns to my other nipple, rolling it under his tongue, then sucking again.

Arching instinctively, I clutch at his back, raking my nails over the cashmere of his sweater. "I really need this . . . oh, Malcolm, *don't stop.*"

"I'm not stopping." He drags his teeth over my nipple and then licks. "I want your hands on me," he quietly tells me as he forces my hand to curl around the front of his jeans, where he is thick, pulsing, and strong as steel. My mouth dries up and I lick my lips as I stroke him over the fabric, and a low growl rips up his throat. "Look at you Rachel," he husks out, looking at my nipples. And then he dips his fingers into the pie and rubs chocolate mingled with whipped cream on each of my puckered nipples.

"Saint!" I gasp, shocked and jerking with arousal.

He ducks his head to tongue-fuck my ear, and as he does that, he asks, "Do you want me to eat you?"

Electricity crackles between us as his eyes trap and hold mine. I nod.

"What part of you?"

Ohgod.

Every part.

Every part on the outside, every part on the inside. I want to be devoured by him and I want to devour him right back.

Nervous and so ravenous my throat hurts, I reach out and add chocolate to my lips. "Here," I whisper shyly.

He grins. "Here?" He leans over and teases the chocolate into his mouth, lapping it gently up from the corner of my mouth.

White-hot lightning streaks through me and I think I make a sound; a needy whimper. He pulls me close and then, then, he kisses and tastes the pie from my lips, every part of my body feeling his kiss.

His eyes are heavy-lidded as he runs his fingers over the chocolate he just spread on my nipples, lightly caressing. "And here? Rachel?"

"Oh, God, Malcolm," is all I can say, clutching his shoulders. He leans in to lick and taste me where there's chocolate. My mouth. I moan softly. My nipple. I moan more. My other nipple. I throw my head back and just hang on to his hard shoulders.

"Delicious. Don't move . . ." he husks out. One strong arm circles my waist to hold me on my feet.

"Never," I whisper, taking the back of his head when he comes back to kiss my lips. I kiss him hard, our mouths tasting of us, and mint, and chocolate and whipped cream and so much desire that the air between us is *more* than warm, it's *calescent.*

I nip his lower lip as the need for him starts consuming me from the inside out. I've never been so brazen, so reckless, but he . . . he *does* this to me. Sexy as hell. He teases me. He eludes me. He makes me wonder what he's thinking. He's nice to me. He's hot for me. God. Look at me.

I kiss him back rather ravenously, so he knows that today meant a lot to me. So much more than I imagined it would. His kiss is just as intimate, slow, savoring, no more chocolate now, just us. And when he speaks, he sounds so turned on I ache inside. "Don't move," he says again. His gaze lowers, just like his voice did, and he unwraps the drawstring of my skirt with slow, deft hands. When I see my panties flutter as they follow it to the floor, my heart flutters too in anticipation.

Securing me in place with one hand on my waist, he sucks on a breast again. He laps up the remainder of the chocolate and the whipped cream but it seems that the thing he wants to reach—to taste, to eat—is me. My puckered nipple *throbbing* under his kiss. Wondering where he'll touch me next is so very thrilling that he's making me crazed with arousal.

"Don't move," he murmurs against my skin, as he reaches out and scoops a little more pie.

Though my senses are in chaos, I manage to stand stock-still.

"Good girl," he whispers huskily. Although Saint's moves are deliberate and his voice is contemplative and controlled, there's a black fire in his eyes right now as he rubs the chocolate over my clit. He looks really turned on, but more than that, he looks determined to devour me. He smears more pie around my belly button. Bends down to tease his tongue around my navel. Then lower, breath scalding hot, lips soft and moving, and then . . . tongue. Leisurely licking my clit. He takes the flesh between his lips and gently sucks it into his mouth while his tongue teases little circles over me.

My knees buckle, but his arm is there, keeping me on my feet.

As he kisses his way up to my belly button, arousing me beyond measure, he lifts his free hand and brushes his thumb over my jawline. "Does it feel good, Rachel?"

I nod.

As he straightens to meet my gaze with so much passion in his, the fire in my stomach hikes up another notch, he pauses as if deciding where to taste me, touch me, next.

It's agonizing.

He trails a finger up between my legs. "This is where you want it. Isn't it?"

I chew on the inside of my cheek and try not to squirm as he rubs a little. I'm so wet, the juices I hear slicking under his fingers are not pie or cream, it's me.

He's teasing, testing. He leans over and licks my mouth again. *Sampling.*

I groan. "Malcolm . . ."

He pinches a wet, swollen nipple.

As he tends to the other, I dip my fingers into the pie and

before he knows it, I'm slowly drawing a two-finger line along his hard jaw, to the corner of his lips.

He looks breathtaking and before he can move away, I grab him by the back of the head and I bend and taste the flavor, bitter chocolate with minty peppermint, and he opens his mouth.

We both taste like dessert and heat and there's so much hotness we should be put away wherever the nuclear weapons are locked up because we detonate each other so fast, so well, so completely, I don't know if we'll survive.

He lifts me by the ass and I straddle him as he carries us to one of the sofas. As we kiss, he's groaning, past the point of being fully in control. I like him this way, so much. When he's almost, *almost* unleashed on me.

I lick his chocolate-and-peppermint lips as he sets me down and gives me a sex-throbbing, mind-bending kiss, physical and animal, the sure thrusts of his tongue curling my toes and pricking my clit in the most delicious way.

I throw my head back, giving him full access. He presses a series of kisses down my neck, wet and warm. "Need you . . . inside . . . need it now . . ."

"Want me inside you?" He stands up and yanks off his cashmere sweater, tossing it aside.

"Yes."

"Hard? Deep?" He unbuttons and unzips, his jeans following.

"Saint!"

Oh god, this beautiful man, eyes narrowed, muscle jumping in his jaw as he tears open a foil packet and sheaths himself, then comes back to spread his big, delicious weight over me . . . this man undoes me. I undulate as our naked bodies connect, *undone* when his mouth and hands find parts of me he wants to taste.

He whispers a seductive murmur below my ear, kissing

there. Dips his tongue in the hollow at the base of my throat. Bites gently into my neck.

I claw at his shoulders. He's in no rush, but I tremble as he takes my legs by the knees and guides me around him—where he wants me. His stomach ripples; his biceps and triceps flex as he mounts me.

Then he grabs my hips and slides me down an inch or two, so that he pulls me down as he thrusts upward to enter me. His name leaves me on a gasping breath of pure gratitude.

Another thrust. We groan. Another. Closer. Closer. I rake my nails down his back. I feel complete, but needing. Full, but aching.

One nipple disappears into his mouth. One hard suck and I'm thrashing, biceps bunching around me as he thrusts.

All the time I feel the slide of hard heat and power.

My hips roll upward. The room is flooded with the sounds we make.

He wrings out my every breath from my body as he watches me writhe, eyes glowing hotly. His gorgeous face hardens in orgasm, jaws tight, eyes a brilliant, possessive green, teeth grinding from the pleasure as he growls, "Rachel."

It's like my sex pulls him in deeper, milking, sucking him in, not letting go.

His buttocks flex, thigh muscles tightening beside mine, powerful back muscles bunching beneath my fingers as he drives forward, deep and fast, filling me so much there's no room to breathe. No room for anything but Saint inside me. I can feel when he's coming, because he whispers the words *I'm coming* in my ear, groaning.

It's so hot when he comes—the only times that I've ever seen Saint out of control—that my orgasm wrenches through my body, causing his cock to swell and jerk in me one, two, three times. I twist beneath him, my mouth seeking his. He grabs me by the cheeks, holding my face as he slows his rhythm, pressing his lips to mine. We kiss, the kiss slow and languorous as our bodies as we come back to each other.

"Oh my god," I breathe.

He laughs softly, shaking his head. Using his arm, he sits back and shifts me so that I'm the one halfway on top of him.

I lock my hands around his neck. If we weren't on the couch, I'd just stay here, ready to fall asleep from the bliss of my new alpha-male-fuck exhaustion. "You're so good at this," I nuzzle his jaw, feeling warm and gooey inside. "I hate a little bit every woman you went through to get this good."

"It was all fun and games."

"Wow. You don't have fun with me?"

His eyes light up with playfulness. "Fishing for compliments, Rachel?"

My belly feels a little tight and I realize I want his love, I want his tenderness.

"I'm snorkeling for them," I admit, laughing.

He laughs too, rising to his elbows and looking at me, eyes tender, and a hot flood of emotion overflows as we smile at each other. "I respect . . . and admire . . . and enjoy every inch of you, Rachel."

I duck my head slightly, suddenly a little shy and aware of my nakedness. I reach to cover my breasts.

My stomach tingles when he smiles endearingly and runs a hand over the side of my body. He moves down to kiss my belly button, between my breasts, and strokes my thighs, teasing all the parts that are sore and sensitive from lovemaking and looking at every inch with reverence.

He kisses me, tasting sexy and sweaty and minty, before sitting up and lifting me with him so that I end up on his lap.

"I like the look of you, I like the smell of you, and I definitely like the feel of you. Now, be a good girl," he pats my ass, "and cover up so I can get some work done."

"If you let me borrow your shower, I'll take a bath." I kiss his lips.

He follows me up and I watch him walk in purely glorious sinful nakedness to the guest bedroom's bathroom to clean up.

I'm so well fucked that my body doesn't feel solid just yet. But I somehow make it to his room.

Once inside his shower, I squeeze my eyes shut and hum and mull over our evening. Maybe I should have said I loved him right now. Or in the car, when I blurted out that he didn't. He went to my mother's. I should've trusted that he would say something reassuring to me, if not a flat out *I love you.*

Tell him, tell him, *tell him.*

But what if he doesn't want to hear it yet? He still hasn't even asked me to be his girlfriend.

Will he ever?

On a soft, wistful impulse, I put my fingers on the wet marble of his shower, and even though rooms separate us, I can feel Saint through it. I feel his chest under my fingertips and his soft hair and the energy of his being, like a constant stream of lightning running through my veins.

People celebrate his reckless side, the one that makes the news, they celebrate his powerful side, the one that sets the standards, but right now nothing is more noteworthy to me than the fact that Malcolm came to my mother's and won her over, just like he did me.

WATCHING ME SLEEP

I wake up in the middle of the night, disoriented by the darkness. I'm not in my room. A leg lies beneath mine and my cheek is resting on hard flesh. Squinting, I look up and Saint is watching me, and I feel myself blush.

"Hey," I say.

He smiles lightly as I tug the sheet up to my chest and sit up, the arm around me moving to lightly caress my back. "Hey."

When he sits up a little too, I edge closer to lean my shoulder back against his chest.

He used to be my 1 a.m. I-can't-sleep text. Now he's my I-can't-sleep comfort item. Like a blankie. But he's alive. And I think I'm his 1 a.m. can't-sleep comfort thing too.

But then, he's wide awake so I'm not doing a good job, am I?

"Can't sleep?" I whisper, gazing at him.

He shakes his deliciously bed-mussed head, running his hand down the back of my hair. "Watching you's even better."

I glance around. "What time is it?"

I'm about to search his room for any indication of the time, or about to feel for my phone nearby, when his voice stops me.

"I'm going to ask you now."

"What?"

"There I was, meeting your mother. And I wanted to hear that I was your guy."

I blink as it dawns on me. I'm so absolutely awake now that a frisson of nerves and excitement starts crawling through my veins.

"I'm going to ask you now." The caress of his thumb across my lips makes me realize my mouth is parted and how fast I'm suddenly breathing. "I've been ready for far longer than you have, Rachel. You weren't ready . . . maybe *nobody* can be ready for me." He smirks, but there's a gleam of sheer purpose and determination in his gaze.

I stare, helplessly aching. "Ask me," I breathe.

"No half measures. I might be difficult—"

"Nothing can be more difficult than not being with you," I say, cutting him off.

"I'm ambitious," he calmly continues. "I ride my people hard, and I'll ride my girlfriend harder, what with everything I want from her—but I'll give her back everything she gives me tenfold."

"Sin, ask me," I breathe.

"Do you want to?"

"I *do* want to—"

"Be my girlfriend, Rachel. Officially. Exclusive and monogamous."

I can't talk at all. Right this second Malcolm has *officially* taken my power of speech. Will there be anything left that I don't willingly give him?

"I want to be that guy you can't ever take out of your head, Rachel. The one you've been waiting for. I want you to have eyes just for me and smile just for me and a tone of voice only I will ever hear."

I'm nodding in the dark and then I whisper, "Yes. I've been your girlfriend for a long time, title or no."

He nuzzles the side of my jaw. "Does a piece of your soul belong to me?"

Oh god. *My article.*

I really and truly can't speak, *now*, when I'm supposed to be screaming my answer. I'm a thief. If he never touches me again, I'll have stolen the way he smells and feels right now.

He pulls me closer. "Say it," he coaxes. "I liked your article very much. I was mad, but I know you, Rachel. I know you wrote that to me. You challenged me to come after you. I'm meeting your challenge now. You wanted to know if I'd catch you? I will. I've got you.

"Say it," he demands. "Does a piece of your soul belong to me?"

His eyes are not green ice, they're green lava.

I duck my head, and I think he can see my blush in the dark. "Yes," I say. And somehow, that's enough. Just one word.

He ducks his head too, in search of my lips, and now *he's* the thief, stealing a kiss from me.

"Dibs," he whispers.

TOTALLY DIBS

*C*loud nine isn't enough; there's no number for the cloud I'm on.

At drinks on Wednesday, Gina declares, "You still have girlfriends, you know. You can't spend all your evenings with your new *boyfriend* without some sort of punishment for neglecting us."

"Fine! The drinks are on me," I assure them.

So my friends drink and talk and try to force some information out of me. But I'm not talking. There are no words to explain what's happening between us. No number for this cloud, no words, just him and me, and his dibs on me.

At night—if he works late, or I'm stuck on deadline and can't come over—we talk on the phone for about two hours.

Sometimes it's just a text, like our latest ones.

Thinking of you ☹
Is there even a cure?

Come over

It's 1 a.m.

Unlock your door

I'm in my first official relationship, and the girls want more details. I meet up with them on Monday. Then on Tuesday, Saint flies to New York for a day on business, and I have one more interview at the *Tribune*. It's nerve-racking. When I come out, I'm close to defeated.

That Tuesday after work, I realize I've lost my little R necklace. I scour my room like mad, I scour Gina's room; I even empty the vacuum cleaner. I got it from my mother for my fifteenth birthday, the only real gold item that I have.

"Oh god, I can't even bear to tell my mother I lost my R," I tell Gina. It's not in my cubicle either. In any of my bags.

The next day I get a delivery.

Inside is a box, and a note.

THE CREW FOUND THIS IN THE TOY. SHE LOOKED PRETTY LONELY.

M

I open the box and pull out my R necklace, and beneath it, identical to the R, is an M.

I call his cell phone.

My heart is a melted ol' mess by the time he answers. "My necklace has a tagalong," I tell him somberly.

"That's right," he chuckles.

"What's the M for?" Though my smile hurts on my face, I make myself sound genuinely confused as I stroke my fingertips over the M's smooth lines. "Millionaire? Motherfucker? Manwhore?"

His laugh.

I get high listening to the deep rare sound. "Little one," he chides with mocking disappointment. "The M stands for Malcolm."

"Oh! *You. Malcolm,*" I tease. "I'm glad that's been cleared up then."

"That's right," he fairly purrs, and after a moment, he sounds deathly serious too. "It also stands for *mine.*"

I'm not sure if he can hear the way my breath catches in my throat as it gets caught in my windpipe, but I hope to god he doesn't. This man is cocky enough as it is. So, like it's no big deal, like I get a thousand gifts every day, I say, "Okay. I guess I'll *try* not to lose it in my boyfriend's yacht."

"Lose it all you want; it'll be just as quickly replaced."

Though he issues it as a warning, I can hear the smile in his voice too. Noticing that Sandy, in the cubicle next to mine, is staring at me with a big dopey smile, I cup the speaker a little bit and swivel my chair around, giving her my back.

"Thank you . . . Malcolm." There's a peaceful silence between us. The kind that's comfortable, not the kind that you need to fill with anything at all. I stroke the M again quietly, closing my eyes when he speaks.

"I'm thinking of you, Rachel."

My voice softens when I admit, "I'm thinking of you too."

I'm not sure what it is about him. If his effect on me is due to his rare ability to turn me inside out with just a glance, a word, an act, or if it's because I never lived this, not in my teens, not until now.

I just never thought you could feel such delicious intimacy while miles apart, with nothing but each other's voices as we each hold the receiver to our ears. I imagine him at his desk, leaning back all cocky, with one of his smiles on his face—the one where his lips are curled so lightly it can barely be a smile but yet it *is*. I'm warm inside as I tuck the phone closer to me as we talk a little. I ask about New York and tell him how frantic I was to find my necklace. I also notice the R is perfectly polished and realized he must've sent it to the jewelers who made the M so that the R looks just as new.

As new as *we* are. Him and me.

When we hang up, I go to the bathroom and slip them out of the box, then I brush my hair aside to expose my throat. I put on the R first, and then I take the M gently out of the box and latch it around the back of my neck. The letters nestle perfectly together near that crook between my collarbones. Strange, how breathless I feel when the M falls into place. I feel like he's kissing that spot again. Permanently.

Letting my hair fall down my back again, I stare at the girl in the mirror—she's not lost. She looks confident and a little flushed, a little breathless and a lot happy. The necklaces—sparkly, shiny-new and double—rest at her throat, and you can see in her gray eyes—gray eyes that almost look silver, because they're gleaming to compete with the gold at her throat—that she happens to think that R + M have never looked so damn good together.

On Thursday I have an interview at *Wired* and I arrive a little late at *Edge*. As seems to be the new norm, my link to Malcolm is nothing anyone wants to touch. The interview didn't go that well at all. There's always someone in the company who knows Saint, is friends with Saint, or maybe even hates Saint—and they don't want the infamous girlfriend in their newsroom.

They seem to prefer the news to come out of their newsrooms, not actually be *sitting* in their newsrooms.

We spend a dream weekend together. On Friday, Gina offers to sleep over at Wynn's on Saturday and Sunday—Gina has gotten a makeup-artist complex (thank you, free samples that she gets at work), and Wynn has offered to be her test subject all weekend while her boyfriend, Emmett, visits his family—so I invite Sin over to make both my bed and me squeal.

I wake up with him two nights in a row, the second one with little sores on my body, in places he used to exhaustion. I don't even mind the fact that neither of us is getting much sleep because my bed and I have never known such a good time.

"God, it's morning already?" I groan, still refusing to move.

He disappears into the bathroom, and I pull the sheets back up to my chin, and I wonder, did I leave my sink clean or did I leave it messy? I think of Sin's beautiful apartment—perfectly organized—and stress a little about what he may think of my girl chaos.

Then I realize if it's messy, he's already seen it yesterday. Relaxing back in bed, I hear him turn on my shower. He's a far

earlier riser than I am; he also gets to M4 usually before most of
his employees do. I'm not yet late for work so I stay in bed and
enjoy all my sore spots as he comes out with one of my towels
hanging low on his hips.

I watch him slip his arms into his button-up shirt and then
fasten it with sure, easy flicks of his fingers.

"Leaving for work," I say dejectedly.

"You could come with me?" His brows raise in humor, and
there's the devil's twinkle in his eye. "I sense you want to come.
Again."

"Malcolm." I can't believe this man. "I'm liquid, and look at
you. You look ready to tackle a dragon. I'm tired thanks to you.
And you want me to come to M4 with you? What? To work for
you? Think of what your investors will think if you hire your
girlfriend."

"They revere me. They'll know I believe she's a word god-
dess and they'll trust my judgment."

"No. I mean yes, I'm all that, but no, I'm not going to work
for you."

He looks down at me with undisguised delight. "You're a
cocky one, aren't you?"

"Me? Cocky? Malcolm Kyle Preston Logan Saint . . . did
you just hear yourself talk about how revered you are?"

"No, Rachel," he purrs arrogantly as he buckles his designer
belt around his lean waist, "I was too busy looking at the way
you're looking at *me* now."

He comes over to drop on the side of the bed, edges my little R necklace aside along with the M, then he leans his dark
head in, and his lips replace the necklaces as he presses them
hotly into my skin.

Gone mush, I wrap my arms around his shoulders and tell
him, in his ear, "I really, really like the things you do to me, Sin."

His voice husks out when he sets a kiss on my chin, and then, satisfyingly, gives me one on the mouth. "Not as much as I like doing them to you."

He reaches for the tie I had taken off him and left on my nightstand as he comes to his feet. "I won't pressure you. This is the last time I put this out there. Take as long as you'd like to reply. Look as long as you want, Rachel. You have a job at Interface."

Considering how difficult it's been to get an actual callback, mainly because of my relationship to him, his words give me a brain orgasm—some much-needed relief on that front.

"I'm truly grateful for it, Saint. But the media has a picnic with me as the main course already. I'd never get respect if my boyfriend got me my job."

"I didn't get it, your skills got it, I simply want the best. I want what I want. Come to Interface with me."

He knots his tie and slips into his jacket, looking at me expectantly.

"I would," I quietly say, *if I didn't care so much*. "But no. It has to stay separate."

He waits a moment without a word, and then urges, "Let me make some calls for you, little one."

"Sin!" I laugh, then sober up. My heart is near exploding right now. "Thank you. But I have to be sure I'm being hired for the right reasons."

"You will be."

"With a call from you, I'd be hired if I were a duck!"

"God, you're stubborn, Livingston."

"You're worse, Saint."

When he finally nods in understanding, I think I love him just a little more than I did just a second ago. He's a man used to getting his way, so my position can't be easy for him. Having his kind of power but wielding it carefully because he respects my wishes to stay independent means so much.

"And you, Mr. Saint," I get to my feet and smooth a hand over his tie, going up on tiptoes to kiss his hard jaw, "go get the moon."

After this weekend, I'm officially the president of Saintaholics by the time I'm finally at work. Helen asks me to go with her to the offices of the Clarks, the family who has owned *Edge* since its inception.

We head up the elevators, down a carpeted expanse, and into an office that is as quiet as a church and the complete opposite of the bustling newsroom below.

Seated at a long table are the Clarks. Mr. Clark is in a light blue suit and a black shirt, and is topped by a full head of white hair. Mrs. Clark is in a light yellow sundress, her dyed black hair wrapped in a tidy little bun.

They usher us to take a seat and I tensely follow to sit down next to Helen, right across from the Clarks.

"Rachel, we've been extremely appreciative of your loyalty to *Edge* since bringing you on board. Your contributions have been and continue to be invaluable," Mr. Clark says.

"Thank you so much, Mr. and Mrs. Clark."

"The reason we asked to see you today is because, as you may have been hearing, we have a very interested buyer for the company and we're keen on selling, for personal reasons. However, this buyer is very explicit that his interest in *Edge* is exclusively tied to whether you remain with it. We've asked for his assurance that our loyal employees will be kept on when his management takes over, and he won't make that guarantee unless *you* guarantee to stay."

"I'm sorry, Mr. and Mrs. Clark, I wasn't planning on staying. Also for personal reasons."

"I see." Mr. Clark rubs his chin, exchanging a worried glance with his wife.

When nobody speaks, some kind of switch goes off in my chest, triggering a bomb countdown. *Tick, tock, tick, tock* . . .

I ask, suddenly concerned, "Are you implying some of my colleagues will be let go if I don't stay?"

I'm gripping the armrests as I wait for an answer.

Tick, tock, tick, tock . . .

"Well, yes. Everyone would likely be let go," Mrs. Clark responds, looking pained as I stiffen in my seat. "We've tried to secure some positions but the buyer has been very firm. Rachel, please consider staying at *Edge*. We can tell the new owner would be very interested in growing your career, and your colleagues would be able to remain."

And kaboom.

Ka-fucking-*boom*.

"Mrs. Clark!" I gasp from the blow, then shake my head, stupefied. "I have a *very* powerful reason for leaving. I *beg* you not to allow my colleagues to be fired. Some of them have been here through every lean time, working hard to see the magazine through. Everyone depends on their salaries."

Xavier Clark cocks his head at my plea. "It's not *me* doing or not doing anything. It's the buyer's demands. I would urge you to consider staying at *Edge*, then, Miss Livingston."

He pauses and takes a long look at me.

"I personally will offer you a year's salary as a bonus if you do. You have to understand," he leans forward, suddenly looking older, tired. "This is our one chance to see a dime back of the life savings we've put into the business. This is a new start for *Edge*, and could be a solid future for both you and your colleagues. Think about it."

"Mr. and Mrs. Clark, what's going on here is absolute . . ." I struggle to find a word, but I'm so outraged, I can only think of a thousand colorful ones to describe this. "This is *blackmail*."

Mr. Clark reels back a little, stiffly. "No, Rachel. This is business," he says. "And I hope we have a businesswoman in you." He nods to Helen, and we stand up when he does. "This must be settled by next Monday for our buyer. Try to help Miss Livingston see the win-win in this circumstance—for her *and* everyone else—Helen?" he asks.

"I'm sorry, Rachel," Helen says when we're out of earshot. For the first time her features are genuinely etched with concern as we walk back to the elevators. "I was afraid this was coming."

I fist my hands at my sides, outraged, impotent, and so damned angry I want to yell even though I try to keep my voice down. "I made a promise that I'm keeping, Helen."

"Oh, pfft. Don't be so innocent. People break promises every day, Rachel."

"Not this promise—not me."

We step off the elevators. My insides are roiling with anxiety and frustration as I go and sit down at my computer and watch Helen head into her office.

The newsroom makes its usual noise, the keyboards, the chatter, the phones, every one of my colleagues working as usual, and I wonder how many will be here by the time Noel Saint is through. Nobody here knows they're hanging on to a lifeline—one I'm holding right now.

Instinctively I pull out my phone and look for *my* lifeline.

I look at the name in my most recent text—SIN—and I

want to tell him. I desperately want to tell him that I'm still leaving, that I'm keeping my promise, that I love having his trust again, but that my friends are at stake. But if I tell him about this, *what will he do?*

Tonight we're supposed to go to a fund-raiser. We're supposed to spend the weekend together after. I could tell him, but I'm not sure that it wouldn't be falling into some sort of trap Noel Saint has set up to goad Malcolm into retaliating.

I lower my phone and find myself looking at *Edge* with new eyes.

Edge, which gave me my start. Gave me some kind of voice, a chance to reach people, a story that I wanted that broke my heart, but that led me to love. After everything, for the first time I'm truly realizing that *Edge* and I are done.

I won't stay here, a sitting duck. I won't be a pawn. I won't be bullied. I love my colleagues and this place, but I can't be responsible for absolutely everything. The Clarks are selling for personal reasons, and I have to act in my own best interests too.

I won't break my fucking boyfriend's heart again. I do have truth and loyalty, and a pair of green eyes owns both.

I find myself walking to Helen's door that afternoon, knocking three times,

"Yes, Rachel?"

I hand out the paper in my hand.

"And that's . . . ?"

"My two weeks' notice."

SIN AT THE DOOR

When I text, Hey Sin. I'm having a tough week. Is it ok if I skip the benefit? he calls me in record time.

"Hey. You all right?" Behind his voice, there are noises and clinking forks in the background. I probably caught him at a business lunch.

"I'm okay. But tonight . . . I want to stay in. Come by later or tomorrow?"

"I'll come by tonight. You all right?"

It's the second time he's asked. He's too sharp not to know.

"I will be," I promise. "I can't wait to see you."

"Hang tight, I'll be by later."

"I'll leave a key under the mat."

I'm not expecting him until after midnight, so while I wait, I lie around in his dress shirt and my white purple-lettered "Peace"

socks, eating popcorn with Gina, exhausted after telling her about my day and trying to tune out with a little bit of TV, when Saint arrives only a little past 8 p.m. He seems to have come straight from work, still in his business suit, exuding testosterone, and I notice the first thing *he* notices are the R and M necklaces on my throat.

He looks bigger right now. Harder. And like something I want to hold on to so much, I feel dizzy.

Dizzy and . . . safe.

For the first time today, I feel safe.

"Sin . . . I . . ." I signal down at myself, and as I do, his eyes move over me and heat up every inch they cover. "I'm not dressed, I was staying in."

"I'm staying in with you." He shuts the door. "Hey, Gina."

"Oh, groan. Are you guys gonna . . ." Gina sets down the popcorn bowl on the table and trails off delicately, looking from one, to the other, for an answer.

Neither Malcolm nor I bite.

Then, plainly, she growls, "Do I have to leave?"

Yes! my body screams. But I can't make her leave for us to fool around; that's just bad friend etiquette. "It's fine, Gina."

"I'll be in my room. Bye, Saint." She heads over and shuts the door, and I glare at him playfully.

"I told you to go to the benefit and come after," I chide.

"Ahh. See . . . I'm good at giving orders, but unfortunately I don't follow them well."

He takes off his jacket, jerks off his tie, unbuttons the two shirt buttons near his throat, then settles down on my couch and I'm not sure if I'm the one who presses up into him or he's the one who grabs me close, but we kiss a little, softly but with tongue.

"What's going on?" he murmurs when he eases back to investigate my features with that keen gaze of his.

I caress the arm he's got curled around me with my fingers, and the muscles of his forearm buzz with strength beneath the sleeve.

"I gave my two weeks' notice today at *Edge*."

A part of me listens to my own voice as if from a tunnel.

I'm *jobless*.

I know that Malcolm can help me and has offered his support but I desperately want to do this on my own.

Especially now.

Already my relationship with Saint is complicated enough. First, his natural playboy tendencies, my own inexperience in regards to relationships, the social media hanging on our every move, and even, maybe, what happened between us. Working for him, I'd be completely dependent on him and I'm too scared. I'm *more* scared of that than of being jobless right this moment.

He watches me with clear, observant green eyes as the words sink in. "You gave your two weeks' notice. Did you get a call back?"

"I'd have told you if I had," I assure him.

For a moment he only studies me. He looks at my face unhurriedly, feature by feature, the tensing of his jaw the only sign of frustration. "You gave your two weeks' notice without having anything lined up?" He tips my face back and regards me in puzzlement. "Are you coming with me?"

"Yes, I don't have anything yet. And . . . no. Please understand."

His eyebrows are still slanted low over his nose. I'm sure he's wondering why I jumped the gun and quit all of a sudden, so I search for the right words, but there's just no other way to say it than plainly.

"Today Mr. Clark offered me a bonus to stay along with a guarantee that my friends would be able to stay as well."

His voice is feather soft. "He threatened you?"

His thumb caresses my chin where he holds my face securely upward to meet his gaze. A ruthless gleam appears in his eyes, the kind of gleam that makes him exactly who he is. Ruthless, unstoppable. I'm afraid to see it right now, when all I want is peace.

"No, no, it was nice." Curling my hand around the hand holding me, I give it a reassuring squeeze. "They were grateful and wanted me to stay, but . . . your father wants me to stay. He wants to assure the Clarks if I stay, he won't can my colleagues. Malcolm, I wasn't going to let him get to you."

There's a darkness roiling in the depths of his gaze. He stands and eases his hands into his pockets. The move is casual, but the energy surrounding Saint all of a sudden is so intimidating I don't know what to say.

A long silence stretches.

"Sin, I can start up freelancing . . ." I point at my laptop, trying to sound positive. "I've spent all day scouring my favorite magazines to figure out what it is I like about them and I made a list. I like those who deal with people. Not things or cars. Not with the trendiest clothes. What gets me are the pieces that talk about a living thing, our strengths and weaknesses, our wins and its losses. That's what I could have done with *Edge*—pieces for the modern reader." I look at him. "I research how other freelancers have started. Usually with capital, and it takes years to build a steady income. I could maybe do it."

He walks to my living-room window. He stares out for a long moment. His back literally looks like a rock wall. "You can do anything you want to."

I don't want him to feel like I'm throwing his generous offer in his face, but I'm a little panicked wondering if he does.

Unless this is about something else entirely. Like his dick *father*.

"Well, what do you think about me freelancing for this one blog . . . ?" I try to turn my computer so he can stare at the blog, but he's not interested.

He turns, but he's looking just at me, directly and narrowly. "Why do you think *Edge* is not hitting its market?"

Exhaling, I close my laptop and shift on the couch so I can face him fully.

It's a good question.

"*Edge* is a bit too broad for a magazine of our size. It needs to find a niche and offer things in that context that no one else does. Helen has been onto that for a while, but the owners have always shot her down whenever she's tried to direct a tighter focus. Every single one of my colleagues that remains is very good at what they do. If only *Edge* were steered more clearly and precisely."

He makes no comment, but he's folded one arm and is rubbing his chin thoughtfully. His lips are curled, as if my answer pleased him intensely.

Frowning, I tell him, "What do you think your father's plans for it are?"

"Absorb it into his other companies, take it apart; keep only what he wants." He starts walking around, still frowning in thought. "I don't believe for a moment his main interest is *Edge*."

Something in his stride is too controlled, too deliberate, the look in his eyes too shuttered, cool as fucking ice, as if that very ice is running through his blood.

I can almost hear him thinking; the energy around him almost shooting sparks.

I know enough about this man to know that he's a genius at self-control. That he's methodical, that he thinks through his every action—that though he has a temper, he rules it, it does not rule him. He doesn't display anything on the outside, but I know that temper is tightly under control right now, and whatever is causing him to turn glacial inside, I'm almost scared on their behalf.

As if he reads my mind, he lifts his head and stares at me across the room, his tone chillingly matter-of-fact. "If my father wants *Edge*, he's going to pay dearly for it. Regardless of whether you're no longer employed at *Edge*, his pride won't let him back out now."

"Back out from what? Buying? Malcolm, it doesn't matter anymore."

"It matters to me." Eyes suddenly growing hot when he looks at me, he comes over and takes me by the chin again. "Do you trust me?"

With his free hand, he reaches out for his jacket. The energy shifts in the room as he puts it on, every cell in my body is aware. *Danger*, it screams.

When Saint frowns down at me and puts on his jacket, I feel like he's suiting up for war. I don't like it.

"Malcolm," I call when he heads for the door without an answer.

His voice is rough but completely uncompromising. "Do you trust me, Rachel?"

Entranced by the war-like gleam in his eyes, I nod.

He swings open the door. "Then don't look into anything just yet. See how things play out first."

God, this man. "Are you leaving for the benefit?"

"No. I'm visiting my lawyers."

"Lawyers see you at this hour? It's eight p.m."

He shoots me an obvious look and I roll my eyes. "Of course they do!" I laugh and groan at his high-handedness.

"Trust me."

"Malcolm, didn't you hear me? I quit!"

He closes the door.

WAR

Later that night he texts me, Free tomorrow?

I answer this because I want him to tell me what's going on: Depends on where we're going or who's asking. What's going on? I've been anxious, waiting to hear something ever since he took off.

But he ignores my question and instead answers: So it's a no for everyone except me.

Someone's cocky! I write back with a laugh.

Wear something comfortable.

With a delighted sigh, I resign myself to the fact that my mystery man will remain a mystery on this night. Whatever he's up to, I trust he knows what he's doing, though.

The next day he picks me up in BUG 2, and once he tells me we're going to a polo match, I keep asking him to tell me what he is up to. But he just chucks my chin and says, calmly and unhurriedly, "Next week."

His calm makes me relax about it as he leads me into the grounds. He's wearing skintight white riding pants that hug an ass as perfect as a baseball player's and a navy blue polo that hugs his torso, riding boots up to an inch below his knees.

Callan and Saint are playing, so Callan meets us and greets us before Saint leads me to a small, round white table with a perfect view of the field, kisses the corner of my mouth, and heads toward the stables.

For hours I sip my mineral water and watch the match, the thundering hooves hitting the ground, shuddering the stands. My hair flying in the wind. All I need is a hat and I'm absolutely in *Pretty Woman*.

I'm hooked on the game. Saint straddling a black thoroughbred horse, charging across the field, swinging a mallet in his hand, his muscles rippling, sweat glistening on his forehead. His horse has red ankle wraps on all four legs, and between the way it thunders down the field and the way Saint rides powerfully on it, I can't see anything else.

But I can hear the whispers of the ladies at the tables behind mine, about the guy on the black horse. *Who is he?*

That's Malcolm Saint, you dodo.

Shh, his girlfriend's right there!

Carmichael's on the white horse . . . do you see him?

I smile privately to myself.

Callan and Sin come over when the match is done. The tables behind me fall utterly quiet. They won 10 to 5, and I kiss Saint on the jaw and congratulate him and then I congratulate Callan.

"Gotta golden swing, this man of yours," he says as he pats Saint's back and they drop into their seats. Then it's "Hey, ladies," as he greets the girls behind us.

They titter.

We stay talking for a while, my curiosity peaked about the polo game more than ever.

"'Fess up, Saint. Does your horse have four names, like you?" I ask.

"He only came with one." His green eyes twinkle and his lips curl as he sips his water with a hand on the back of my chair. "He already had a track record when I purchased him at auction." Then he adds, "Matrix."

"And Callan's horse?"

"Swear to god, Saint, if you poke fun at my girl again . . ."

"His horse came with a name too." Malcolm leans his head to me and laughs when Callan shoots him a deadly look. "Tinkerbell."

On Sunday, he surprises me by sending Claude to get some Garrett Popcorn—my favorite caramel that I love—and I chomp it down while we both sit and read in his comfy library. After I've licked my fingers good and clean and forced a few kernels past his lips, loving how he playfully tries to draw my finger into his mouth along with the popped corn, I curl up to his bare chest as he reads Michael Connelly while I read what stuck to me from his office bookshelf: an Agatha Christie, *Destination Unknown.*

I keep getting up to change my book for a few other Agatha Christie offerings even as Saint flips his pages.

Settling back down with a collection of Miss Marple stories, I peer into his book and make him share the page with me so I can skim through what he's reading.

"Why does he suspect his brother's death wasn't a suicide?"

"Read it." He tweaks my nose and tells me, "Get back to yours."

"I like yours better."

"No. You like distracting me better."

"That too."

We laugh, and I then determine to ignore him, so I pull up my book and shift on the long couch to set my feet on his lap. He takes one foot in his hand and holds his book with the other, reading for another half hour.

Before long, he's leaning over to peer at *my* book. "Where are you?" he asks, his voice gruff from not speaking for a while as he skims the page. "Ahhhhh."

I slap his shoulder with the book. "Don't spoil it for me. What do you mean, ahhhh? Is he the bad guy? Tell me."

He chuckles low, then pries my book away, sets it aside, and we kiss, slow and easy. And I end up lying back as my body grows soft as cotton, him hard and strong above me, and we take a reading break to make love.

Later, he orders home delivery for us and we read some more while we wait. I study the look on his face as he turns the pages of his book. So *intellectual* today.

Once again, as I have over the entire weekend, I try to wheedle out what he talked to his lawyers about only for him to simply say, "Next week," without even lifting his eyes from his book.

I sigh and reluctantly let it go, cuddling against him, Saint automatically raising his arm around me as I do.

Holy crap. It's scary, how much I like it here.

With these arms, who needs red slippers to come home?

I arrive, exhausted and satisfied plus a million, at work at nine on the dot on Monday. Before I enter the elevator, a man with the most intimidating vibe, the harshest look on his face, and the biggest group of minions around him steps out.

I start when he looks at me.

Noel Saint. Like he crawled out from the internet and the endless harsh photos of him there ended up right here.

Right in this building.

Shock paralyzes me for a moment. Tall and dark-haired . . . he's almost as beautiful as Malcolm. But there is nothing even remotely playful about this man.

Where Malcolm's presence buzzes with energy, Noel Saint feels like a bomb about to explode right now when he sets his eyes—completely unlike Malcolm's—on me.

"You," he says. In the most contemptuous tone I've ever heard.

He steps over to me and, out of self-preservation, I step around as one of the young production interns boards the elevator.

"Are you coming?" she asks, holding the door open, like she's offering me a lifeline.

I hurry inside and Noel Saint turns to stare at me, and I stare back at him unflinchingly. Inside me, a ball of pure loathing starts burning in my belly, and I shoot him a look more hateful than the one he is sending my way. More hateful than I've ever given anyone in my life.

And he says, with a sneer, "He won't win," before the doors roll shut.

A morgue-like silence settles in the elevator.

"Whoa. Who was *that*?" the intern asks, blue eyes wide in concern.

I look at her, wishing I could remember her name so this would be less awkward. "My . . . boyfriend's father."

"Oh wow." She pats my shoulder regretfully, and I exhale shakily.

Was he here visiting the Clarks?

He didn't look too pleased.

Did he find out I'm not on board with his asshole blackmail plan?

He seemed so beyond mad, I can't believe anyone would get this riled up about anything, much less a measly employee leaving her job.

I'm still feeling a ton of dread sitting like a brick in my stomach as I step out cautiously on my floor and look for any signs of gloom and doom.

And I'm surprised that there's not. In fact, everything is normal, on Red Bull. Almost too much noise. Too many laughs.

I head to my desk.

"Rachel, Helen wants to see you immediately! And then report back to me," Valentine instructs with a very wide smile when he spots me.

I walk to Helen's office, glad to see Valentine looking happy, wondering if maybe he found a new job. Helen waves me in and I immediately start, "I am very firm on my decision, Helen—"

"Are you really? Because the entire office is thrilled!"

When I only stand there in growing confusion, she adds, "As you know, Noel Saint has offered for *Edge*." She claps her hands together, clearly delighted. "But . . . your boyfriend didn't seem to like that."

I inhale painfully. "I know."

"In any case, there's a bidding war going on." She nods. "Noel Saint versus M4." She eyes me. "Malcolm's taking on his father for *Edge*."

I'm pretty sure the world just stopped turning.

"Did you hear?"

HEART. FUCKING. ATTACK.

"He's upping the ante."

Half in anticipation, half in dread, I ask, "Who's winning?"

"I don't know but . . . I'm rooting for your boy." She finishes that with a mile-wide smile. "You know that love letter you wrote to him?" she asks as I head to the door in a complete state of shock and confusion. She winks. "This might just be Saint's reply."

Me: a woman of words.

Him: a man of action.

Shit. I cannot, cannot, let him buy *Edge*. Not because he'd be my boss, that's not even an issue anymore. But because I won't let him throw his money away into something he's never believed in. I won't let him be reckless because of me.

"*Edge* isn't worth what they're offering for it," I tell Helen. "You know that."

"They're not paying for *Edge* now. They've got a long-standing rivalry and they're going to do this to the end. Your boyfriend's father wants *Edge* with you in it, your boyfriend is not letting him take you on."

"But I quit, Helen."

"If Saint wins, you'll come back," she says assuredly.

When I step out of the office, nobody is working. At all. They're all leaning in groups around their cubicles and when I come out, they hoot.

"Hey, we're Team Malcolm!" Valentine calls.

"Team Malcolm!" Sandy says.

"TEAM MALCOLM!" the chants begin around the office.

"Guys . . ." I start, groaning.

Fuck. I laugh nervously, and go back to my seat and text him. SAINT! *Edge* is in an uproar?!

We'll talk later.

What? Malcolm Kyle Preston Logan Saint!!! I reply.

Later.

Please tell me you know what you're doing.

You shouldn't even have to ask.

God I LOVE you! I want to text. *You're unpredictable and you drive me crazy and I love you.* But the next time I say it, it will be looking into his green eyes, and that's that.

I sigh at that and then sit at my computer, look up Noel Saint's image, and give him the finger.

"Take that from us at *Edge*. Asshole."

He promised to come over after work. I shut the door, breathe, and look at all my things. Almost everything I love is within these walls.

I'm safe, right? The water feels a little rocky but it's not going to turn my boat.

I grab my laptop and head to my room. It's my baby. It's the one thing I'd take in the event of a fire. It's who I talk to, my laptop. And it's who talks to me.

It's all I need to work, really. It can feed me, feed my mother, as long as I have the will.

I can leave *Edge* and while I still have my laptop, there's still hope for me.

But Saint is out for blood and it's all because of *me*.

I search for this bidding war online as I wait for him.

His social media is quiet. But I see a couple of articles posted yesterday and today that catch my eye.

> M4 stock dropped more than 5% after hours . . .
>
> Shareholders are deciding to sell after Saint's decision to invest in Tahoe Roth's oil well, not the only bad business decision he's made in the past quarter . . .
>
> Rumors about entering a bidding war for *Edge* have sent the stock plummeting even further . . .
>
> Sources say M4 Chief Executive Officer Malcolm Saint's head is just not in the right place after his involvement with columnist Rachel Livingston, who exposed the universally loved magnate only recently in an article for a local magazine . . .

I click the links and stare at the pictures. We're out having dinner together, in one. In another, he's getting into his car. In another, he's standing in a sea of men, looking detached and somehow . . . alone. Thoughtful.

I swear. In all the articles about him online, few of them tell you how Saint is actually generous. How come no one writes about that? Or writes about the bad side of his fame? What it might be like for a person so exposed to the world, someone continually judged—even by his girlfriend. Someone who can't help but see skewed mirrors of himself thrust up by the media.

Does he see himself as the media sees him? Or what other people see?

The Malcolm Saint you hear about in the news is reckless and intense—he doesn't save a close friend's business. The Saint in the media wouldn't buy a mural to support a cause that I believed in, he wouldn't come to my campout. The Saint in the media wouldn't offer me a job regardless of what happened between us, just to keep me away from someone he knows could do me harm.

The Saint in the media is a powerful legend, but my boyfriend is a mysterious, thrilling man who I want to peel open and then kiss all the way inside to whatever wounds made him.

I think of his father. How frustrated Saint has been, trying to get me out of *Edge* and into M4. Suddenly I understand his position.

Would I want my boyfriend in harm's way? No. Just knowing M4 is taking a hit because of some allegedly bad business calls—partly because of me—I want to comfort Saint. I want to take my measly thousand-dollar savings and go buy the three shares in M4 I could afford, just to show him I believe in him.

I just want to hear him reassure me that he won't throw his hard-earned money on a lost cause, on revenge on his father, on revenge for me, on saving all my colleagues.

He's a man who's been asked for many things by people who want to use him. I want him to know all I want is his support and his love. He doesn't have to save everybody to prove himself to me. He doesn't have to prove anything to his dad anymore. He is Malcolm Kyle Preston Logan Saint, intense, relentless and ambitious, ten times more powerful than any other man in Chicago, capable of building a thousand *Edge*s from scratch, and his father can go straight to hell.

When Malcolm arrives at my apartment late, I charge over to him, take his hand while Gina keeps watching TV, and lead him to my room.

"I saw him today. Noel," I say, knowing by instinct he'll want every detail of our encounter.

When his green eyes flash protectively, his eyebrows slant over his eyes, and he opens his mouth, I lift my fingers and press them to his lips.

"He stepped off the elevator before I could go in. He said you won't win, and then I rode upstairs. That was all. From what I've seen of him, he's big on insults but that's all the game he's got."

Still frowning, he takes my wrist and lowers my hand. His voice is low and deadly. "He went to *Edge*."

I nod and lace my fingers through his, somehow wanting to calm him. "Probably meeting with the Clarks."

"Funny," he says with perfectly moderated anger, "because the Clarks are kissing my feet right now for starting the price war."

"But they need that second buyer for the price to rise, don't they?" I say.

He shrugs off his jacket and walks over to the corner chair, tossing it over the armrest before he unknots and pulls off his tie. "Even without any assurance of you staying, my father's ego won't stand backing down to me. Like he said, he doesn't want me to win." His lips curl as if he's savoring the fight.

He shoves the tie into his jacket pocket and stands there, in that white men's shirt, looking at me as if making sure that I'm all right, and my heart is quivering when I add, "You're bidding on *Edge*."

"M4 is."

"M4 is you, Saint. You're bidding on *Edge*? Why?"

"I'm not bidding on *Edge*. I'm bidding on you."

My entire body resonates with shock and emotion at his words, the violently tender expression on his face. I drop my gaze. "It hurts to think that you're doing this for me."

"Don't say that. You have no idea what you've done for me."

He holds my face in one hand as the other gently cups the back of my neck. His eyes are like daggers of heat and truth, ruthlessness and loyalty as he peers down at me, his lashes halfway over his eyes.

"Do you know what I'd do for you?" A huskiness enters his voice as he circles my chin with his thumb. "You're the only heaven I will ever know, Rachel"—he looks into my eyes—"and if you were a hell, I'd sin my whole life just to stay with you." His eyes are intense one second, and the next, they're smiling down at me as he scans my face and adds, "I would kill for this one . . . ear." He takes it between his thumb and forefinger and tugs it playfully, and when I finally smile, his expression becomes sober again, his voice low and smooth as steel. "My father won't touch you, Rachel. He won't play with you, threaten you, so much as breathe on you."

"Saint," I protest, "I don't want him to touch *you*."

As if that's inconsequential, he kicks his shoes off, settles down on my bed in his shirt and slacks, and opens his arms. I go there. And he asks, very plainly, "Do you want me to buy you *Edge*?"

"What?"

Ohmigod. Saint did not just ask me this!

But he did. He did.

"You said . . ." I clear my throat, shaking the daze off. "You once said you didn't see your money going there. You don't be-lieve in *Edge*."

"But I believe in you." He watches me. "I'm not bidding on it for myself. I'm either giving you your magazine back, or draining the demon who spawned me of every last drop for dar-ing to attempt to toy with you." A ruthless gleam appears in his eyes, his voice dropping. "If you want it, I won't back down until I break him and *Edge* is yours. Yours to do what you want with, your platform." He studies me in both silence and appre-ciation, his eyes missing no detail. "Is *Edge* what you want?"

I'm struggling to control my emotions, stumped by his con-tinued generosity to me. "I love *Edge*," I admit, "but I want . . . I want to be somewhere with potential and that doesn't remind me of what I almost gave up for it. Somewhere with freedom. I'd love for my friends to have jobs, of course. Have a way to earn more, work more. Maybe I want something more, I'm . . ."

He looks at me—both patient and expectant—as if he's still waiting for more.

"Malcolm, back down," I finish.

"Do you or don't you want *Edge*? Tell me." He tilts my face up so those keen eyes absorb every inch of my expression.

"No," I hear myself say, painfully realizing this is true. "I don't. I hadn't realized until now how much I want a fresh start. *Edge* is in my past now. I want . . . I want the best for my friends but maybe we each have to find our own way . . ."

"I'll make sure your friends don't lack for opportunities."

"You will?" My eyes widen, and I grip his shoulders. "Then back down."

"Not yet." He leans back and crosses his arms behind his head. "We still have a way to go."

"How high are you raising the price? What if Satan backs down and leaves you as the purchaser?"

"He won't back down. He's been wanting to go head to head for years. He wants to show me who has the deepest pocket and after I'm done with him it will undoubtedly continue to be mine." God, his smirks are killing me.

I laugh, then groan. "Malcolm, you're too bloodthirsty. Back down now."

"Once your two weeks are up, when he can't touch you," he calmly assures.

"Malcolm," I groan.

He laughs and pulls me close, staring into my eyes. "Don't you trust me? Take that leap, Rachel."

I sound a little scared when I ask, "Are you going to catch me?"

"It wouldn't be a leap if you knew that for sure, it'd be a step. In steps, you go by facts, you leap on faith."

In me, I read in his gaze. *And in you.*

I nod, breathless under his touch, the look of complete ruthlessness and determination I see. "Okay. But . . . back down please."

"Rachel, I will."

"Promise me."

He laughs tenderly over my concern, but then he falls sober, extremely so. "You want me to promise?" he asks softly.

I remember he doesn't make promises. So I bite my tongue and say nothing.

Then he leans forward, slowly, achingly slow, "I promise you," he suddenly rasps out, with a firm nod, "I do. I promise you." He seizes my face to look at me and kisses the corner of my lips. "The moment you've stepped out of *Edge* for the last time, you come to me. Whatever I'm doing, you come to me. I want you to always come to me."

I'm still reeling as I nod, and then I just lie there in his arms—Malcolm mentally planning his strategy, and me, learning to trust.

THE FINAL LEAP

My last day at *Edge*, I cry. My friends cry, and Helen, she sucks it up. Valentine brings a pie and tells me, "I'm still rooting for Malcolm."

"Don't, Val," I whisper. "What's happening shouldn't be happening. I'm not staying . . . *Edge* and I are done. Wouldn't you like to start new?" I glance at Sandy, who's also at my cubicle eating pie. "Maybe start up something like *Bluekin*, edgier, where we can all maybe own shares of our start-up—motivating us to really make a killing for it."

Valentine looks around, then says, "Dude, I can't forgo my salary for months while we try to get the online thing going."

"I know, but—"

"And Sandy barely makes rent. She can't afford to freelance while also working on our own website, just hoping it's a success."

"Let's at least think about it. Maybe talk about it a little more. If you're let go by . . . well, if Noel Saint lets you go or proves impossible to work for, please don't just take shit from him. Move onward—to something better. Even if it doesn't seem like that at first. It's scary, I know. Hell, I'm still scared but I also know I want something more."

"You? Not playing it safe? I'm . . . stunned, frankly." Val nods admiringly.

"I can't play it safe now. I'm taking a leap and if I find something good, I'd love you guys with me. I can't have this guilt of you guys losing your jobs because I left—"

"Hey, it's not *you* who'd can us, it's that asshole."

"Still—"

"Rachel, get out of here. Go and get a life. A different one. One where you can look back and all this," he spreads his arms to encompass the newsroom, "was just a part of it. A big part, but only *one* part."

I really had hoped Valentine would consider us maybe striking out together, giving ourselves a platform for our stories. I really wish they weren't so understanding and kind, and so hard to leave. I really wish Helen had been an asshole all the time, so I could walk away with my box of things without tears in my eyes. But of course that's not the case. It never really is, in real life.

So I do sniffle—a lot—and give out more hugs than I've given out in a while, and then I walk out of *Edge* and dump my box of things outside, keeping only the portrait of my mother I used to have on my desk and a little pen that I got at a motivational conference that says GO FOR IT, and so I am.

Without a call.

Without a text.

Without any kind of forewarning . . .

I head to M4.

Saint asked me to come to him, but the truth is, I need to. I just need to look at him and be inspired by all that strength of his and maybe, I just need to hear him tell me everything will be all right.

I'm leaving the old me behind at *Edge*.

I'm leaving all my mistakes.

I'm leaving the scared girl behind.

This is me taking the leap.

And I need to know that he won't let his father goad him any farther, that he won't be acquiring *Edge*.

Because Malcolm Saint has done enough for me.

I'd let him do anything else now, I realize, because I *trust* him—he can love me, protect me, help me—but not go to war over me.

At reception, the ladies are surprised to see me—but I can tell they've seen the social media. They know I'm the "girl-friend" now.

"Miss Livingston, what a surprise," one says. "I'm sure Mr. Saint will be pleased—if you'll let me ring you up?"

I thank her and then head up in the elevator. *Breathe, Rachel.*

Catherine is already on her feet when I get off, also a bit flustered by the surprise visit. "He's with some of his board, if you'll just take a seat for a moment." I smile weakly and grip the M in my fist, tugging it and rubbing it against the R.

As I wait, I listen to his four assistants take calls and type on their keyboards. I smooth my skirt down my thighs when the door to his office opens and a pack of businessmen emerge.

They're all screaming confidence and power. "Good day, Mr. Stevens, Mr. Thompson," Catherine calls to the business-men as they head to the elevators.

And then I hear *his* voice from within the room. It's so deep—familiar—I feel it like a low hum, vibrating in the deepest part of my body.

"He should've known if he wanted to play hardball, I'd be game. I'd strike a home run before he even realized he made a mistake throwing a ball my way," he says decidedly to the man with him. Then he spots me and lifts his eyebrows and the ruthless smile he's wearing—the one directed at the person he means to crush—starts to fade when he sees me sitting here, my eyes maybe a little red as I struggle not to show how crestfallen I feel.

"We'll settle this once and for all tomorrow at two," he tells the businessman in a lower voice.

The man nods and leaves. My gaze is caught—my heart is frozen—as Saint slowly stalks forward. Directly toward me. He takes me gently by the arm as I stand, and leads me to his office, and I know by his gentle but firm grip that *he* knows I'm not okay.

Inside his office, he pulls me into his arms, tells me, "Breathe."

I grip his tie and nod.

"You came to me," he groans then, in my ear, as if that thought undoes him.

"Always," I whisper, still gripping his tie.

"Mr. Saint," his intercom beeps. "Your one o'clock just arrived?"

I watch him walk with that confident stride of his to his desk as I try to hold myself together. With a press of a finger, he tells her, "Reschedule. I'm going to need an hour."

I shake my head. "Don't, really. I'm all right. I just came to let you know . . . I'm out. I leapt."

I spread my arms out and turn to stare out his window, not sure how I feel about my next words. *Scared? Hopeful?*

"I'm a free agent."

"Then turn around and look at me, Rachel," he whispers.

Hearing the raw emotion in his voice, I turn.

Holding my gaze with fierce intensity, he lifts the phone on his desk and dials a number. "We back down," he says, and then, he hangs up, very slowly. *Click.*

"I didn't mean to interrupt," I admit. "I just wanted to . . ."

"Know that I kept my promise," he finishes.

"Yes, but . . . no. I wanted to see you, Saint. I always want to see you when I'm happiest, or saddest, or . . . I just always want to see you."

I watch a dozen emotions skid through his eyes. "I'm here for you, Rachel."

"I know," I say. And for the first time I believe it, 100 percent.

Maybe no man has ever been there for me before. No father, brother, boyfriend, and now, I believe Malcolm Saint is here for me because he wants to be. My chest hurts with love.

"So you just backed out?"

"That's right." He shrugs dismissively. "There's a binding agreement running through the auction, legally binding the winner to go through with the purchase. The bragging rights will cost him a fortune."

My body's shaking. I didn't realize, in my haste to come here, that when I dumped my old stuff outside of *Edge*, I also dumped my sweater. *Really Livingston?!* The air-conditioning is blasting as high as these top business corporations always keep it. I'm shivering so much the last part of what I say is through clenched teeth.

"I know you said I could work at M4 but—"

"But you're right, it's not ideal for us," he quietly admits, eyes probing me in silence. "I won't be holding you back, Rachel. Tying you down where you're not happy."

My teeth chatter. "You know my reasons are because I want us . . . more. I'm going to start freelancing . . ." I stop talking when he crosses his office to a familiar, pristine white, smooth space on the wall.

With a tap, he opens the hidden closet and takes out a jacket. "Here."

"I don't . . ." He puts it over my shoulders and the brush of his fingers on the back of my neck triggers a tremor down my spine. "Saint, don't," I say. I'm afraid that his touch is going to make me crumble from the inside out.

His eyes look liquid on me as he touches the R and the M necklace resting at the base of my throat. "What happened to Malcolm?" he teases me.

I can see he's trying to make me happy and it makes me love him all the more.

"Malcolm," I then say, with a smile. His eyes go liquid with heated tenderness as he takes my hand. "Come with me now."

"I'm sorry you had to butt heads with your father for me," I tell him as we board the elevator.

We stop one floor down, and Saint tells the pair of businessmen about to board, "Take the next one," and they instantly retreat.

He looks at me once we're alone again. "You grew up without a father. In your mind, he would've cared for you, appreciated you, he would've talked to you. I *had* a father, but every time I threw a ball, he threw it farther just to show me how short my range was. Every time I built something, he smashed it in the simplest way he could, to show me all the flaws in my plans. Not all fathers lift you up. Some stick their foot out to trip you." He speaks without inflection, as if it's only a fact of life. "In the beginning, you try harder just to show him that you can. Then, you do it to prove to *yourself* that you can. Until there comes a day when you simply do things because you can. I'm not doing this for my father. I wasn't backing *Edge*."

He opens a room on the eleventh floor. "I was backing you, Rachel."

I glance around at a dozen computers, high-tech equipment, the offices in the corners. It looks like a . . . newsroom.

"This is where Interface started. Before we went corporate. When it was just an idea, the start." He signals around, and as I take in the impressive room, I feel him eyeing me with a gaze that is both achingly gentle and silently contemplative. "So you see, it's standing here . . . just waiting for another great idea. Another great start."

As I look at all of the high-tech computers and chrome desks, I have a déjà vu moment of the time he took me to the Interface building and kissed the *fuck* out of me.

"You can take this floor. *Yours*," he emphasizes. "I'll fund your start. You can build your own team. Your board. You'll make the choices. And you'll give yourself the platform you need to write whatever it is you want to write."

He looks at me with a twinkle in his eye and hope, as if he wants to see me smile, as if he's hoping this will be it.

"You'd have more responsibilities than writing, true. But you're smart, you can bring in your team. If you get stuck, I'm sure you'll think of someone who can help you. You can build your own *Bluekin*. Even better."

His stare is so admiring and respectful and loving, I can't breathe.

Oh.

God.

Epic love. This is it. Want it or not. Do you take the leap? Do you take it?

Saint did. He believes I can do something more than what I do—he believes he can give me freedom and help me build a platform to see me soar.

My eyes water a little and I duck my head and try to wipe a tear. He reaches for me. He puts one hand on my face, forcing my gaze to stay on him.

I feel a pull of heat in my belly.

"Let me give you this." His eyes are completely mine, but at the same time, they swallow me. I've never felt his energy so powerfully wrapped around mine. Have never seen such pure, undiluted, raw emotion in his eyes. My chest hurts.

"You don't know how much I admire you, Rachel." His eyes glow with the force of his emotions. "How you care for others. For me. I appreciated your words before, but this . . ." He takes something out of his pocket, and I hold my breath when I recognize the magazine cover for the article I wrote. "This was very brave, Rachel. Putting yourself out there like that for me. This was a leap on its own. You're right." He lifts it up for me to see, then sets it aside on a nearby desk and starts coming forward. "It was our story, but not our entire story. It was only the beginning."

I cry freely now. "I love you, Malcolm."

"Do you really?"

"Yes, really."

He frames my jaw in wide, warm hands, tilting me to his line of sight as he dries my face. "The first time I heard it, I couldn't think of anything else. Even when all the shit came down, I'd think of those three words. I've loved you for a while, Rachel. All the fortune I've amassed and I'd never wanted to lay it out there for someone the way I want to lay it out there for you.

"You wanted your world to go still, stand still with me. I may be thirsty, ambitious; I'll charge out there, but this . . . what we have. Let's stand still here, you and me."

My throat closes when I remember what I told him before. I've never been held like this by anyone else. I've never had a man's arms around me in comfort, making me feel so utterly safe. I never imagined that I could stand in the middle of the storm that is Malcolm Kyle Preston Logan Saint, and truly feel like my world is finally becoming still.

His smile.

His. Damn. Smile.

I forget its effect on me.

My stomach is in a wild swirl.

"Malcolm," breathlessly, I stare. "You'd do this for me?"

"I'd do more."

A silence full of meaning falls between us. I want to say so many things but I can't find my precious words. His actions won over this time, for real.

"I love you, Malcolm."

"And I love you, Rachel. Very much."

My throat closes. "Hold me for a hot second."

He already is holding me as he whispers, "I'll hold you for four." Then, in my ear, he adds gruffly, "Go home and think about this—"

"Yes," I cut him off, and this time it's me who grabs him by the collar and kisses the fuck out of him.

"I've got to get back to work. Let me take you to dinner?" he asks me.

"I've used up all my no's with you," I say quietly, kissing him as I speak.

He kisses me as he speaks too, voice husky with male pride. "So it's another yes."

"Definitely."

"Not good enough, Rachel. Say it."

I laugh. "Yes, greedy man. You freaking woman-wizard. Yes, yes *yes*!"

That evening I call my ex-coworkers and tell them if they're leaving *Edge*—I want them with me. I'm having lunch with a few of them next week, including Valentine and Sandy. Then I talk to Gina and we call Wynn.

"Rachel!" is all Wynn can say. "I'm . . ."

"Speechless, I know. This dude leaves me speechless all the fucking time now," Gina jumps in to say.

I sit here speechless too, or rather wordless, feeling warm and fuzzier than my socks. They're both getting hung up on the fact that he's supporting me and my dreams. I'm hung up on the fact that—despite his upbringing, loving his variety in women and business ventures, and the fact that it seemed fairly impossible to do—I'm very, very sure that Saint loves me.

When Malcolm arrives, I'm wearing a little black dress and ballet flats, my hair down and hardly any lipstick.

The door of his Pagani Huayra flies open, and he holds my hand as I slip inside, and soon we're speeding off.

"Hey," I ask. "How was your day?"

"Good now."

He reaches out to give me a brief, but delish corner kiss, and I reach out to take his hand after he changes gears, leaving it there.

We go to a private room at a five-star restaurant called Tableau. Behind a set of velvet curtains, we're alone, just Sin and I, talking about today. I guess I'm the one talking the most, but he's listening to me like he always does with a charmed amusement that spears into my heart and melts me.

"I called my ex-coworkers. I told them if they're leaving *Edge*—I want them with me."

"Your mother?"

"I haven't told her yet."

"You realize she can hand-paint your covers if you wanted her to?"

"Yes. And I do want her to."

He sits across the table from me and I just want to lean over and eat him up with kisses. I feel cherished. Protected. Safe.

"I'm so excited."

I laugh lightly while his boldly handsome face smiles warmly across the table. I love when his full lips soften with humor and his part-smile, part-smirk goes all the way to light up his eyes.

"So your father has officially bought *Edge*?"

He nods.

"You knew he wouldn't back down to you."

"He's as proud as me. He told you he'd win, didn't he?" He leans back and eyes me quietly. "He was obsessed with my mother. They were perfectly in love until I arrived. He couldn't stand that his perfect wife gave him an imperfect son. He resented that she became protective of me. She loved me more than him. He didn't take it well."

"I never knew." I look at him.

"Now I know."

"What?"

"What he felt. That I'd do anything for you. Fuck over anyone to protect you. Do anything to keep you. Crush the world for you. My mother's gone but he still wants to prove he's better than me. Prove to her how wrong she was to choose me over him. She asked for a divorce but he never let her go."

"It would've been hard. For a mother like yours not to love you hard. Especially if you were stuck with your dad."

"I fared well." He smirks.

"You did," I say lovingly. I think he notices the longing inside me.

"Come over here."

He reaches out for my hand over the table and tugs me around with the lazy confidence of a guy who knows—with certainty—he's getting laid tonight.

"I like this smile," he says as I carefully sit on his lap. I laugh lightly. "And this laugh."

The lights are low. They shine on Malcolm as he moves the little M and R necklaces at the bottom of my throat and sets a kiss on my pulse point.

"Are we to be each other's desserts?" I ask him.

God. I sound so hopeful I laugh after.

The lively twinkle in his eye makes me think that he's planning something wicked. "You're definitely mine."

He dips his index finger into his wine.

"What are you up to, Sin?" I chide and before I can say more, he's dipping his finger into my mouth.

Leaning over, he follows his finger with his kiss.

I lick his finger. "You've liked doing this since the wine tasting."

"You have no idea."

He shifts me on his lap, and looks at me lazily through half-closed lids.

He tugs my dress upward to my hips and slips his hand into the warmth between my inner thighs. My body jolts pleasurably at the touch of his fingers stroking me softly.

I'm nervous someone will come in, but he's looking at me with such heated mischief, I can't resist him.

I put my lips on his neck, my fingertips roaming the flat planes of his chest. The muscles harden under my fingers. My mouth is trailing up to his, and I hear his groan when my fingers start going down his chest, down his abs, to spread my hand over as much of his hard-on as I can.

And then Malcolm's hand is easing off my ballet flats, and they fall with a clatter. He pulls one of my legs until I'm straddling him.

He kisses the tip of my nose, then my eyes, and his mouth takes mine again in another slow, drugging kiss. I inhale as he stops to look down on me. I hold my breath, exhaling as he reaches out one hand to cup my face. And then he kisses the corner of my lips.

"Oh god, don't. I won't last if you do that."

"Why . . ."

I inhale sharply, then hold my breath as he slides his lips across mine and to the other corner of my mouth. My lungs strain as I hold my breath, savoring the ghost kiss until he eases back.

Our eyes connect. My lips tingle from his kiss. I exhale shakily, reaching out to cup his jaw. And I do exactly what he did. I brush my lips to the corner of his mouth. I hear him inhale too, deep and hard. Exhale when I ease back. Green eyes shimmer with desire and need and things he hasn't said to me but maybe I don't need him to. I don't need him to at all. I lean forward and press my lips to the other edge of his mouth. But he cheats. He cups the back of my head to hold me still and turns a fraction of an inch so he can capture my kiss with his lips.

I try to edge back, very aware that the waiter will soon be returning and I need to go back to my seat.

"Did you mess up my lipstick?"

"What lipstick?"

I laugh, and Saint chuckles and holds my hand over the table as I return to my seat.

"I like this laugh," he says, his thumb stroking over the back of mine. "I like this laugh very much."

He wants me to spend the weekend with him, so we stop by my place. We'll be hitting *The Toy* and doing lunch somewhere he wants to take me to, by the lake.

Gina is panicking when she sees me come home one minute and come out to the living room the next. "You have a bag? A *big* bag?" she asks, wide-eyed as she stares at the bag slung over my shoulder.

"It's only one comfortable pair of shoes, Gina, for the gym in his building. One for going out. And one for the office. And my toothbrush, and just a few more things. I'm not moving in, I'm simply being practical. He . . . he asked me to spend the weekend."

"Rachel . . ." she says.

"It's only the weekend, Gina! Maybe one or two nights a week. I'll find a good balance," I promise.

"Dude, you're making me want to get a dog. Someone who gives a shit about when I get home."

"I DO!" I cry, hugging her as my heart squishes a little bit.

How could I not have thought of this? I've been so happy and I didn't think twice about saying yes right now. "I love you, G."

She hugs me back in mopey silence, but then slaps my bum. "He's out there?"

"Yes."

"You know . . ." She pauses, her expression apologetic. "He's no Paul, Rache."

"I know, Gina."

We stare at each other. We've never really been separated in a way that feels so . . . real for years.

"Okay. I'll see you Monday," I finally tell her, heading to the door as she drops back to the couch and glares at the TV.

"Monday is Monday, Rachel, not Tuesday or Thursday," she threatens.

"I *know* what Monday is." I groan and laugh, as I hold the doorknob in my hands, still somehow waiting for a bigger reassurance.

"Don't look sad on my behalf, I'm having an orgy while you're away. Shit is really going to go down here now that the responsible one is gone," she promises, but all too soon, she drops the big bad-girl act and grows serious, her expression softening. "Rache, I'm so happy for you. I love how happy he makes you. I want you to know I'm on board with this, one hundred percent."

My best friend. Unlike Wynn, not a lot of people like Gina. Not a lot of people get her. But I love her all the same. I come back, give her another kiss on the cheek, and leave quietly.

"Monday," I say.

"Have enough sex for the both of us!" she calls.

I come out into the evening breeze, swinging the bag with my things behind my shoulder.

And there he is, leaning against his car, arms crossed, wearing this most perfect smile.

I start forward and I'm truly breathless. I walk up to him and he meets me halfway. His smile, when he sees me, is the kind that stops traffic. And now it stops my heart. This man renders women stupid and I'm officially the most affected, because I've been seeing a lot of his smiles today. And I've been smiling a lot too.

I'm smiling now, a smile that receives a kiss from his smiling mouth as he helps me into his car.

The elevator doors close behind us seconds after we reach his penthouse. The city lights twinkle outside, and it looks so perfectly peaceful and happy as he lifts me in his arms.

Locking my legs around his hips, I grab his shirt collar and let my lips wander up his jaw in search of his. "I'm hungry," I breathe.

"Open your mouth then," he says. He wets my lips with his tongue for a moment before drawing back to look at me with fierce eyes. "That what you want?"

I nod and wrap my arms around his neck. He rubs his nose into my hair and inhales deeply, then drags his nose down mine and starts kissing me. He crushes me between the wall and him, and reaches to slide his hands under my dress. I feel his fingers caressing my flesh, up to my bra, and I hear him unhook it.

I'm shaking as he frees me, and then he takes my dress in one hand and pulls it over my head in one smooth yank.

I fist his T-shirt in my hand and tug, and he helps me, grabbing it in one fist and pulling it over his head. His hair ends up even more mussed than usual, and he looks so sexy that my airway constricts, and I can hardly talk as I rub his smooth skin with my fingertips.

"Malcolm." I dive to lick a beautiful brown nipple while rubbing the other one.

I cling as he lifts me up in his arms and carries me to the bedroom, our mouths never unlatching. He doesn't carry me elegantly like Rhett Butler in *Gone With the Wind*, because I'm not as hard-to-get as Scarlett, but he carries me with his hands on my ass and my legs around his hips, his delicious hard bulge pressing to the apex between my thighs as his mouth works on mine. My body trembles with his nearness and my mind races at the mere thought of us heading straight toward our happily ever after.

"Fuck me fast." He sets me down on the bed and I stretch my arms over my head, moving sensually to tempt him. "Fast, then slow."

"Shh. My bed, my rules. Strip the shoes and those tiny panties." He unbuckles his belt, and at the sight of his sculptured body, I'm dying.

He is perfection. He looks impenetrable in a business suit, as if nothing can touch him. But naked, he's a god, all tanned, toned chest muscles. Dark hair rumpled from my hands, those green eyes liquid. He's everything I never knew I wanted and more.

My mouth waters as I edge back in bed and watch him unbuckle.

He watches me too, and I get a sense of both weakness and power as I start to take off my panties in slow, teasing movements of my legs, loving the way he watches me kick them in the air.

He looks at me with a smile that slowly turns wolfish.

Something about me giving him everything, my every wall shattered, seems to make him more possessive. Before I know it, he's spread my thighs apart and is licking between my legs, his big, beautiful muscles bulging between my parted thighs.

Reveling, I pump my hips up to his mouth, every flash of his tongue knotting me up. I clench my teeth as I try to hold back my orgasm for a little longer. I'm about to combust when he raises his head and looks at me heavy-lidded.

"I love you, Rachel." The hard emotion on his face as he looks down at me is so powerful, I shudder to my core. He strokes his hand up my side so that he can touch his thumb to the corner of my mouth. "I love you like nothing else in my life."

"I just melt when you say it."

He laughs softly, and I lie here and smile, feeling like goo.

His mouth covers mine, his kiss gentle and loving as he spreads over me. He fills my mouth with his tongue and my body jerks from the pleasure, watching him above me. I've never seen a guy look at me that way before, his eyes hot and proprietary and meltingly hungry.

He slides one hand down my abdomen, circling my belly button then caressing my sex lips with his fingers, until finally sticking his middle finger inside me.

"*Malcolm*," I moan, rocking my hips and thrashing.

He takes my mouth, and I kiss him.

"No condom," he murmurs, looking at me.

No condom . . . just him and me.

It involves a high level of trust, this thing we're about to do. And neither of us hesitates as our lips fuse again. I grab him to me, curl my legs, and undulate welcomingly as he drives inside me.

He groans as I moan and before I can climax instantly from

the feel of him, he pulls out. And I'm there, shivering, suspended in the pinnacle of both physical and emotional pleasure. Gasping for air, I look at him, panting, burning, and his chest is heaving as he holds himself up on his arms above me.

He likes prolonging. I close my eyes and savor the way he does it. His lips once again tug on my nipples then trail along my abdomen. Up my neck. He smells me. Tastes me. Relishes me. Experiences me. I grab his hair, undulating beneath his hot, hard body. Savoring him back. He's my obsession and my addiction, the only place I feel both safe and exhilarated.

"Sin," I beg.

He pulls free from my kiss and growls, "I am obsessed with you." Then, he grabs my hips and fills me, whispering, "I adore you," filling me completely, watching me with those smoldering green eyes I can feel in every part of me, building up a new orgasm, cupping my breasts in his hands, and bending to lick and lave both tips.

I thrash beneath him, unsure if I can survive so much of him. So much pleasure. Such total, consuming pleasure. But I do—and he goes deeper in me.

I sigh in relief every time he thrusts back in. Sigh his name pleadingly. He takes my mouth with his, his kiss ravenous.

"I am . . . crazy . . . about you," he rasps, moving in me so deep I can feel him in my heart. His face moves to my ear. "Let me own you, Rachel, and I'll let you own me right back. You're my lady now." He kisses my forehead, my nose, and my lips.

"Don't close your eyes; look at me," he says, and when I lift my lashes, his eyes are luminous in his face, and he's the hottest, sexiest thing I've ever seen, watching me as he fucks me as if transfixed.

He rams his hand into my hair and makes a hard fist as he

moves his body over mine, pinning me down for leverage as he watches me come for him.

I give myself over. Sin. Saint.

Malcolm inside me, Malcolm watching me with his green eyes, Malcolm clenching his jaw as he makes love to me, Malcolm who has my heart.

We spend Saturday on *The Toy*. He orders food from a delicious French restaurant before we sail and then the crew cleans up as we head upstairs.

We're in the top-level sitting area now as the yacht moves through the water, sated from swimming, making out in the water, doing it in the cabin shower, and then in the bed. Relaxed from all the sex, Malcolm works for a while on a couch and I lounge nearby, with my feet on his lap and one of his hands stroking them absently as I surf my phone a little bit.

I'm steering away from anything that could be a downer. So no Saint social-media-digging shit for me. No Saint social media about his father. I hear him take a call and am happy to overhear that M4's stock had a huge rally after the news broke that *Edge* went to Noel Saint's corporation. And now I can't stop dreaming of my new career. My new office space. My new life.

I'm thinking of all the things I want to do as the wind drags by and Malcolm finishes up, and when he shuts his laptop and I hear the unmistakable silence of powered-off electronics, I close my thoughts too as he pulls me up by the waist, then scoops me up in both arms and takes me to bed.

"I have legs," I whisper sleepily.

He gives me one of his toe-curling smirks. "Long, lovely ones too."

His king bed is waiting for us, sprawled in the center of the room, kind of big like him.

He sets me down in bed, but I crawl away and slip into one of his shirts as he strips, while exhaustion weighs me down after the day.

We settle into the bed a little bit; I crawl in and I plump the pillow and slide under the covers, and he joins me, flipping onto his back, pulling an arm above his head, relaxing as his free hand curls around my shoulders and presses me to his chest. I'm warm and soft inside, settling against him. The safe, warm nook in his arms. Gathered against his large, warm male body. Contentment and peace flow through me even as his body buzzes like it always does. With that never-ending thirst of his that I try to quench with *me*.

And we kiss a little. And as the kiss starts to heat up, we end up fucking slow and easy, not talking, only the noises of kissing and skin touching, our breathing and the yacht engines. I almost choke when I orgasm—the pleasure is so intense I hold my breath for forever, then exhale and lie limp, surrounded by all of Sin.

He kisses me passionately when we're done. Like he's grateful for my affection and my companionship and my desire of him.

Then we cuddle and I set my cheek against his chest and fall asleep fast and easily, like only the warm and safe do.

HIM +1

I wake up in Malcolm's arms Monday morning, and though I see there's a bit of light stealing through the drapes, I can tell there's still maybe ten or twenty minutes to dress for work . . . maybe I'll just stay right here forever.

He's still in bed, his eyes closed, his dark hair in a delish rumpled mess. I shift my hip, lightly trailing my fingers up his chest, noticing the claw marks of my nails on his pecs.

My eyes widen. What . . . holy shit, did I do that?

Welcome to the land of the crazy in love, Rachel. This may have been why you were so reluctant to move here?

Grinning, I rub my fingers over the marks, and his hand slides up my back. I lift my head in surprise. His lips are curled as he watches me.

"I actually clawed you last night?"

His voice is husky with sleep. "No, the girls who came in while you were sleeping did."

I smack his shoulder and he catches my hand, his voice deepening. "Come here."

"Saint . . ." I breathe as he rolls over me.

He reaches between us, sliding his hand down to cup me between my legs. "Hmm?"

Shivers run through me. "You had me a thousand times last night."

Gruff whispers as he kisses and nibbles my ear. "Did I? It doesn't seem like enough."

"Malcolm"—I push at his shoulder a little and edge up to sit—"in five minutes I need to get dressed for work."

"You *own* your work."

"Not yet. I haven't signed anything, and last you told me, it's today at two p.m. In the meantime I'm going to meet with my possible future team and start getting to work."

"All right, Rachel," he says, clearly indulging me. "I'll only take four minutes and fifty-nine seconds." He pulls me back down.

"Malcolm!" I laugh, then look at him, my smile fading. "Are we really going for this? Your first monogamous, exclusive relationship?"

His grin remains, but the glint in his eye turns serious. He nods, kisses my shoulder, then smiles softly down at me, brushing his thumb over my skin. "We're doing it. And I've got an eight-thirty."

After a quick shower where it's hard to focus on just showering, I find myself sitting on the corner of his bed with a towel wrapped around my body, just watching him—not even caring I'm going to be late. He's got a thousand and one identical shirts and ties and jackets, and as he buttons the one he plucked off the hanger, I watch him become Malcolm Saint before my very eyes. My eyes taking in his every move, his nimble fingers zipping up his slacks, his muscles flexing as he slides a shiny leather belt around his narrow waist.

He looks at me when he feels me watching, a dent appearing in his forehead as he frowns. As if he doesn't realize I'm just sitting here drooling my face off. Why can't it be like the cavemen times, when all that mattered was getting food and then we could gorge on each other and lock ourselves in here forever?

But he doesn't want just the food; he wants the world, the moon.

And, apparently, me.

"Come here." He pulls me up and I close my eyes, my toes curling when he sets a kiss that's almost chaste on my lips. "We're meeting the lawyers at two to make it official. Start planning your board; one that'll help you make your new venture whatever you had once dreamed *Edge* could be. Give yourself a team that will help you build the platform you need to put what's here," he taps my temple, "out there." He signals out the window.

Laughing with a combo of pure raw nerves and excitement, I nod.

He chucks my chin. "Have coffee with me before I go?"

"Yes."

"I'm knotted up." He twists his neck side to side as we walk out. "You really know how to tangle up a man in bed," he says, patting my butt affectionately as we walk to the kitchen.

I inspect every inch of him leisurely as he makes coffee and—trying to be a good girlfriend—I reach out to massage his hard shoulders.

It doesn't last long. Easing behind me instead, coffee in one hand, me in the other, he stares out at Chicago like an overlord surveying his land. I lay my head back on his shoulder and let him rock me slightly as we look at the city. The city, the world, the horizon. I sense he has most of that, but he wants more, *everything* we see out there, and what we can't see.

Everything he thinks he can accomplish, he's going to get.

When I go pour my coffee, I spot a crisp, white, posh-looking invitation on the kitchen island near one of his sets of car keys. It reads:

Malcolm Saint + 1

I smile when I read the invitation to one of the city's grandest galas. "Are we going?" I ask his back.

"We're always going." He brings his coffee cup to the sink, his eyebrows drawing together as he looks at me. "And that smile?"

"I was just thinking that . . . it's nice."

He kisses my temple. "Get a dress."

"Saint, I have a dress."

"Get one on me."

He sets down his credit card. I leave it on the granite counter, knowing he'll kick up a fuss when he sees that I didn't take it. I'm humming as I put the invitation back in place.

I can't wait to see where our relationship is going. People speculate on what I am. His girlfriend, his four-month girl, his lover, his fling, his obsession, his one sole error in judgment, his mistake. They can call me whatever they'd like, it doesn't change anything.

I'm his plus one . . . and he's my everything.

EPILOGUE:
OUR LIFE NOW

I t's a busy day at *Face*.

Face is my baby—brand new and still taking its first steps into publishing, both online and in print. I teased Malcolm about calling it that as a play on Interface, and when he chuckled in that amused way of his that tells me he kind of liked what I just said, I knew it was the perfect name.

Valentine, Sandy, and twelve other reporters are busy outside my office today.

It's great. But it's difficult to be in the same building as the guy I'm dating.

Sometimes I spot him leaving out the window, his hair and suit dark as the gleaming Rolls-Royce parked outside. Sometimes I watch him arrive from a business lunch, a conference, a board meeting at one of the multiple companies he advises—it's hard to keep my Saint hormones from running wild.

Sometimes we accidentally meet in the elevator as I ride up to my floor . . . and he rides to his. He's good at showing no emotion. But when our eyes lock, there's that inevitable spark I see light his green eyes. Our companions move as though by instinct to let him get close to me. We don't touch. At least, I don't. But he sometimes stands so that our hands graze. Sometimes his thumb comes out for mischief, brushing the back of my finger—the tiniest bit. Other times, he laces our fingers for a heartbeat.

A most delicious, achingly sensual heartbeat.

And there was this one time when he hooked his pinky to mine and rode the entire way up to my floor standing there, tall, quiet, among the bustle of people, nobody but *me* knowing that this man—this man really loves me.

Sometimes I go up to his office or he comes down—and somehow we both know why we're there. To talk, sometimes.

But sometimes to be quiet.

Superduper quiet as he kisses my mouth red, and red, and red, and simply coaxes me to promise him that I'll come over to his place tonight.

At his place, we fuck all night long.

In mine, we fuck quietly so that Gina doesn't hear us.

It's perfect. I wouldn't change a single thing.

Not of him, not of us.

I took the leap, and Malcolm caught me.

So we have this arrangement. During the week, we generally sleep at my place because I don't want Gina to feel lonely. The weekend, we're in his. This Thursday he has offered to drive me home, but he makes a five-minute stop at the bank. I stay answering some last emails on my phone and then peer curiously out the window when he comes out with one of the managers, who shakes his hand goodbye, then he climbs on board and asks Claude to take us to his building.

He's holding a suspicious envelope in one hand as he settles into the seat across from mine and slowly gets rid of his tie and tucks it into his jacket pocket.

"This is so not the arrangement, mister," I chide him, scowling.

He smirks. "Are you mad at me now?"

"So absolutely mad," I exaggerate.

"I'll make it up to you easy." He leans forward and runs the pad of his thumb down my jawline. "I have a surprise." He waves the manila folder in his hand in the air, and the butterflies respond.

"What is that?" I pry.

"Something."

"It's clearly something. But what?"

"Patience, grasshopper." He leans back in the seat with this infuriating smirk, the very image of patience itself, and stretches his arm out behind him, a very self-satisfied look in his eye as he watches me squirm to find out his surprise.

We head to the top of the building. At the very top, there's a pool exclusive to the penthouse. It's an infinity pool, where the water seems to blend out into the twinkling lights of Chicago.

We've used this pool a couple of weekends, but this evening, the luxurious white chaises have been removed. They have been vacated to make room for one lone table at the center platform that crosses the pool. Connected, also, to the pool is another platform featuring the only lounge area that seems to have been left untouched.

The one Saint and I always sit in to enjoy the view.

The paths toward both the table and the lounge are littered with electric candles that glow quietly as we pass.

It's so breathtaking—and so unexpected—that I spin around with wide eyes.

"So this is how you're making it up to me?" I catch him watching me a little too closely, and I kiss his jaw and whisper, "I like it. Make me mad again."

His hand engulfs mine, then he leads me forward to the lounge. "Dinner comes after the surprise."

He sits me down on the larger couch and settles next to me, and then draws the envelope to his thigh.

"If my mother couldn't meet you, I thought you could still meet her." He pulls out a 5 x 7 color photograph from inside and extends it to me.

I feel a visceral reaction to the image of the woman I see, and the handsome teenager standing beside her, letting her wrap her arm around him even though he's already taller. I recognize him instantly.

How can I not? I love him to pieces. Every part of him. And I love that woman in the picture simply because of the smile she's wearing and how lovingly she's holding him.

"She was reckless, spent money like her life depended on it," Malcolm tells me. "She was passionate, and brave, and she loved me. Despite everything."

He reaches into the folder again, and this time takes out a box with the name Harry Winston on it. He snaps it open. And there's this lovely, exquisite ring sitting proudly at its center. It's a round stone, super classical.

"When I was born my father told her to go buy the biggest rock she could find to celebrate the birth of what could now only be their only son. She didn't buy the biggest rock, she bought the most perfect: D, internally flawless, 4.01 carats. She took off her engagement ring and wore this ring for as long as I can remember. When her leukemia was diagnosed, she told me she wanted to give me this ring. This was symbolic to her for me, and she wanted my bride to have it. I told her there would be no bride, to keep it. When I . . ."

He pauses, his expression troubled by the memory.

"When I came back from my skiing trip with the guys, I was given a folder with that picture she kept on her nightstand. A trust fund. And this ring."

As he lifts the ring, it refracts all the lights around us, sparkling rainbows.

"So I went to the bank, got it the biggest box I could find, and stored it, having no intention of ever opening that vault. But all I've been able to think of lately is getting this ring out of that vault . . ." He kisses my hand and slips it on. "And onto your finger."

The ring slides easily onto my finger. It's a little big, and suddenly my finger feels just as heavy as my chest. Sin surveys my adorned hand, then looks up at me with this hopeful, loving gleam in those eyes of his. Eyes that used to be cold, when I met him for the first time, now look at me with the heat at the core of the earth.

There's a smile on his lips too, a smile so adorable it's almost boyish.

"Tie the knot with me. Be safe with me. Reckless with me. Be who you are with me. Be my wife, Rachel—marry me."

My eyes get blurry and my lips are trembling as I purse them painfully because of his story. Because I'm wearing a ring on my finger.

And he speaks: "You once told me you wanted the world to stand still, you wanted a safe spot to stand still. I want to be that place for you." His hands are almost swallowing my face, but it's his stare that swallows me most—swallows me whole. "Even if I'm spinning through life, the spot beside me will be the eye of the hurricane, and nothing there can be touched or harmed. I want you here with me, beside me."

My breaths have become ragged and I'm shaking all over in disbelief and happiness and emotion.

"Have you wondered what a man in love looks like?" As confident as ever, he kneels, ducks his head and kisses my naked hand. "*This* is what he looks like."

I break down and duck my face and bury it in his hair as a sob escapes me. I'm melting. Swooning. Dying. I should probably speak but I'm struggling with a wet face and a clogged throat. His mother. The only other woman this man has ever truly loved before me. I feel so grateful to hear about her. I feel so humbled that he thinks me worthy of wearing this ring.

Saint hears my sniffles and straightens back so he can dry my tears.

I love my mother so much; I can't imagine how it must've hurt him to lose her.

"This . . ." I struggle to explain, "is what a woman in love looks like when the man she loves shows her he loves her too."

There's a deep texture in his voice when he lets out a breath and says, "She looks lovely."

He starts to straighten and tucks his hands under my armpits. "What are you doing? What is—what are you—Malcolm!"

Laughing, he lifts me up to his eye level as he stands—lifts me up as if I weigh nothing—kisses me on the mouth. "What does she say?"

He waits a little, eyes searching, impatient, anxious, claiming, primal, male, Malcolm's. "Rachel?" he prods softly.

I'm hyperventilating. "We never . . . we never . . . you never told me you wanted . . . you were thinking . . ."

He takes my hand. I feel him rub the diamond under his thumb in a slow, languorous circle. "I'm telling you with this." He looks at me somberly.

My reaction is visceral, instinctive, there is no doubt in my mind as I grab his shirt, boost up and I'm shaking all over and press my mouth to his, answering with my wet kiss. He lifts me up by the waist and my skirt hikes up as I curl my legs around him.

"Yes," I breathe, grabbing his jaw in my hands and drowning in the lights inside those green forests of his that I swear to god contain the sun right now.

He nuzzles my nose. "Yes?"

"Yes, Malcolm. Always yes." I press my lips to his, no tongue, just lips, and I squeeze my legs and arms around him as tight as I can as we hug . . . for a long time. Simply hold each other. For a long time.

The wind teases my hair, and I feel it wrap around our faces as we lean our foreheads against each other.

I'm crying and laughing and, suddenly, raining wet kisses all over his jaw, his temple, his forehead, his nose, his lips again . . .

He stops me with his hands to look into my eyes. "Two more times."

"You want me to say yes four times?"

God. What do you do when the man you love asks you something?

You say yes.

Four times yes.

What do you do when a Saint loves you? You love him with all that you possess.

What do you do when Sin comes calling?

You do *him.*

Well, ladies, it's official @malcolmsaint is off the market, aka ENGAGED. From now on @racheldibs gets both the Saint and the #sinner

FUCK THAT BITCH I GIVE IT A MONTH

WHATTTT!

Seriously there's no way Saint can get sated with just one! EVER!

Is anyone else in mourning now that Saint's engaged? I'm having a severe case of blues!

Are you still going to throw those big parties of yours @malcolmsaint? The city won't be the same without you!

@malcolmsaint and @racheldibs Congratulations to the hottest couple I've ever seen!

Please, please post pictures from the wedding! Post pictures of the honeymoon! Rachel, post pictures of Saint!

From @gggina:
So happy for my best friend! I'm still going to kick @malcolmsaint's ass if he hurts her.

From @wynnleyland:
My boyfriend and I are toasting tonight celebrating.

From @CallanCarmichael:
Well, like they say, never say never. Cause guess who said never? #SaintSaidNever @malcolmsaint

From @TahoeRoth:
Now that Saint's off duty @Callan Carmichael and I are
doubling up on our duties to you ladies.

And then again from @TahoeRoth:
While our man & his bride have a honeymoon sexfest in a few
months, we're having a sexfest & everyone's invited—THIS
MEANS YOU GINA @gggina

And from me:
Fear not @gggina My fiancé knows how to take a woman to
heaven and keep her there! #HighInHeaven #HighOnSin

ABOUT THE AUTHOR

Katy Evans is married and lives with her husband and their two children plus three lazy dogs in South Texas. Some of her favorite pastimes are hiking, reading, baking, and spending time with her friends and family. For more information on Katy Evans and her upcoming releases, check her out on the sites below. She loves to hear from her readers.

Website: www.katyevans.net
Facebook: https://www.facebook.com/AuthorKatyEvans
Twitter: https://twitter.com/authorkatyevans
Email: katyevansauthor@gmail.com

ACKNOWLEDGMENTS

I have to give a special shout-out and thank you to all my early readers, who read my stories in the rawest form and still somehow like them enough to read them again when I'm finished. You guys are pure angels on earth (angels who are in love with Sin!). All my thanks to you, Angie, Cece, Dana, Emma, Elle, Jen, Kati, Kim, Lisa, Mara, Monica, and my childhood friend Paula. Special thanks to my agent, Amy, and my daughter, both of whom always read first and last and in between, as fast as I get them the pages. I love you!

And to Kelli C. and Anita S., my polishing masters.

Huge thanks to everyone at Gallery Books, including my funny genius editor, Adam Wilson; my publishers, Jen Bergstrom and Louise Burke; the art department, production department, and the publicists; to all the bloggers, booksellers, Sullivan and Partners, everyone at Jane Rotrosen Agency, my foreign publishers, and to my family.

And to my readers, who give my book life in their minds and hearts.

Thank you!